Six Yea

Phillip Strang

BOOKS BY PHILLIP STRANG

DCI Isaac Cook Series
MURDER IS A TRICKY BUSINESS
MURDER HOUSE
MURDER IS ONLY A NUMBER
MURDER IN LITTLE VENICE
MURDER IS THE ONLY OPTION
MURDER IN NOTTING HILL
MURDER IN ROOM 346
MURDER OF A SILENT MAN
MURDER HAS NO GUILT
MURDER IN HYDE PARK
SIX YEARS TOO LATE
MURDER WITHOUT REASON

DI Keith Tremayne Series
DEATH UNHOLY
DEATH AND THE ASSASSIN'S BLADE
DEATH AND THE LUCKY MAN
DEATH AT COOMBE FARM
DEATH BY A DEAD MAN'S HAND
DEATH IN THE VILLAGE
BURIAL MOUND

Steve Case Series
HOSTAGE OF ISLAM
THE HABERMAN VIRUS
PRELUDE TO WAR

Standalone Books
MALIKA'S REVENGE

Copyright Page

Dedication

For Elli and Tais who both had the perseverance to make me sit down and write.

Chapter 1

Marcus Matthews knew of three certainties as he looked out of the room's small window. The first was that he was at the lowest point in his troubled life; the second, that he was the wealthiest he had ever been; and the third and most crucial, he was dead.

How had this come about, those who had never met him might have asked, but to Matthews life had always been a challenge.

The circumstances of his birth: a homeless shelter in the north of England, a mother who was a heroin addict when she became pregnant at the age of sixteen. He was six months old when she died, prostitution the only way she knew to feed her habit and her child.

When the teenage Marcus reached the age of sixteen, a woman had knocked on the door of his adoptive family's home. Her name was Molly, the effects of a hard life all too visible.

'Gwen, that was her name, although you must have known that,' Molly said. That much Marcus knew.

'She loved you,' Molly continued. 'I was there when you were born, when she died.'

An adolescent teen who had developed a penchant for graffiti and wanton vandalism did not respond to 'love', but he was interested enough to listen to the woman as she talked.

Marcus's adoptive parents, Brenda and Gavin, sat quietly. They had always known that one day he would learn something of where he had come from; where he was heading back to if he did not mend his ways.

Brenda ruled the household. Marcus liked her more than Gavin, a well-meaning pen-pushing civil servant. Each working day, he would depart the house, and each night as his wife watched the numbingly boring television with its quiz shows and their inane questions, there he would be at the dining room table, checking figures, fretting over them. And then the money he brought home each week, a pittance. Marcus knew this because he was a thief, and he regularly helped himself to some of the contents of his mother's purse, his father's wallet. Not once did they complain, which meant to the unruly Marcus one of two things: either they overlooked what he did, or they were stupid.

On his twenty-fifth birthday, his luck had finally turned. He'd had a succession of pointless jobs, a result of failing to take notice at school. A fish and chip shop that produced the worst tasting food in the world, each and every day spent sweating over the hot fat, and the potatoes cut into chips, the fish that tasted of anything but fish. From there, a job in a metal fabricating shop, the constant hammering having almost destroyed his hearing, and even a turn at driving a taxi, but he got lost too often, eventually wrapping the vehicle around a telegraph pole late at night.

And then, there she was, two weeks later, next to him at the bus stop, his driving licence having been suspended. The bus trip was short, but they had started talking; he, a man with little prospects; she, a vision of loveliness in his eyes. Three months later, Marcus and Samantha were married in a registry office, with a reception at the pub, an argument later that night, a baby in a cot within seven months.

It was Samantha's father, Hamish, who had made the decision about the wedding. 'No daughter of mine is going to have a child out of wedlock,' he had said, but he didn't attend the wedding.

Hamish McIntyre was in jail for a botched robbery; there was no way that he was getting out of prison to do his duty by his daughter.

'You made her pregnant, you marry her, and if you harm her, just once, you'd better hope that you can be like a chameleon, because I'll find you, no matter how long it takes. Do you understand me?' McIntyre had said when Marcus had visited the depressing prison to ask his permission to marry his daughter; a formality as a phone call from the prison a week earlier had sealed Marcus's fate.

'I understand,' Marcus had replied. He would have said that he loved Samantha with all his heart, but the father was not a man for sentimentality. Apart from his daughter and the ugliest dog that Marcus had ever seen, he loved nothing else.

'One word from Samantha and you're dead meat, don't you forget it,' the parting words as Marcus left the prison, words audible enough to be heard by the other prisoners and the prison officers. McIntyre was a violent man; he did not intend to let anyone forget that fact, especially in a maximum-security prison. Marcus had left through the prison gate, his legs still shaking, needing a stiff drink to calm his nerves.

Marcus saw the love between him and Samantha as eternal. And her father's offer of a job, once the man had been released, and enough money to buy a small place, was just what he needed.

For two years, peace reigned, but Samantha was flawed. An indulgent father, a husband who was at work, or only wanting to be at home with her and their child, was not what she needed: she needed a life.

A violent psychotic was how Marcus had come to see her father. No one could do what he did to a fellow human being and be sane. He had witnessed the slaying of a rival, the knifing of the man, the smile on Hamish McIntyre's face when he had finished.

'No other bastard is going to cheat me,' he'd said to Marcus. As strange as it was, Hamish enjoyed Marcus's company, and the two would spend time together. One patting the other on the back, telling him to drink up; the other frightened that one wrong word and he'd be minus a part of the anatomy that wasn't getting much attention from Samantha, and none at all for the last five months.

Hamish had not yet been told of the fancy man that Samantha preferred over her husband. He was eventually when, after a few too many beers, Marcus had opened up to his father-in-law.

The fancy man skipped town, or so the story went. That was what Samantha was told when her father instructed her to return to the marital bed and to do her duty.

4

It would be three years before the man's body was found. By then, Samantha was still honouring her marital vows, and Marcus had become Hamish's right-hand man.

***

Outside the small room at the top of the house, the sun was setting. It was going to be a clear starlit night, the night that lovers crave. However, Marcus Matthews was sure that it would be the night that he would die.

He had been a day and a night in that room, and apart from visiting the bathroom, he had not left it. He knew that he could; the door was not locked, and there was no one watching the house. No one would question if he left the city or the country, and he had money. Others might have questioned his reason for staying, but he did not.

He sat down at a small table and opened another chocolate bar, his diet since he'd made his way to the room, climbing stairs that were almost too narrow for a person to navigate. Samantha had been back with him for fourteen years since her lover had vanished, and, on the whole, they had been good years, he reflected.

A creaking on the stairs, the door opening. Marcus stood up as the person walked into the room.

'A man who could always be trusted to keep his word.'

'A man's word is his bond,' Marcus replied. He felt a sense of unease as a gun was pointed at him. 'Come in. There's always time to talk.'

'It would be best if I do what I must and leave.'

'Why so soon? We have much to talk about, you and I.'

5

'It pains me to do this.'

'It is what was agreed.'

The two men sat down at the small table. Marcus produced a bottle of wine and two plastic cups. He poured the wine into the cups and handed one to the man who was going to kill him. 'Here's to you,' he said.

The other man laid his gun on the table and held his plastic cup up. 'Here's to better times,' he said.

The air was charged with emotion, the tension palpable, yet the two men, one a murderer, the other a victim, passed the time talking and laughing and reminiscing about people they had known, people that had died. For nearly ninety minutes the conversation was animated and emotional, and then the bottle of wine was empty.

It was Marcus who spoke first. 'It's time,' he said.

The man opposite offered his hand, which Marcus shook. He then picked up the gun and shot Marcus twice in the chest and once in the head. He then put the weapon in his jacket pocket and left the room.

If anyone had seen him, they would have seen the tears in his eyes. If they had been able to hear, they would also have heard, 'I did what had to be done.'

With that, the man closed the door to the small room and descended the stairs.

Chapter 2

It had been the mother of one of the youths who had phoned the police after her son came in screaming about what he had seen. Billy Dempsey, the more daring of the two boys, a skinny youth with bad acne, had been the first through the window at the back of the house; the preliminary details relayed to Homicide by a Constable Hepworth who had answered the call.

'We've had trouble with him before, stealing from shops, so we didn't believe him at first. That's why we checked before we called you,' Hepworth said.

A pair of amateurs was what Gordon Windsor, the senior crime scene investigator, had called Constables Hepworth and Lipton, although he had added a few angry expletives. 'They're told there's a body, and still they have to stick their collective noses and feet in.'

Detective Chief Inspector Isaac Cook, the senior investigating officer in Homicide at Challis Street Police Station knew that Windsor was right. A phone call in the late afternoon from Katrina Dempsey, Billy's mother, and Hepworth couldn't resist the chance to take the initiative and go with his offsider, a drinking buddy when off duty, to have a look.

'It doesn't look as if Constables Hepworth and Lipton have much of a future in policing,' Isaac said after Windsor had calmed down.

Windsor had seen the damage the two men had done when they had forced the back door, and then their footprints in the house, not even having the sense to keep their hands in their pockets either.

'It's time we'll waste. Was it made clear that there was a body?' Windsor said.

'According to Billy Dempsey and his friend, Andrew Conlon, that's what they said. It was Dempsey's mother who had caused the confusion, questioning her son's veracity, and Hepworth had had dealings with the youth before. It appears that Billy Dempsey has a sense of the dramatic; lying and exaggerating come only too easily to him.'

Pathology had conducted a post mortem within twenty-four hours of the discovery of the body. Nothing had been found apart from an approximate date of death determined by what was left of the corpse, an empty bottle of wine, and an old newspaper on the table in the centre of the room, and that the man had been shot three times at close quarters. The crime scene investigation team had been over the room, checked for fingerprints. The two boys had not entered the room, neither had the two constables, a plus in that the murder scene hadn't been contaminated.

Forensics had checked the bottle of wine at the crime scene, examined the cans and boxes of food in the cupboard and a plastic bag. The date of the wine's purchase had been confirmed at a local off-licence.

'It was on special,' the licensee said. 'Good value for the price, although it could have done with a couple of more years' cellaring.'

The identification of the dead man wasn't a problem either. Marcus Matthews had a criminal record: fraud, robbery when he was younger, fencing stolen goods when he got older, and then there was his known association with Hamish McIntyre.

***

A murder had been committed, but Isaac Cook did not feel comfortable with the reports he was receiving. There was no violence, and clear signs of two people sharing a bottle of wine: one of the two a murderer, the other a victim. It was as if two friends had sat down and decided on a course of action that resulted in the death of one of them.

Murder was not conducted in such a manner, Isaac knew that. The man who had died had remained in his seat. It couldn't be an assassination: that required surprise, and usually a crowd to hide the assailant while he got close enough to take the shot, and then pandemonium for him to make good his escape. In that room, there had only been two people. The idea of an arranged killing had been considered, the victim dying of a terminal ailment, the pain such that the man had preferred death to life, but Marcus Matthews was found to be in good health, and his bank account had shown no financial difficulties. And the background checks had not revealed a man with a depressive outlook on life.

On the contrary, he had been a cheerful man, in spite of being a crook who had had more than his fair share of brushes with the law, even spending time in prison on two occasions as a young adult.

Larry Hill sat still, saying little. It was early, not yet seven in the morning, and as the team had expected, a new murder case meant that early-morning meetings were again the norm, and working long days and weekends was to be expected. Larry, a man who enjoyed a greasy breakfast at a café on Portobello Road in Notting Hill when he could, and one too many pints of beer of a night time, sat quietly as Isaac went over the case so far.

'It's murder, no matter the reason,' Isaac said. He was standing up, looking out of the window of his small office, his carefully honed team watching him. Sergeant Wendy Gladstone, closing in on retirement but not there yet, did not like the rigidity of the office, certainly not the reporting, and computers to her were anathema. Bridget Halloran, a great friend of Wendy, was the office supremo and computer expert: if you needed information from the internet or from the various police databases, she was the best person for the job.

Larry Hill wasn't too fond of computers either, but he could struggle by with them. He, like Wendy, preferred to be out on the street, and working his contacts, more often than not the local rogues and villains; drinking with them of a night at one or another pub was par for the course. Isaac understood that, so did Larry's wife, a woman who looked for better in her life than a detective inspector's salary could give her and who continued to remonstrate with him to be more ambitious, to improve his qualifications, to become a detective chief inspector, a commander. Not that she was going anywhere else, as regardless of her remonstrations, and Larry's apathy, they were a couple still in love, still able to show affection for one another – but not on the nights when Larry came home having had a few too many beers.

Isaac was tall, dark because of his Jamaican heritage, and fit. He'd exercised every day before a recent trip to Jamaica with Jenny to visit his relations. He had proposed to her there – she had accepted as he knew she would – and now they were married, the blonde-haired wife with the porcelain complexion and the black man. Jenny ensured that he continued to exercise regularly.

***

Isaac's penchant for the early-morning meetings did not sit easily with Larry; he was a late-to-rise, late-night person. The meetings did not suit Wendy Gladstone either; she still struggled with her arthritis, and the cold, damp mornings exacerbated the problem, not that she'd complain openly as ill health would be the quickest way to early retirement. Bridget Halloran had no such issue with the early starts, and the chance to be in front of her computer screen filled her with joy, not dread.

As was the custom, the meetings were an opportunity for all present to put forward suggestions, no matter how foolish and obscure they were. This time what they appeared to have was a murder by agreement. It baffled all of them, and one thing that Isaac did not like was uncertainty.

'Marcus Matthews was married to Hamish McIntyre's daughter,' Larry said. 'The word on the street is that McIntyre's not involved.'

'A name to strike fear into anyone who knows him,' Isaac said. 'You've seen him around?'

'Once or twice, but he moves in elevated circles now. He's not the sort of person to get down the local pub of a night for a pint with his cohorts. Strictly upmarket is McIntyre, a box at Ascot during the season, seats at the opera, the best of everything.'

'When I was younger, he was a rough man who swore profusely, maimed anyone who got in his way.'

11

'He still is,' Bridget said. 'I've compiled a report. The relationship with his daughter is tortuous, and it's believed they've not spoken for several years.'

'Wendy, any more to add?' Isaac asked.

'I'll check out where McIntyre goes, get a feel for the man. You'll be off to meet with Matthews' widow?'

'We will.'

'Hamish McIntyre didn't kill Marcus Matthews,' Bridget said, looking up from the folder in her hand.

'Why's that?' Larry said.

'If the date of death is confirmed as 13 September 2013, then McIntyre was not in the country.'

'Where was he?' Isaac said.

'Majorca,' Bridget said, smug because she had the facts. 'I've checked, and he exited England on the twenty-fifth, returned on 14 October 2013.'

'Long enough to establish an alibi,' Larry said.

'Hamish McIntyre had a broken leg. He'd been in a car accident, and the hospital records haven't been falsified. He couldn't have climbed those stairs with his leg in a cast.'

'Where is McIntyre now?'

'He rarely comes into London, preferring to stay at his house in Kent.'

'If he wants to pretend to be the country squire, it doesn't alter the fact that the man's a criminal.'

'No one's been able to prove that conclusively for a long time. His last conviction was in 1996, served two years for robbery, a building society in Croydon,' Bridget said.

'Two years? That's not a long time,' Larry said. He had seen it all before, a smart lawyer, a villain with money, the ability to intimidate witnesses, to pay them off if necessary, and murder became a minor and unfortunate affray.

'One of the other gang members was sentenced for seriously wounding one of the building society's employees with a baseball bat,' Bridget said. 'Everyone in the place, employees and customers, gave statements at the scene that the man had spoken with a Scottish accent, whereas the man who was convicted was from London, full-on Cockney.'

'A travesty of justice?'

'No one would stand up in court and repeat what they had said at the crime scene, and the gang members had all been masked.'

'Two years, why not an acquittal?' Wendy asked.

'A police car had been passing by. They saw McIntyre pull away from the scene, two others in the car. There was no denying he was involved. He stuck to his story that he had been outside in the car, and yes, he admitted to his part in it.'

'He couldn't get out of it totally,' Larry said.

Chapter 3

It wasn't often that houses stayed unoccupied in Kensington. For one thing, their values were so high that whoever owned them rented them out, renovated them or sold them.

136 Bedford Gardens, a detached Victorian house, was an exception. There was nothing to mark it out from the other homes in the street, apart from its advanced state of decay.

Charles Stanford, the owner, had been traced to an address in Brighton, a seaside resort in East Sussex.

It was the second day of March, and as Isaac and Larry drove along the seafront in Brighton, saw the waves and felt the blast of the cold wind coming off the English Channel, they were not in the mood for ice cream or candy floss.

Isaac had brought Larry Hill into Homicide after they had met on a previous case. Larry had impressed him, not only with his professionalism but also with his astuteness in seeing through the evidence presented and drawing alternative conclusions; conclusions which had turned out to be right. It wasn't a burglar or a predator who had killed a woman in her apartment, her naked body untouched apart from her head being thrust into a bath filled with water. It was her older lover, a man who never saw justice, becoming the victim of an ordered assassination.

Isaac knew Larry to be an asset, but the man came with baggage, not known initially. Detective

Inspector Larry Hill was an alcoholic. It could be controlled by Isaac reading him the riot act and his wife withholding favours in the bedroom, making him sleep on the sofa downstairs.

'Stanford's a man who lives off the grid. A place in Kensington worth millions, yet he appears to live a reclusive existence. That's according to what I could find out from his local police station,' Isaac said. His words proved to be accurate; Stanford had an upmarket address to the north of the city, in Preston Village, named after the manor house that had existed since the thirteenth century and had been rebuilt in 1738 in the Palladian Style. The manor house, reputed to be one of the most haunted buildings in Britain, did not interest the police officers; although a dingy and rundown house three streets away did.

Isaac and Larry could not believe the aberration. Amongst the elegant houses in that area was an unpainted and unloved building. At the side of the house, a driveway with an old wooden garage at the end of it, the doors falling off their hinges. In the front garden, the detritus of years.

Isaac, a fastidious man, did not want to go any further, but he had no option.

Larry raised the large brass knocker on the front door and slammed it down hard. After what seemed an eternity, a voice came from inside the house. 'What do you want?'

'Detective Chief Inspector Cook, Detective Inspector Hill,' Isaac said. 'We have a few questions for you.'

'I've broken no laws. Go away!'

'Are you the owner of a house in Bedford Gardens, Kensington?'

'I own a lot of houses.'

'Your name is Charles Stanford?'

'I mind my own business; I suggest you do as well.'

Outside the house, on the pavement, an old woman stood. She was dressed for the chilly weather, in a warm coat and a woollen hat.

'He doesn't come out often,' she said. 'You've seen around the place. You're from the council, another order to clean up, is that it? Not that you'll have any more luck than the others. The only way is if you come here with a gang of men and do it yourself.'

'We're here to see Mr Stanford,' Larry said. 'We're not from the council; we're police officers.'

'If it's as bad in there as it is out here, then the best of luck,' the woman said as she continued walking down the street.

Isaac knocked on the door, this time with more gusto than Larry had.

'I'm coming,' an exasperated voice shouted. 'Can't a person be left alone?'

The door eventually opened. 'Now, what do you want?'

'136 Bedford Gardens, Kensington. Are you Mr Stanford, the owner of that property?'

''It's one of mine,' Stanford said. A dishevelled man, he looked destitute and without a penny to his name. But Bridget Halloran, the department's internet aficionado, had found out that the man owned at least twelve such properties.

'It's been empty for a long time.'

'More years than I care to remember.'

'May we come in?' Isaac asked.

Outside on the street, another woman and her dog had appeared.

'Don't let that mutt defecate on my pavement,' Stanford shouted.

Not that it would have made any difference from what Isaac and Larry could see.

Inside the front room – entry had been granted – the curtains hung in shreds. At the rear of the room, magnificent in its heyday with its decorative ceiling, stood a bookcase full of books, some neat and in rows, some thrown on top of each another. An open fireplace held centre stage in the room; in the past, a log fire would have burnt there, but not today. The room was freezing cold, and Isaac and Larry both hunched their shoulders and buttoned up their jackets. Stanford made no reference to the cold, dressed as he was in tracksuit bottoms, a tee-shirt that had possibly been white once and a dressing gown.

'What is it with Bedford Gardens?' Stanford asked. He had sat on one of the sofas in the room; a cat, previously asleep on a window sill, taking what heat it could from the weak sun shining through the window, came up close to him, wanting to be allowed to get on his lap. 'Get away,' Stanford said as he pushed the animal roughly to the ground.

'How long has it been empty?' Larry said. It wasn't the first house of a recluse he had been in; it was the worst, though. The smell of the cat, flea-infested as Stanford had said, was overpowering. Cobwebs hung from a chandelier in the centre of the ceiling.

'Ten, maybe twelve years,' Stanford said. He kept his head low, avoiding eye contact. He had not proffered a hand when the police officers entered, and no cup of tea was likely to be forthcoming.

'Do you live on your own?' Isaac asked.

'I don't like people. State your business and leave.'

'Marcus Matthews. Does the name mean anything to you?'

'Not to me.'

'We found him on the top floor of your house in Bedford Gardens, or what remains of him. He's been dead for six years, and you're the only one with a key to the place.'

'It's the land I want, not the house.'

'You could have demolished it.'

'Why?'

'How else could you get the land?'

'Buy cheap and wait my time.'

'Twelve years?'

'I'm in no hurry, and if you'd checked, you would have found out that 136 Bedford Gardens has structural problems.'

'Why land? Why not fix the house?' Larry asked.

'I don't see why I'm telling you this, but you're here now. Planning permission won't allow me to knock it down, too many rules and regulations, preserving England's heritage and whatever else. Nonsense if you ask me, but then again, I suppose you're not interested. Why should I spend money fixing the place up when it's easier to sell the land unencumbered?'

'The question remains,' Isaac said, 'as to why you're not concerned that Marcus Matthews is dead on the top floor of the house?'

'You're asking the wrong person.'

'Who would be the right person?'

'I'd find myself a smart police detective and ask him. Why don't you just do that and leave me alone?'

'A smart police officer would ask the owner, wouldn't they?'

'Then you've had a wasted trip. I don't know how he got there, and as to why, I don't care.'

Chapter 4

A visit to Stanford's local police station and a conversation with Inspector Wally Vincent, a smartly-dressed man in his early forties, had revealed the following about Charles Stanford. He was eccentric, he only left the house every ten to fourteen days, he was the bane of the local council and his neighbours.

'He's not a murderer,' Vincent said. Isaac instinctively liked the man, a professional; Larry did not. Although what Larry didn't like, which Isaac could see, was that Larry Hill and Wally Vincent were, in terms of experience and age, very similar, but one was lean and fit, the other was suffering the effects of alcoholism.

To Larry, Vincent represented a threat.

'How can you be so sure?' Isaac asked. The three of them were sitting at Vincent's desk in the police station. The top of the desk, as the man, was neat, not a thing out of place. The impression that it gave was that this was a man on top of his game.

'We keep an eye on him. Not me particularly, but there's a file as long as your arm, the times a neighbour made a complaint, the times he has. There's not much we can do, and as long as he's not violent, there's not much that can be done. And if he wanted to get some barking dogs, then the neighbours can complain all they like. We're paper tigers to him, and he knows it.'

'You know that the man's wealthy?'

'We do.'

'We found a body in one of his houses,' Larry said. 'We believe there must be a connection between the dead man and Stanford. We need him to open up.'

'What you need and what you get are two vastly different things,' Vincent said. 'I apologise for my flippancy in this matter, but there's one thing that separates Stanford from the other eccentrics and troublemakers we've all dealt with.'

'What's that?'

'The man has been a barrister, a QC, a judge. He's highly educated, knows the law better than we do. Fifteen years ago, he started causing trouble. Up until then, we didn't know anything about him. The man has never committed a crime apart from local violations, arguing with his neighbours. How he got to be that way is not our concern.'

'You're just dealing with the consequences, not the cause.'

***

It was eight in the evening when Isaac and Larry drove into the car park at the back of Challis Street Police Station in Bayswater. Up on the second floor, the lights still burnt; burnt as they were going to for the next few weeks until the murderer of Marcus Matthews had been apprehended.

Sergeant Wendy Gladstone was the first to welcome the two men as they entered Homicide. A veteran of the police force, it was Isaac who had brought her into the department. Even after thirty years in the south of the country, her Yorkshire accent was still strong. An earthy woman in her fifties, her enthusiasm was boundless, although her mobility was suffering because of her arthritis and her health was of concern. Bridget Halloran was also present.

A few of the ancillary staff that a police department always has too many of, or increasingly too few as technology and cost-cutting take effect, beavered away in the background. Most had left for the evening; their work could be done the next day. However, Isaac was an acknowledged workaholic, even by his wife, though she had lasted the distance in their relationship when others hadn't. An attractive man, he had had more than his fair share of women over the years, and while others had not been willing to accept the hours he spent away from home, Jenny had.

Bridget handed over her preliminary report, a copy to each of the people in Isaac's office.

'A summation,' Isaac asked. It was another late night, and Jenny had already been on the phone, understanding when he said he'd be home in a few hours.

'Charles Ernest Stanford, 86 Knoyle Road, Preston, Brighton, East Sussex. The man is aged sixty-eight,' Bridget said.

'We were told he was a judge,' Larry said.

'It's all in the report. He graduated from Oxford University. He was a barrister before becoming a Queen's Counsel, taking the silk as they say. A judge at the age of forty-nine, a recluse two years later.'

'Recluse? Is that known?' Isaac asked.

'There are no marks against him. He presided over a couple of controversial cases in his time as a judge; defended a few villains as a barrister, got some of them off. One of them had his case dismissed for murder on a technicality, the police putting forward false evidence. The freed man went on and killed another man two days after his acquittal. Charles Stanford copped a lot of flak in the media for defending him.'

'The murderer?'

'In Broadmoor for life. The man should never have been on the street in the first place. But if we locked up everyone who's a threat to society…'

'…there wouldn't be enough prisons to hold them all,' Wendy completed the sentence.

'Does that explain Stanford?' Isaac asked.

'The last case that he judged was another murderer, this time a woman on trial for murdering her husband. The woman was convicted, although the case and the judgement were controversial,' Bridget said.

'Give us the précised version.'

'Yanna White, a Romanian immigrant, forty-three years of age, an internet bride. She had married Douglas White, a man twenty-one years older than her.'

'A desperate misfit?' Larry asked.

'That wasn't put forward at the trial. They had been married for thirteen years; two children, a girl of ten, a boy of eight. On the face of it, the family had been happy. That's according to those who knew them: neighbours, work colleagues from where the husband worked as an engineer; from where Yanna White worked as a store manager.

'Yanna Nastrut was degree-educated in Romania, and her English was flawless. She had been attractive when she had met Douglas; still attractive when she appeared before Charles Stanford. The media were against her from the start. Douglas White was not a misfit, as Inspector Hill referred to him. He was a man

23

whose first wife and children had died tragically in a car accident.

'In despair, five years after they died, he entered into the dating game again, but Douglas had aged, the weight was coming on, and he had never been a sociable man, more content at home with his family.'

'So he turned to the internet?' Wendy asked.

'He signed up to one of the more reputable companies. They gave him three women that matched his profile, and he started an online correspondence with them, soon rejecting two of them, choosing Yanna. They met and married in Bucharest. Douglas White's family liked Yanna; she loved them,' Bridget continued. 'She had grown up in a small village in Bacâu County, a poor area even by Romanian standards. A father that had beaten her, a mother who was distant and uncaring. In time, the father and her brothers had driven Yanna out and to the capital city. She revealed that much to Douglas's family.'

'Any history of sexual abuse from her father and brothers?' Isaac asked.

'Yanna would never talk about it, not even in her defence.'

'Why did she do it, kill Douglas White?' Wendy said.

'She hadn't been sex-trafficked in Romania, all too common from where she'd come from. At least, she'd never answer to that possibility,' Bridget said.

'It would have helped her defence if she had been.'

'She was the best witness the prosecution could hope for. Douglas White's family came forward at the trial and spoke for Yanna, told the judge and jury that the woman was of exemplary character, that she loved her children, was a credit to both her and Douglas, and that the dead man had worshipped his wife and if she had killed him, then the reason would never be known.'

'No question of her guilt?'

'The knife was in Douglas's chest, Yanna's fingerprints on it. She signed a confession that she had killed her husband in a moment of weakness. Apart from that, it was up to the defence lawyer who only had character witnesses, no substance.'

'Charles Stanford had no option but to sentence her for first-degree murder,' Isaac said.

'No option. The woman had sat silently through the trial, had shown no emotion, only showing sadness when her two children were mentioned.'

'What happened to them?'

'They were taken in by the family of Douglas's elder brother. Both of them are adult now and married; the boy's an engineer, the same as his father, the girl is a qualified doctor. Neither will talk of what happened, only that they miss their parents.'

'Yanna White?'

'She was sentenced for her crime and imprisoned in Holloway. It's closed now, but then it was a high-security facility for the more violent. She had never shown violence before killing her husband; none after.'

'And where is she now?' Wendy asked.

'After three years in the prison, a model prisoner, although she rarely spoke and never interacted with anyone, she found an open door that led to the roof of the main building. She just walked off the edge of it, fell fifteen yards, breaking her neck on impact. She was dead. Douglas's brother legally adopted the children, and they were told of their mother's death. By then the eldest was fourteen, the youngest, twelve.'

'A tragic story,' Isaac said, 'but what's it got to do with Stanford?'

'He had walked away from the law before then, six months after he had handed down judgement on the woman. There was no criticism of his handling of the trial, and on appeal, with mitigating circumstances, the woman's sentence could have been reduced.'

'Was there an appeal?'

'Douglas White's brother wanted to, but without Yanna's cooperation, what could they do. She never saw her children again after the end of the trial. Just a brief hug as she was led away. She never shed a tear.'

'She condemned herself,' Isaac said.

Chapter 5

After Stanford's home in Brighton, the home of Samantha Matthews came as an agreeable surprise. It was in one of the better streets in Hammersmith, once a suburb where those who couldn't afford Kensington lived. But now it was affluent and the houses, mainly terraces, were well maintained and worth into the millions. Larry Hill knew this better than most, as his wife had dragged him around enough open house viewings in the area. He'd admit that his wife did keep their house spotless, their children clean and tidy, although when she wasn't looking he'd often put their clothes on hangers in the wardrobe, pick up their dirty plates – they preferred to snack in their rooms – and even close the toothpaste tube in the bathroom for them.

Larry was a contented man, and whereas promotion to chief inspector was once important, he just didn't have the necessary drive. He knew his drinking was starting to get out of control again, but he knew he could not stop, nor did he want to.

Not that he was an alcoholic, he'd not believe that. He had even gone three months with no more than a couple of pints of a night, so he couldn't be addicted to the drink. It was just that he had a thirst that needed quenching, a love of the taste of beer, and enjoyment of the camaraderie and jovial banter that a pub offered. Not like his chief inspector, Isaac Cook, who was comfortable with one pint of beer on occasions, although most times he would have a glass of wine instead.

'Someone's already been around,' the lady of the house said as she opened the front door, the smell of cooking coming from the kitchen at the end of the long hallway.

'Detective Chief Inspector Isaac Cook, Detective Inspector Larry Hill, Challis Street Homicide. May we come in?' Isaac said as he and Larry showed their warrant cards.

'I've done my mourning, six years ago, so don't expect me to be the weeping widow.'

'Mourning?' Larry said. He looked at the woman, saw that under the apron she was dressed in designer clothes.

'You're right, it wasn't. One day he's there, scoffing down his eggs and bacon for breakfast, and then nothing. I thought it was another woman at first, but he wasn't the type, never was.'

'He's been murdered,' Isaac said as he and Larry sat down at a table in the kitchen. Samantha Matthews opened the oven, checked the roast beef and potatoes inside.

'I take it you want a cup of tea?' she said. She had put on weight over the years; a photo on one wall of the kitchen showed her as a young woman with a svelte figure and a pretty, not beautiful, face. The pretty face remained, and she looked like a decent woman, someone who'd be at the church helping out of a Sunday, playing cards with her circle of friends, drinking coffee at one of the cafes in the area. Yet she was the daughter of a violent man, the widow of a murder victim and minor villain. It was hard to see her in that light as she busied herself in the kitchen, preparing tea and freshly-baked cake for two men who would not be liked by either of the two men in her life, her father or her husband.

'The last time you saw your husband, could you tell us about that,' Isaac said.

'He was a good father. He spent time with the youngest, asked her what she was going to do at school that day, not that he could have helped much. You see, Marcus wasn't an educated man, yet I was fond of him.'

'You're obviously well educated.'

'My father ensured that. My mother died when I was in my teens, but my father was always there for me. I can't feel sorry that Marcus's dead, not as much as I should; I've had six years to get over him and time has moved on.'

'Your children?'

'The oldest, Grant, is twenty-one, his own man now, living with his girlfriend. I've told him that his father has been found. He took it philosophically. He knows of Marcus and his criminal record. He's not so keen on my father.'

'Yet you don't disapprove?'

'The men who walked through the door at night were family men, men who loved their children and provided for them. I didn't disapprove or approve. It was for the women to not ask questions or lecture and demand. My mother accepted that fact, and so do I. Don't expect me to offer further comment; my father did time for a robbery back when I met Marcus. After that, he was never in trouble with the law again, although he was in court a few times for one reason or another, never convicted.'

'He has a reputation as a violent man. A man who, it has been suspected, has killed, given orders to others to kill on his behalf. Does that shock you?'

'I've heard it all before. He was a hard-nosed businessman who did business with other hard-nosed men back in the past. Sure, some of his businesses were skirting the edge of legal: gambling clubs, one or two strip joints, a couple of pubs, but none of them was illegal.'

'Not socially accepted ways of making money, were they?'

'People don't care if you've got money, and my father has, so have I. No one asks questions around here or sticks their nose in the air as I walk by.'

'If they did?' Larry asked. He hadn't said much so far, preferring to eat the cake on the table in front of them, the third slice so far.

'They don't, that's all I know,' Samantha said. 'Let me go back to the day he left.'

It felt strange to Isaac. In another time she would have been referred to disparagingly as a gangster's moll, yet Samantha Matthews was the perfect hostess.

'He left the house that morning. He said he'd be back by five in the afternoon. I had no reason to doubt him. I was angry when the days and the weeks went by with no sign of him.'

'What did you do?'

'My father was better than anyone at finding missing persons.'

'The police?' Larry said.

'What could you do? Issue a missing person's bulletin. Marcus was not on your list of someone important, to be found at all costs, and you know I'm right.'

'Sadly, I'd have to agree with you,' Isaac said. 'Very little would have happened, no team of police officers checking known haunts, asking questions in the street.'

'At least you're honest. My father looked high and low, got people asking questions, sticking their noses in.'

'In time?'

'The weeks stretched to months, and I got used to the fact that he wasn't coming back. Life moves on whether you want it to or not. I resigned myself to the situation, had the occasional fling, but nothing more. The only one who never came to terms with it was our daughter, the youngest. Annie was only ten years old when Marcus disappeared. She's sixteen now, and I haven't told her yet that her father has been found. She's a sensitive child. I'm not sure how to broach the subject, and there's bound to be waterworks from her, sorrow from me. I'm sure we'll huddle in a corner together and cry our eyes out. Strange, isn't it. Marcus was nothing special to look at, not good at anything much, and if it hadn't been for my father, he'd have struggled to find decent employment, and we'd not be living here in this house. Yet we all loved him; even Grant and our other son, James, and he's more than a handful, more like his grandfather than Marcus.'

'What is it with James? He's eighteen now, any trouble with the police?' Larry said. He was looking at an empty plate now, having scoffed down the last piece of cake. Isaac had looked over, knowing that once again he and his detective inspector would need to have a serious talk.

31

'My father was violent in his younger days, and well, you know that. He spent time in the cells for brawling as a youth, and then in his twenties it was drunken fighting outside the pub of a night time. Petty by today's standards and your contemporaries back then didn't have the rules and regulations they have now. He was a troublemaker, I'll admit to that, so would he. He'd even admit that the police taking him round the back of the station and thumping some sense into him did him good, made him see the errors of his ways.'

'Or made him wise enough to make sure that his violent outbursts were committed away from prying eyes.'

'You're not here to talk about my father,' Samantha said brusquely, her pleasant demeanour temporarily absent.

'We aren't, not yet,' Isaac said.

'What does that mean?' Samantha replied.

'We know that whoever killed your husband would have been an agile man, at least agile enough to climb the stairs up to the top of the house where he had died. We've checked, and your father had a broken leg at the time.'

'My father wouldn't have harmed Marcus, no matter what.'

'Because he liked him?'

'He wouldn't have done anything to make me sad or angry. My father and I were always very close, even more so after my mother died.'

'When did your mother die?'

'When I was thirteen, cancer.'

'And your father looked after you from then?'

'We always had someone or other in the house to look after me. Good women from a reputable agency, but it was my father who was always there for me. He never missed out on spending time with me, helping me with my schoolwork, attending open days, making sure that I went on all the school trips overseas.'

'And then you get tied up with Marcus, a man of no great worth and certainly not educated or cultured to your level.'

'He had hidden depths, did Marcus.'

'What do you mean?'

'He had a kind heart. We met one night after he had lost his job and his driving licence, and I was upset after a broken romance. My father was in prison, the last time as you know for that robbery.'

'If your father had not been in prison, would you and Marcus have spent time together?'

'It's unlikely. My father always ensured that whoever I went out with was of my class, no criminals or ne'er-do-wells for me.'

'Considering your father's reputation, that's a surprising statement.'

'As I said, my father is a businessman, but one with a criminal record. He knew what that entailed, the sort of men that he associated with. He didn't want that for me. And as for those that I went out with before Marcus, the sort of men my father approved of, some of them were total bastards. But with Marcus, it was different. As I said, he had a kind heart even if he did not have the sophistication of the others. He treated me well, and he loved our children. What more could a woman ask for?'

Isaac could not discern whether it was a good story woven by a smart woman or a pack of lies. Further checking of Samantha Matthews and her history was needed.

'Can we come back to the last time you saw Marcus?' Larry said. He sat upright, or as upright as his protruding belly would allow; the tabletop and his stomach were too close to one another for him to be at more than an incline.

'He left here, and I never saw him again. It was a normal day, no arguments, no issues with the children.'

'Were there arguments?'

'How long have you been married, Inspector?'

'Eighteen years.'

'Then you know the answer. We argued, but no more or less than any other married couple. Marcus wasn't the sort of person to bear a grudge for too long, and I couldn't see the point in staying angry. A flaring of tempers, some harsh words, that was all. And Marcus never hit me, not like some of those that my father vetted. And now, if you don't mind, I think we've exhausted our conversation. Annie will be home soon, and I need to tell her about her father.'

Isaac had to concede that the woman was correct – there was no more to be gained by prolonging his and Larry's time in the house, surprisingly pleasant considering the reputation of her father.

Chapter 6

Isaac had to admit to some trepidation as he and Wendy drove up to the front door of the mansion: the man they were to meet had a frightening reputation. Larry was confined to Challis Street. After the cake-eating episode at Samantha Matthews' house, Isaac could only feel disgusted with the man. After all, he had gone out on a limb when he invited him to join the Homicide department at Challis Street.

Larry was heading for trouble, and whereas he had presented himself well in the past, now the skewed tie, the shirt hanging out, was not the image that Isaac wanted his team to portray. He prided himself on his personal appearance, each morning re-ironing the shirt that Jenny had ironed previously, always taking care to ensure that his short-cropped hair was brushed, his shoes freshly polished. To him, a good appearance was a sign of professionalism; Larry did not portray that in any measure.

On the front door of the mansion was a large brass knocker shaped like an elephant's head, which Isaac duly raised and dropped. After a short time, the door opened, a man standing there, dressed in a dark suit. It was not Hamish McIntyre, Isaac knew that from having seen the man in his teens, and Bridget had sent a current photo to the team, as well.

'Mr McIntyre is expecting you. If you'd follow me.'

'And you are?' Wendy asked.

'Not Jeeves, if that's what you're thinking. The name's Armstrong, Gareth Armstrong. I'm Mr McIntyre's butler.'

Isaac recognised the surly attitude of someone who had spent time in prison.

The two police officers followed Armstrong through the house and out to a conservatory at the back.

A man was leaning over flowering plants that were in pots on a raised platform. He looked up. 'Orchids,' he said. 'What do you know about them?'

'They're beautiful,' Wendy said.

'You must be Sergeant Gladstone.'

'That's correct.'

'Forgive me, an old habit of mine. I like to know who I'm meeting in advance. I checked you both out, nothing detailed, just entered your names on an iPad. And you must be Detective Chief Inspector Isaac Cook,' he said, looking over at Isaac.

The man removed his gardening gloves. 'I'm Hamish McIntyre. You're here about Marcus, am I right?' He was dressed in a suit, a lighter shade than that of his butler.

A firm grip, Wendy thought as the man shook their hands.

'We spoke to your daughter about Marcus,' Wendy said.

'Unfortunately, the relationship between my daughter and myself has soured somewhat in the last few years. You're aware of my love for her?'

'She made it clear that you were always there for her, especially after her mother died.'

'Tragic, Maureen dying like that, but it was quick and relatively painless. Ill health, none of us know when our number's up, do we?'

Isaac could see where Samantha had acquired her charisma. How much of her father's was feigned or real was unclear, but one thing was sure, this was not an uncouth man, not a fool, and although he had no academic qualifications, he was clearly exceptionally bright and streetwise. He wasn't going to fall for any police interviewing techniques, any attempts to disarm him, to confuse him, to make him say things he didn't want to.

'Your butler was precise when we met him, although not pleased to see us.'

'Gareth spent time in jail courtesy of your people. He has no love for the police.'

'How about you?' Wendy said.

'A drink, you must have a drink. I'll have Armstrong prepare us a pot of tea. I'm afraid we only have Earl Grey.'

'Earl Grey will be fine,' Isaac said.

The three moved into the house and sat in the expansive living room.

'Beautiful house, you have here,' Wendy said as Armstrong poured the tea.

'Continuing from where we were,' McIntyre said. 'Gareth was one of the gang at the building society. You know all about that, so we don't need to discuss it, and besides, it was a long time ago. Unfortunately, he didn't leave it at that. He's spent a few more years in prison since then, once for robbery, another time for selling drugs. He turned up here a couple of years ago, repentant for a life misspent. I took him in, gave him a job. I'd trust him with my life.'

'And your silver?' Wendy asked flippantly.

'It takes a crook to know when another crook has decided enough is enough. Or in my case, an ex-crook. Gareth's got what he wants here, a calm life, no need for any more. All the striving to better yourself, what's it worth in the end? Peace of mind is what you treasure in your declining years. That's what I've got.'

'Mr McIntyre, if you don't mind me saying, you have a fearsome reputation,' Isaac said. 'Yet you are as charming and hospitable as your daughter.'

'I'm sure you know how I made my money. I wasn't dealing with the Boy Scouts. You were either on top, intimidating others, not by violence but by the perceived strength of character, or they would walk over you. Believe me, I pushed the envelope, but I didn't break the law.'

'Some of the businesses were nefarious, socially unacceptable,' Wendy said.

'The strip clubs, that's what you mean. They were good earners in their days, but they've gone now, at least they are for me. A more permissive age now, no need for the titillation and the harmless fun they provided.'

'Were the girls selling themselves?'

'Not in the club, they weren't. If they were outside, then that was their business. As you say, nefarious, not illegal.'

'And now?'

'The clubs have gone, although I own the buildings. My money comes from owning real estate now, a less traumatic way of earning money. But you want to know about Marcus. Maybe we should talk about him.'

'Very well, tell us.'

'Samantha was mad for him. I don't know why. She could have married someone of substance: a doctor, a lawyer, even an up-and-coming politician. Still, there's no accounting for taste, and she chose him. I'm in jail for the robbery, a blot on my past.

'The next I know she's pregnant, and Marcus is almost wetting himself in the prison when he comes to ask for her hand in marriage. I'll give him his due, he did the right thing by her, and he always loved her. She could have chosen worse, but he was a petty criminal, not the person I would have chosen.'

'It was her decision,' Wendy said, remembering that her father had lined up a wealthy farmer's son in the remote part of Yorkshire where she had grown up. They had been out on a couple of dates, and although the man had been pleasant enough, and he was never going to be short of money, his conversation consisted of the weather, what crops to grow, and where to buy the best livestock. In short, the man was a bore. The problem was solved when she went to Sheffield, a large city not far from where she lived, eventually meeting her husband there. Wealth had never been an issue with him; he had none. But he had never bored her and had given her two sons. He had since died, barely knowing who she was at the end. A blessing when his time had come, and now she and Bridget shared a house, pooled their resources and headed for the sun whenever the urge took them.

'Samantha's turned out alright, and her children are a credit to her. The eldest, Grant, is hoping to be a doctor, although James is an angry young man, the same as I was at that age. But then, I turned out alright.'

'Annie?'

'Very sensitive, a lovely young woman. The spitting image of her mother at that age.'

'The day Marcus disappeared?' Isaac said.

'I met up with him, gave him some chores to do. He wasn't the ideal employee, not bright enough, but he was married to my daughter, so I made allowances. I liked him, a thoroughly decent man, although if he hadn't had Samantha and me, he would have ended up like Armstrong, in and out of prison.

'Anyway, we meet at nine in the morning. There's an issue at one of the clubs, a burst water pipe or something like that, plus one of the bartenders was helping himself to some of the money. Marcus had to check on him and take the appropriate action.'

'What sort of action?'

'The sort that gives you a sore head and a few days in bed. You can't let them get away with it, or else they'll all be trying it on. A few of the girls were into drugs, and they were always after extra money.'

'He was beaten up?' Wendy said.

'It wasn't a police matter, and if the man took his medicine, I'd let him back in the club, give him his old job again. No one ever cheated twice.'

'And if they did?'

'Hypothetical. They never did.'

Isaac knew that wasn't the truth, but it wasn't the reason they were at the mansion drinking Earl Grey.

'Marcus left you and went to the club?'

'It wasn't until that night when Samantha phoned to say he hadn't come home that I thought any more about him. I went around to her house, and then I got some of my people to start making phone calls, to make visits to the clubs and premises I owned, to trace his steps. It wasn't like Marcus to do anything silly, and Samantha thought it was another woman, but that wasn't Marcus. He wasn't the sort to fool around, not even with the girls in the clubs, and some of them were easy. The days went by, and then the months. Eventually, we all start to move on with our lives, even Samantha.'

'You never suspected that he may have been killed?'

'Suspected, I would have. But I never really believed that to be possible. Sure, I dealt with some rogues at the time, but murder wasn't part of their modus operandi. Acting tough, being tough were part of it, but kill someone and the police would start sticking their noses in, and we didn't want that. We looked out for ourselves; your people would have only got in the way.'

'What did you think had happened to him?'

'I assumed he had just vanished, the reason never to be known, but I had no reason to believe he was dead. At least I didn't want to think that, not for Samantha, not for their children.'

'The rift with your daughter?'

'Occasionally, the subject of Marcus would come up. It eats at you, not knowing what has become of him. It was a couple of years back. I was at her house and Marcus came up in conversation. It had been four years. I might have said something unkind about him.'

'Might?' Wendy said.

'Did. I told her that he wasn't worth waiting for and that she should find herself another man.'

'How did she take that?'

'Not well. She started accusing me of never liking him, and she wouldn't be surprised if I hadn't done something to him.'

41

'Had you?'

'I couldn't do that, not to Samantha. I think that's where our conversation ends,' McIntyre said. 'It's time to make peace with my daughter.'

Chapter 7

The days passed in Homicide. Isaac busied himself with reports and continued the daily routine of the early-morning meetings, the evening meeting to discuss what had resulted from that day.

Detective Chief Superintendent Goddard, Isaac's mentor and friend from the early days of Isaac's policing career, when Isaac had been a sergeant and Richard Goddard an inspector, made his presence known in the office daily.

Matthews rated low on the crimes that needed solving, so much so that inertia was threatening to permeate the department.

Bridget was to provide the renewed impetus. 'I've been checking through a history of crimes that Hamish McIntyre is suspected of.'

The consensus in the office was that Samantha Matthews had been open with the two police officers when she had been interviewed. However, Isaac, the more cynical of the two of them, wasn't yet one hundred per cent convinced that she wasn't involved in the death of her husband. A person without flaws, and considering what her father did, was always suspect; dig deep enough and the skeletons would fall from the cupboard. Yet none had fallen so far.

The quick arrest which every police officer hankers after, good for the record, wasn't going to happen this time. And murder by consent was a new crime for them to consider.

A conviction for first-degree murder seemed unlikely, and even second-degree was a long shot. Conjecture on Isaac's part as he had spent time going over the circumstances in that small room at the top of that house, trying to imagine the scene, as if he were a fly on the wall: two men enjoying a glass of wine together, reminiscing, and then one shooting the other dead.

Marcus Matthews did seem to be unique, and maybe Samantha Matthews was right that he had a kind heart and was a decent man. Isaac knew from his association with villains and his seniors, even politicians in Westminster, that education did not always make a good man, and authority, especially a lot of it, did not always make for an honest person. And give a man an aristocratic title, especially if it was inherited, then villainy, carefully concealed, was always a possibility.

It was not like Isaac to philosophise inordinately about such matters, but the death of Matthews was bizarre and unprecedented. It had even given Jenny cause to comment on a couple of occasions because of her husband's apparent detachment from her. It was true, Isaac had to admit. He always could come home of a night, late usually, leaving the work both mentally and physically back in the office, but not this time.

Isaac sat at the head of the table in the conference room that adjoined Homicide, Larry over to one side, Wendy to his right.

Bridget was standing. She pressed the key on her laptop for her PowerPoint presentation to commence. 'You can see that I've detailed all investigations into Hamish McIntyre over the years,' she said.

'His conviction for the robbery?' Wendy asked. Her right leg ached, arthritis causing her trouble, not that

44

she'd complain, although at home with Bridget she would; the reason she had drunk more than the usual two glasses of wine the night before.

'I've continued from then. Hamish McIntyre was a minor player back then. Now, he's an exceptionally wealthy man, almost a pillar of society, although as I intend to show you, he may not hold that elevated position for too long.'

'What do you mean?' Isaac said. He had to admit to being impressed by Bridget's ability to find new avenues to explore when he and the others were floundering. He believed himself to be competent with computers, but Bridget was in a league of her own. He had speculated about what she could have achieved if she had turned to crime. No need for her to rob a bank or break into a house; all she would have to do would be to open her laptop, make sure there was a cup of tea to one side, and hack into wherever she wanted, to access bank accounts and company records. Industrial espionage, blackmail, banking fraud, all from the comfort of a warm room.

'We have to remember that Hamish McIntyre is a smart person, and he always adopted a hands-off approach when violence was being meted out. The second slide gives a list of suspected acts committed on his behalf, but nothing directly linking back to him.'

'He ran night clubs, strip joints, there must be something,' Larry said.

'Disputes with the licensing authorities, local councils objecting to his activities, competitors; yes, there is. He was tough, and the councils felt the force of his anger and his legal team on more than one occasion. Not necessarily illegal, although a competitor's night club burnt down mysteriously one night.'

'Hamish McIntyre?'

'There's no direct evidence, but he was the main beneficiary in the upsurge of customers to his place. The local police suspected he was involved, but no proof, no cameras in the street or in the night club, none that worked, anyway. There's no doubt in the police's mind that it was all well organised, and the club burnt to the ground almost before the fire brigade could get there.'

'The owner of the club?'

'Overseas at the time. He never came back, no need to. The man had plenty of money, and the inconvenience of having to deal with McIntyre was probably deemed not worth the effort. And besides, there was an inference that the club had been a front for underage girls out of Ukraine and Russia.'

'Sex trafficking?'

'Prostitution, at least. Nothing was proven.'

'Any suspicion that McIntyre was involved with running women?'

'It's been put forward on various police reports, but never proven.'

'But you've found something.

'I ran a check on vehicles owned by Marcus Matthews and Hamish McIntyre over the years. I then set up a search of their movements over twenty years. There are an estimated half-a-million surveillance cameras in London alone, although I couldn't access all of those, and going back twenty years, a lot less. I ran an automatic number plate recognition on all the records I could access. A lot of them are no longer available, but some are, especially if there's a criminal investigation in the area. There was the murder of a known drug dealer back in 1999. The owner of the night club that burnt down was implicated, and by default Hamish McIntyre. Nothing was proven against either of them, and the case remains open, although long buried in the files.'

'Where's this leading, Bridget?' Larry asked, impatient to be out of the room. He needed a cigarette, and the police station was strictly no smoking.

Bridget moved forward one slide.

'It was missed at the time, and besides the dates don't correlate. Twelve days before the drug dealer, a low-life by the name of Devon Toxteth, was dragged out of the river, Marcus Matthews' car was in the street where the man stashed his merchandise. No connection to Toxteth but where we're going is more interesting. Two days after Matthews' car had been in the street, a car owned by Hamish McIntyre was there.'

'The occupants?'

'On the second occasion, Hamish McIntyre and Marcus Matthews. The resolution back then was not as good as now, and it's grainy, probably not good enough to hold up as evidence, but I'm convinced as to the car and the occupants.'

'They're in the area, what does that mean?' Wendy said. She had to admit admiration for her friend.

'On the 15th January 2002, this is three years later, a warehouse close by to where Toxteth had kept his merchandise, even sleeping there most nights, was opened by the owner. He'd been in a battle to get the land rezoned as residential. One day earlier he'd secured the permission, and he was there with another man who was going to demolish the warehouse and then build luxury

47

apartments on the site. Inside, something that was going to delay the work: a body.'

'Murdered?'

'It took some time, but eventually the man was identified as Stephen Palmer, a used car dealer. He was thirty-one years of age, and his death had been violent.'

'Hamish McIntyre and Marcus Matthews?'

'Nobody made the connection at the time. The condition of the body and the date of his disappearance – need I tell you the date?'

'The period that the two men had been in the area of the warehouse?' Isaac said.

'Exactly. They were involved. I've emailed you all a copy of the investigation into Palmer's death, including photos of the dead body. Not even his mother would have recognised him.'

'Any known associations with either McIntyre or Matthews?' Larry asked, the need for a smoke abated temporarily.

'The report will show that Stephen Palmer was a man with no criminal record and that the vehicles he sold were in good condition. There appears to be no connection to either of the two men. He was a man about town, plenty of girlfriends, but no issues there either. Some of them were interviewed, as well as some of his male friends; the man was regarded as a decent person who caused no trouble.'

Isaac could see another flawless character, but the man, he knew, would have skeletons in the cupboard, the same as Samantha Matthews had.

Chapter 8

Bridget's work had established a high degree of probability that Hamish McIntyre was a murderer and that Marcus Matthews had been his accomplice, willing or not. Although police records had shown that Matthews was a shady character, the label of violent had never been pinned against his name, not surprising considering that the man had been neither particularly tall nor muscular. In fact, the general consensus from those who had known him was that he was an insignificant little man, decent to talk to, to buy you a pint in the pub, and that he couldn't hold his drink. 'One pint was his limit,' said one of the men in the pub where Larry had conducted enquiries. The man, a burly labourer with tattooed arms, was red-faced and angry; he was also drunk and looking for trouble.

'A direct approach to Hamish McIntyre will have all the wolves out,' Isaac said as he sat in Chief Superintendent Goddard's office on the top floor of the police station. 'They would be wanting us to present our evidence, threatening legal action, and claiming that the police vendetta over many years is just that.'

'You're referring to his lawyers?' Richard Goddard said. An ambitious man, frustrated that he had not risen higher in rank in the London Metropolitan Police; down to political manoeuvrings by others he would have said. He'd not mention that he was an adroit political animal, always attending one conference or another, making sure that he was present when there were politicians in

Westminster to woo, his mentor now wearing the robes in the House of Lords. The problem for Goddard was that the dislike between him and the current head of the London Metropolitan Police was instinctive, mutual at their first meeting.

'We've no proof against McIntyre. Stephen Palmer did not die quickly, and whoever did it either enjoyed the experience or had a reason to hate the man.'

'What's the connection between McIntyre and Palmer?'

'From what we know, the two men never met each other.'

'What do you want from me? You're experienced enough not to need my advice,' Goddard said as he leant back in his black leather chair.

'I'm updating you. Palmer's murder is twenty years old, that of Marcus Matthews is more recent. And we don't know if there is a connection. If Hamish McIntyre killed Palmer, that's one thing, but he didn't kill Matthews, not because he wouldn't have been capable, but because it wasn't possible, the man had a broken leg. He would never have negotiated the stairs.'

'So trying to pin a twenty-year-old murder on McIntyre, for which you have only circumstantial evidence, doesn't help in solving the murder of Marcus Matthews.'

'That's about it. We'd never prove Palmer's murder was the handiwork of McIntyre.'

'Then find the proof, make the connection between the two men. Until then, keep away from Hamish McIntyre. The moment you go in heavy with him, you're in for trouble, we all are. You've met him, what's he like in person?'

'Exceedingly polite and charming, well-spoken, no more the rough accent and the bad language; in other words, the archetypal upper-class Englishman.'

'And the upper-class Englishman has surrounded himself with the establishment. The man has some impressive contacts. If, as you believe, he is guilty of murder, then make sure you can make it stick. I don't want our noses ground in the dirt over this one. Palmer died for a reason, find that reason. It may still be a red herring, nothing to do with McIntyre and the death of Marcus Matthews, and you may just be wasting everyone's time.'

'That's the problem. I know that we could be, but there are no leads on who killed Matthews.'

'No one in the area remembers anything suspicious from six years back?'

'None that we've found. We thought we had a lead, an old man down the street recollected someone entering the building, but he was just keen to be involved in the investigation. He couldn't tell us who he had seen, which year it was. Quite frankly, I don't think we can solve Matthews' murder with what we've got.'

Isaac had not needed to speak to his senior about the course of action he was contemplating. As an experienced police officer and the senior investigating officer in Homicide, the decision on how to proceed was his. But Richard Goddard was a friend, a mentor, a sounding board.

***

Two floors down, on Isaac's return the team were busy going over the evidence. Wendy was, as usual, struggling with the paperwork. Isaac knew that Bridget would help her out when she had a free moment, which didn't look to be anytime soon. Larry was propped up in a chair, the weak sun coming in through the window gently warming him as his eyes closed.

'Larry, my office, now,' Isaac said, brusquely. Wendy looked up from her laptop, looked over at Larry, looked up at Isaac; her expression showed that she knew what was afoot. Bridget continued tapping away at the keyboard on her laptop, the monitor to her right-hand side.

'Larry, you're letting the side down,' Isaac said inside his office.

The detective inspector rubbed his eyes, fiddled with his tie, skewed at the neck as usual. 'I've got a few things on my mind. I'll do better, believe me.'

Isaac didn't.

'Larry, you've got a good family, a supportive wife, and a good record in this department, but you're an alcoholic.'

'Admittedly, I like a few pints once or twice a week, but I can give it up anytime I want.'

'You can't, and you know it, even if you won't admit to it. I can either reprimand you, file an official report, or you can sort yourself out.'

'It's the pressure at home, to bring in more money, to study, to become a chief inspector.'

'Most people thrive on pressure. What's wrong with that?'

'Nothing for others, but it's not for me.'

'You're of little use to me at the present time. It's moderation that is needed, not abstinence. You've got to break the cycle.'

'I'll try.'

'You won't. I'm sending you for a full medical and fitness evaluation. I want to know that you're fit enough, mentally astute, and able to either stop the alcohol or to temper your need for it.'

'I need to drink. It's the one way the villains open up to me. If they see me as one of them, then they talk. I can't be there in the pub with them drinking orange juice, can I?'

'I'd agree. Getting drunk every time is not vital, though.'

'You're right,' Larry said.

In spite of his reply, Isaac could see a man in denial.

'Tomorrow at 8 a.m. you're to report for your medical. Bridget will give you the details of where to go.'

'Does the department know?'

'Not from me. It's up to you, and this is the last time we'll have this conversation. In the past, you've pulled yourself together. This time I'm not sure that you can. I suggest that you get a good night's sleep, and present yourself for your medical tomorrow.'

A sheepish man left the office. Although optimistic by nature, Isaac could not help but hold the view that Detective Inspector Larry Hill was a lost cause.

***

Gareth Armstrong drove the Mercedes from Hamish McIntyre's country mansion to Hammersmith. McIntyre was in the back seat enjoying the luxury of the vehicle, the smell of the leather, the air of respectability that it afforded him.

As McIntyre prepared to knock on the door of the house, it opened.

'I know you didn't kill Marcus,' Samantha Matthews said.

'I would never have harmed him, why would you never believe me?' McIntyre said as he moved forward to embrace his daughter, the one constant in his life, the person he loved more than any other.

'You've harmed others, why not him?'

'Because he was your husband, the father of your children, my grandchildren.'

'You'd better come in; loitering on the doorstep will only have the neighbours gossiping.'

McIntyre breathed a sigh of relief; his daughter's sarcasm meant that the rift between the two had healed.

Inside the house, an air of tranquillity ensued. It was as if nothing had occurred between the two, so fond of each other that they were. The gangster, honest enough with his daughter to allow that appellation to be applied to him, was confident in knowing that she would never condemn or criticise him for what he had been in the past, the actions he had committed, the violence he had meted out.

'Annie?' McIntyre asked.

'Better than I expected. There were tears, but she was always closer to her father than the others.'

'I misjudged him when you married him.'

'He cared for us.'

'I know.'

'Who killed him?' Samantha changed the subject.

'I've got my people looking for clues, checking old acquaintances, visiting places they'd rather not.'

'And?'

'Nothing so far. It seems he waited in that room. Why would someone wait to die?'

'Marcus had strange ideas of right and wrong.'

'Still, it's bizarre. Why give your life on a principle, an agreement made in the past?'

'There was always a side to him that I didn't understand.'

'I'll not relax until we find out who killed him.'

'The police?'

'They can conduct their investigation; I'll conduct mine.'

'And if you find out who it is?'

'He answers to me, not to a judge and jury.'

Hamish McIntyre left the house later that night. Before leaving, he spent time with Annie, sat with her as she did her school work, spoke to her about her father, her hopes for the future. Samantha watched the two of them with affection, seeing herself there with her father instead of Annie. She knew that she loved her father intensely, the man who had brought her up single-handed after the death of his wife, her mother. She knew she'd never lock him out of her life again.

***

Larry presented himself for his medical, only to be told that it was not a cursory examination: blood pressure, cholesterol, a check on his breathing. Instead, as the doctor informed him, he was to have the full medical examination, as well as a fitness and substance misuse test. He knew that he could never pass, especially the fitness test. He was an overweight man of forty-three, not a junior recruit.

Isaac would later admit that the comprehensive medical and fitness examination and tests were for his inspector's benefit. He wanted Larry back on the team in excellent condition: stamina restored, the enthusiasm of the man unbound, the good sense to look after his own well-being.

The examination and tests were a disaster, as both the doctor and Larry had expected. Isaac received a report within the hour of Larry leaving the doctor's office: blood pressure – 140/90 mmHg, cholesterol level – 230 mg/dl, body mass index – 29. The one high point in the report was that Larry's eyesight was excellent for a man of his age.

The fitness test, known as the multi-stage shuttle run test, was the worst. It consists of running between two lines fifteen metres apart, the electronic bleep progressively speeding up with each run stage until the participant reaches the required speed. Larry failed to complete the test, having to sit down and catch his breath, almost lying on the floor.

In the second stage of the fitness test, Larry fared better, in part because he still retained strength in his upper body. He managed to complete four of the five pushes of a 34 kilo (push) and 35 kilo (pull)

Isaac knew that if he presented the doctor's report to Richard Goddard, he would agree and move Larry out of the department. It was an avenue that Isaac didn't want to pursue, not just yet.

Chapter 9

Larry entered Homicide twelve hours after his reality check at the medical centre. Eight of the interceding twelve hours had been consumed by sleep, the other four with talking to his wife, who knew when her husband had something on his mind. She had wheedled the truth out of him, about how his job was on the line and that his physical condition was not good; not that she needed to be told that. The romantic interludes in the bedroom in the last year, before the children woke, had become infrequent. It wasn't that she didn't want him, but his snoring and belching had destroyed any chance of romance. Even so, he tried to reawaken affection in her, but she invariably started talking about this and that, or else got up and fussed around the house, or, if she really wanted to put him off, discussed furniture and wallpaper.

Wendy made a comment about Larry's freshened-up look, and Bridget smiled. Isaac said no more on the matter; he had lambasted the man enough.

The early-morning meeting continued, Isaac emphasising a change in tactic, an attempt to find the reason for Marcus Matthews' death, not the culprit, as they had no further leads. Charles Stanford, the retired judge and now semi-reclusive eccentric, had not been willing to say more about the house in Bedford Gardens, other than it was only still standing due to luck and not because he wanted it to.

Further discussions with Wally Vincent, down in Brighton, had not added much. Stanford, to him, was a pain to deal with, but he hadn't had reason to visit and remonstrate with him for some time, and he hoped it would stay that way. He had enough to deal with, as murders and crime were not exclusive to London; they had their own villains, drug addicts, and reprobates.

With Larry focused, or as focused as a man could be when he was carrying fifty pounds of excess weight, he left the office with Wendy; their destination, the home of Stephen Palmer's brother. He had been interviewed briefly before, but little had come of the conversation. That had been before the added focus on the case, the hope that there was a tie-in to the death of Marcus, though it was conceded by the department that that hope was slight. Marcus had almost certainly been present when Palmer died, and he had been killed since then. And the belief that if you keep digging long enough, something will turn up was current in the minds of all those in Homicide.

It was a useful gardening adage, but in a police investigation it often proved correct that the flower may bloom up above, but down in the soil, with the worms and the grubs, was where the truth lay. Not that Bob Palmer was a creature of the soil; he was an accountant.

'I know what you're feeling. I've been through this myself,' Wendy said as the two police officers headed towards Palmer's house in Oxford. It was motorway most of the way, and even though the traffic was light, there was steady rain and a light mist. The trip should have taken about ninety minutes, but as they were not in a hurry – the scheduled meeting with Palmer wasn't until 11 a.m. – the two of them stopped at a motorway café for breakfast, Larry opting for cereal and a cup of tea, Wendy enjoying her bacon and eggs, looking over at the jealous eyes of her inspector.

'It's my health,' Larry confided.

'It's your weight, Inspector, and if you don't mind me saying it, your drinking.'

Larry did mind; it was the truth, but the truth sometimes hurts.

'Why is it that what we love often gives us pain?'

'The human condition,' Wendy said, having heard the phrase on a television documentary.

'It's not so easy. I can't stop drinking, and once I start, I enjoy the camaraderie, the atmosphere of the pub. I'll miss it if I stop; if I don't, it's my career and my job.'

'My husband, when he was alive, had a bout of drinking too much, spending too much time with his drinking pals. There was me in his ear at home, and then there were his colleagues, all in need of a good seeing to, egging each other on. It was either them and the drink or me.'

'He made the right decision.'

'Eventually. He stayed at home more often, joined Alcoholics Anonymous. No idea why it was anonymous, everyone knew each other, but it worked in time. Not that he was ever free of the need and there were the occasional relapses, but we dealt with it.'

'I should join if that's what's needed. My wife is supportive, but for how much longer, I don't know.'

'Don't give me that sob story. Your wife's a stayer. She'll even attend the meetings with you if you're ashamed to stand up and admit you're an alcoholic.'

'I think I can do that, Sergeant. Thanks anyway. It's good to talk to someone who understands.'

'We all understand.'

The conversation lapsed, Wendy finished her cooked breakfast, and the two of them left the uninspiring café with its smell of cleaning detergents and greasy food.

At Oxford, the door was opened by a man in his fifties. In the top pocket of his shirt, a couple of pencils and a pen. It was clear to Larry that the man was either a total nerd or, as an accountant, he hadn't embraced the modern age of computers, spreadsheets, and online submission of tax returns. To Wendy, the man had the appearance of someone out of his time, spectacles precariously perched on the end of his nose. He looked at the two police officers, his head tilted down, his eyes raised to look them in the face.

'Come in, come in,' Bob Palmer said, speaking in a rapid-fire staccato manner.

Inside the house, he cleared two chairs covered in papers.

'A lot to do, not enough time, but that's how it is. You're here about Stephen?' he said, barely catching his breath.

'It was a long time ago,' Larry said. 'We've reopened the case, not sure how far we'll get with it. We thought you could help.'

'I didn't see my brother often. We went our separate ways after we had grown up and we didn't have much in common, other than our parents.'

'We were told that he was a sociable man, plenty of friends.'

'If he fell over in the mud, he'd come up smelling of roses, always a girlfriend on his arm, one in reserve. Not like me.'

'Not much success with the ladies?' Wendy asked.

'I would sometimes joke with him to let me have one of his leftovers, but he never did. He just told me to find my own, but I couldn't, too shy, weird.'

'You belittle yourself, Mr Palmer,' Wendy said, although she could see the truth in what the man said.

'It was a traumatic period when Stephen disappeared. Our parents were alive back then, not that they are now,' Bob Palmer continued.

'They died young?' Wendy said. She could feel some compassion for a man who found life difficult. The house, his parents' before they passed away, needed paint and new carpets, and it had been some time since fresh air had flowed through the building, the musty smell evident.

'Our father suffered from a weak heart and bad lungs, a period in the coal mines up north when he first left school; health and safety weren't so good back then. Not that he ever complained, not much, although our mother, a vibrant woman who could argue with the neighbours over any trifling matter, used to tell him to snap out of it, do some exercise, and that what ailed him was all in the mind.'

'Was it?'

'Our mother was a half-full sort of person; our father was half-empty. The day they identified Stephen as the body in the warehouse, he suffered a heart attack and died.'

'I'm so sorry,' Wendy said, choking up with emotion. She was still a sensitive soul, even after so many years in the police. It was rare, she would have admitted, as most of those who saw dead bodies, some mutilated, some minus limbs, even heads, became inured to tragedy. She remembered attending the death scene of a murdered

61

man with her DCI. She had been out at the back of the building, sick as a dog, and there was Isaac in the middle of the crime scene, blood to one side, bone to the other, casually discussing the victim, or what was left of him, with Gordon Windsor, the senior crime scene investigator.

'Thankfully, our mother wasn't there that day when our father died.'

'Why not?'

'She was a good person, tough as old boots, but when Stephen disappeared, and we always knew it was foul play…'

'Knew?' Larry interjected.

'It had to be. Stephen had no enemies, never in trouble. What else could have happened to him? He wouldn't have left the country, not with his business doing well. The office was open, and the cars were lined up outside for sale. He had plenty to live for.'

'Your mother?' Wendy reminded Bob Palmer, who was now sitting down, staring at the floor.

'After Stephen disappeared, there were months of nothingness. You can't believe how it affects a person, the not knowing. Our mother slowed down, no arguing with the neighbours, no complaining at our father. She'd sit for hours on end in the kitchen, a hard chair, not eating, only picking at her food. Five months after my brother disappeared, she was dead. We buried her at the local church, a spot reserved next to her for our father, another for Stephen, if or when he was found.'

'After he was found?'

'I saw what was left of him. Unrecognisable as Stephen, as anyone. It upset me greatly. In due course, the body was released, and he was buried next to my parents.

I was there at the service, so were several of his old girlfriends, beautiful women, all of them.'

'Mr Palmer,' Larry said, 'we have suspects for the murder of your brother, but the link is tenuous. We don't understand why a criminal element would have been interested in your brother.'

'I can't help you there.'

'We're told that he was honest.'

'He prided himself on that, and he was looking to go upmarket, to sell luxury vehicles, and the people who have the money for them don't want a fly-by-night, smart-arsed, glib-tongued hustler to deal with.'

'Let's come back to the women at the funeral. Did you know them? Were you introduced, or did they make themselves known to you?'

'There were three of them. One I knew, Liz Spalding.'

'How?'

'I was in the same class at school with her. I fancied her back then, still do, but it was Stephen who was taking her out. Jealous as hell I was back then, and there she is at the funeral, lovely as ever. She was polite to me, upset over Stephen. She had wanted him to marry her, but it wasn't likely.'

'Why?'

'Stephen was taking out more than one woman at the time, he told me that.'

'The other woman?'

'He'd not say.'

'The second woman?' Larry reminded Palmer.

'Oh, yes. There were three women at the funeral. Liz Spalding, I've mentioned. The second woman was blonde, slim, beautiful face. She seemed a few years younger than Stephen's usual girlfriends.'

'Her name?'

'Bec Johnson. She introduced herself, told me how important Stephen had been to her, how he had helped her to find herself.'

'What does that mean?' Wendy asked.

'I've no idea. You'll have to ask her. As I said, she was younger than him by a few years. At the funeral, she would have been about twenty-two or twenty-three. A pleasant woman with a lovely voice. She wasn't as upset as Liz Spalding who wept profusely through the service, and when they lowered the coffin into the ground, she was on her knees. I had to help her up, and she clung to me tight from then on, something she would never have done at school. Strange, isn't it? All those years, I had wanted her close, and then it was my brother that brought us together.'

'Together? Are you saying that you're still with her?'

'After the funeral, I hoped we would be, me on the rebound, but it wasn't to be. I never saw her again, although I'm told she married a doctor or a lawyer, had a couple of kids, divorced, remarried.'

'Bec Johnson?'

'She's still in the area, never married. I see her occasionally when I'm out at the shops. She always stops for a chat, and sometimes we have a coffee. I've no idea what it was with her and Stephen, and she never opened up about it. No doubt he was sleeping with her, but she never said as much, and I wouldn't ask.'

'Did you ask her out?'

'In my clumsy way. I'm never sure what to say.'

'The third woman?' Larry said, tired of listening to the man. He wanted facts, names, addresses, somewhere to go, someone to question, someone to arrest. Sitting there, his stomach was in contortions – the bowl of cereal for breakfast had only agitated it and a motorway café latte, no matter how expensive it had been or what fancy name it had been given, wasn't a pint of beer. He needed a pub lunch, a glass of beer, a big steak with chips and all the trimmings. He knew he wasn't going to get it.

If he had a drink before he went home to his wife that night, the first night after he had admitted that he had problems at work and he couldn't keep off the drink, then she'd throw a fit, scream at him.

To Larry, he was between the devil and the deep blue sea; he was in hell.

'The third woman?' Larry repeated the question. Palmer had a faraway look about him, no doubt dreaming of Liz Spalding and Bec Johnson, Larry thought, imagining it had been him with the two women instead of his brother.

'She sat at the back of the church, a handkerchief to her face, although I can't remember any tears. And then at the grave, she stood to the back, mouthing some words to herself.'

'What sort of words?'

'I couldn't hear, but I don't think it was a prayer. One minute she's there, and then after I had taken hold of Liz Spalding, I looked around, and she was gone. I've no idea who she was.'

'Describe her?'

'Not so easy. She was dressed in black, and her hat had a wide floppy brim which covered part of her face. It

65

also had some sort of veil. But as I said, I never spoke to her.'

'Did anyone else?'

'I wasn't looking that keenly. I had organised the funeral, and that occupied my time. And if I had been looking at any woman, not that I was that day, it would have been Liz.'

'It's important, the third woman,' Wendy said. 'Think hard, anything else about her. A mysterious woman who keeps to herself at a funeral, not looking at anyone, leaving before the end. It could be important.'

'It's seventeen years since we buried him, 3rd April 2002. He would have been thirty-four on the day of his funeral if he had been alive. Murdered at thirty-one for no apparent reason. It doesn't make for a great epitaph, does it?'

'We intend to find the reason and to bring the perpetrators of this crime to justice. Sergeant Gladstone's right, we need to find this woman,' Larry said.

'Very well. Attractive, as best I could tell. Slim, although starting to put on weight. Average height, well-dressed, not cheap clothes, black stiletto heels. An air of confidence about her.'

'What does that mean?' Wendy said.

'Some people slouch, I know that I do. But this woman didn't. She kept her head down, but her body was upright.'

'Did you see a car?'

'I glimpsed her getting into a dark blue car when she left. It was parked not far from the grave, quick getaway if you're suspicious of her.'

'Any more?

'She wore a wedding ring.'

'Engagement ring, diamonds?'

'I can't say I noticed, but I wasn't really looking. I just remembered that when we left the church to head to the grave, that she had placed her bag on a headstone and her hand was exposed. She'd had black gloves on before, but she had removed them, and I saw a ring. I didn't study her, nor her hand. It's just an observation that came back to me. Important?'

'Could she be the other woman that your brother spoke about?'

'Why would he have messed around with a married woman? He had his choice of women; married women bring complications.'

'Married women bring anger and jealousy and murder, Mr Palmer,' Larry said. 'We need to find her and to talk to Liz Spalding and Bec Johnson. We need your help in finding all three.'

Chapter 10

'It wasn't that he didn't try it on,' Bec Johnson said when Larry and Wendy met her at a restaurant in the centre of Oxford, popular with the local university students, judging by the clientele that day.

'You see his brother from time to time,' Wendy said.

'I can't say I know him that well, not that anyone does, but yes, we meet occasionally. He likes to talk about this and that. He's a sad man. His brother was the total opposite, and I'm not sure if Bob even liked his brother when he was alive. But in death comes the regret.'

'Your relationship with Stephen?' Larry asked. A salad washed down with orange juice had constituted his lunch for that day, and it was now three in the afternoon. Bec, now in her forties, was no longer the sweet young thing she had been at the funeral. The effects of the last twenty years had aged her, although her face was clear and free of makeup. Her hair was cropped short.

'I met Stephen through my sister; we hit it off. You see, he was keen on her, taking her out, wining and dining her, taking her away for the weekend, especially if he had a decent car for sale. He liked to show off if he had a Mercedes or a BMW, and Janice, she was a sucker for men with big cars; equates to something or other, or is it the opposite, I can't remember. Not that it ever concerned me. Janice lives in America now, has done for many years.'

'He wasn't going to succeed with you, was he?'
Wendy said, more perceptive than Larry.

'I like men as friends, not as lovers. That's the way
it's been since I was thirteen. Nothing wrong with it, and
Stephen didn't care either way. I was sixteen when we first
met, before he went to London, although we kept in
touch, spoke all the time on the phone. He liked to talk to
women, sometimes just as friends, other times, well,
you've been told about him. The man was incorrigible,
although always charming and courteous, and generous
with the woman. Some men treat the women as if they're
chattels, but not Stephen. Always opening the door for
them, complimenting them. He was someone I could talk
to when I had a broken heart, a shoulder to lean on. My
parents abhorred what I had become, chastised
themselves for my upbringing, wondering where they had
gone wrong.'

'Your relationship with your parents now?'

'Terse. Nothing said, not any more, but they never
want to meet my partner, and we've been together for
sixteen years, joint ownership of this restaurant.'

'We need your help, Bec,' Larry said.

'How? I'm not sure how I can help.'

'At the funeral, Bob Palmer mentioned three
women. You're one, then there was Liz Spalding. We
intend to have the same conversation with her soon
enough. There was a third woman who kept to herself,
didn't speak to anyone, and left before the proceedings
had ended. Do you remember her?'

'It was a long time ago, and I wasn't in a fit
condition to look at anyone.'

'According to Palmer, you held it together,
although Liz Spalding didn't.'

'Liz, she was a friend of Janice's at school. She was living up in London at the time, going around with Stephen. She's the emotional type, tears at the drop of a hat. As for me, I keep it bottled up, but I was as upset as she was.'

'The other woman?'

'I vaguely remember someone, but that's all. I'll try to think back to then after you've gone, but I'm certain I won't be able to help you. Sorry.'

***

Even after the early-morning meeting, the drive to Oxford, the interviews with Bob Palmer and Bec Johnson, and then the journey back to London in the pelting rain, Isaac still expected the two officers to be in the office for a debriefing.

It was nine thirty in the evening, and even though their DCI had apologised for bringing them into the office, he had been adamant about the need to meet regularly. Wendy had no issue with it, as she had managed to grab a hamburger at McDonald's on the way down the motorway. Larry, determined to eat a salad at home with his wife, was feeling miserable; his body ached, his head throbbed, his throat felt as though he'd drunk disinfectant. If food had appeared in the office, especially one of Bridget's home-made cakes, he knew his resistance would not hold out.

Thankfully for Larry, Bridget had no cakes, not even a biscuit. The most Inspector Hill was going to get was a cup of coffee, no sugar, and a thirty-minute debrief, a run-through on the day's events and what the plan was for the next day.

Isaac's success rate and that of Homicide in solving murders were due to his diligence in leaving no stone unturned, and if that meant further work had to be done by any member of his team before the early-morning meeting, then he expected whoever it was to pull their weight and to do the necessary. Bridget had done a few overnighters, so had Larry and Wendy; none would ever complain, as to be part of a winning team was all-important to them, Isaac knew that. In the time between murder cases, perilously short as it often was, a casual atmosphere pervaded the department: the level of humour elevated, idle conversation, the chance to surf the net, the literal put your feet up on the desk and lean back.

'So, according to Palmer, this mysterious woman was married, probably having an affair with his brother, Stephen. Is that how we read it?' Isaac said after Larry and Wendy had updated him on their visit to the university city.

'It's a good enough motive,' Larry said, hoping that he could soon go home and eat something, anything.

'Then we must assume that whoever she is, there might be a connection back to Hamish McIntyre.'

'It depends if he was paid to kill the man,' Wendy said. She felt tired, and she'd need to eat before going to bed, as well.

'That's not what my research would indicate,' Bridget said.

'You'd better explain,' Isaac said.

'Hamish McIntyre is a killer, although he only becomes involved if it's personal,' Bridget said, glancing down at the paperwork she held in her hand.

'Are there examples?'

'The file that you all have a copy of shows seventeen murders with Hamish McIntyre's name pencilled in as involved. Fourteen of them classified as murder, the other three regarded as suspicious. One victim had fallen out of a building, the tenth floor, another had electrocuted himself, and the third had been hit by a car while cycling home.'

'Which ones are attributed to him personally?' Larry asked, his stomach cramping up again.

'It's in the file,' Bridget said. It was clear that Inspector Larry Hill hadn't read the file that she had given him the day before, not in detail anyway. 'Archie Slocombe. The man owned a club two doors from McIntyre's.'

'The year?' Isaac said.

'1998. Archie Slocombe, a fifty-eight-year-old male, owned a dozen or more strip clubs and gentlemen-only clubs in London and Manchester, financial interests in a dozen more. He had the financial clout, and Hamish McIntyre was eating into his empire, slowly opening clubs near Slocombe's, poaching the girls with more money.'

'And better drugs?'

'Probably, but that's not in the report. One of McIntyre's men had mysteriously died three months earlier, threw himself off a bridge with a couple of concrete blocks attached to his ankles. A suicide note was found at the scene; the dead man had recently left prison, five years for grievous bodily harm. Not one of life's gentlemen, and not missed by anyone, certainly not a man he put in a wheelchair permanently, and another a vegetable after the man with the concrete adornments, Paddy O'Hare, had slammed his head into a brick wall, repeatedly.'

'Charming,' Larry said.

'We've seen his type before,' Isaac said.

'The word on the street was that McIntyre and Slocombe were heading for a violent confrontation and that it was either one or the other. As I said, three months later, August 28th 1998, Archie Slocombe was fished out of the river, fifteen days after he'd gone missing. Either he'd been taken by a shark, or someone had gone at him with industrial tools.'

'Industrial tools?' Wendy quizzed.

'Chainsaws, angle grinders, electric drills. The police checked into it, but the mood on the street was sombre, and no one was talking, more afraid of McIntyre than the authorities. With no evidence against him, Hamish McIntyre soon acquired all of Slocombe's assets, bargain prices by all accounts. No one was willing to argue with the man or debate the price. He cleaned up, secured his fortune, bought the fancy house that Inspector Hill and Wendy visited.'

'Any more?' Isaac said.

'I think we've had enough, DCI,' Wendy said.

'Maybe you're right,' Isaac said, 'but please read the other cases against him.'

'Not if I want to sleep tonight.'

'Then tomorrow,' Isaac said. 'Let's wrap this up, meet tomorrow morning, the usual time.'

'Early,' Larry's final word that night.

'Doing it tough?'

A nod of the head from Larry.

73

Chapter 11

Liz Spalding, one of Stephen Palmer's girlfriends, and the object of his brother's unsatisfied lust, had proved not so easy to locate. In the end, Bridget found her in Polperro, in Cornwall, a small village close to the sea, picture-postcard beautiful, the sort of place that Wendy loved, the kind of place where Isaac would last for a week.

Two days had passed since Larry had gone cold turkey on alcohol and pub lunches, and he had suffered that first day and night, although the second day it had been easier, and Larry, not that he'd tell anyone, had had his wife's loving attention for the first time in a long time.

'Three times, considering another one,' Liz Spalding said as she sat in the garden of her cottage overlooking the sea. Larry looked at the view to his right, then at the woman opposite, but mostly at the woman. Even Wendy would have admitted that Liz Spalding, Stephen's paramour, Bob's fantasy, the wife of three men, the mother of two children, was a stunner. The tan on her face and arms, the perfect hair, the gleaming teeth, the firm bust – even though she was in her fifties, she looked ten years younger.

'This is our weekend retreat,' Liz Spalding said. 'Oh, yes, I remember Stephen, who wouldn't. I was mad for the man, but then he disappeared.'

'He was murdered,' Wendy said. The suntan and the perpetual smile did not sit so easy with her as it did with Larry. She could see that he was enamoured of the woman.

'I was upset when I heard. I never knew the reason he left me.'

'He left everyone. Did you take it personally?'

'At the time, but now we know it wasn't me.'

'His brother believed you wanted Stephen to marry you.'

'And you listened to him?' Liz said.

'We listen to everyone, not necessarily believe them,' Larry said.

'Yes, I wanted Stephen to marry me, although he wouldn't have unless I had been pregnant.'

'Why?'

'Stephen wasn't the settling down type.'

'An honest answer,' Wendy said. 'Now let's get down to the basics, find out about you and what you can tell us about Stephen that we don't already know.'

'Please don't read me wrong. Three husbands, another one soon enough, doesn't make me an empty-headed floozy. I've still got a brain in my head, and your inspector trying to look down the top of my blouse isn't doing either of you any favours.'

Larry averted his eyes, shifted uneasily in his chair. The truth hurt, and he'd been caught out. He was red in the face; Wendy was ready to burst out laughing.

In the end, it was Liz Spalding who defused the situation. 'I suggest we all have a glass of wine and forget what I just said,' she said. 'Shock tactics were needed. I can't blame Inspector Hill for looking, and I can't say I mind. I do, however, get upset when I'm judged, openly or otherwise, of being something I'm not. For the record, my first husband died before his time; the second left me; the third left me for his boyfriend. How I would have fared with Stephen, who knows?'

With Liz inside the house organising the wine, Larry and Wendy looked at each other.

It was Wendy who broke the ice. 'How do you feel? Or is that a silly question?'

'The woman's no pushover; hardly Bob Palmer's type.'

'She's manipulative; used to putting people, more likely men, on the spot, and then coming on coy and innocent, wheedling her way to get any man she wants in her bed. Just make sure you're not one of them, and stop looking down her blouse.'

'Not so easy when she thrusts her breasts at me all the time. She made sure that the sun was shining on her blouse; I could see straight through it.'

'If she's as hard as I just said, then why was she crying her eyes out at Stephen Palmer's funeral. It makes you think, doesn't it?'

'Crocodile tears?'

'Why not? She had Bob Palmer wrapped around her little finger, making him believe in her sadness. What if it wasn't?'

'For what reason?'

Liz Spalding returned with a bottle of wine and three glasses. Larry eyed the wine, a pinot grigio. He wasn't a wine drinker, only when his wife was entertaining the local social-climbing set at his house.

'You'd better have just the one glass,' Wendy said to him. 'You're driving on the way back to London, so you'd better be careful.'

'My second husband had a fondness for drink,' Liz said, having overheard the exchange between the two officers.

'Did he stop?'

'It was either the bottle or me; it didn't stop him, in the end, walking out on me.'

Larry said nothing, careful to avert his eyes. Wendy could see that the woman was a tease. Larry, even if he had been there on his own, would have left the cottage with no more than a handshake and a sore head. A detective inspector would not have kept her in the luxury that she was accustomed to, although Stephen Palmer might have.

'There are several questions that come to mind,' Wendy said as she downed her first glass. Larry sipped at his, his hand shaking slightly: the taste of alcohol was good. The desire to down it in one go and to pour another glass was too tempting. He put his glass back on the table and pushed it to one side.'

'Not to your liking, Inspector?'

'I'm afraid the opposite is true.'

'A beer?'

'Not for me. I'll just sit here while you two drink,' Larry said. 'Bob Palmer said that you clung to him at the funeral.'

'He was the nearest there was to Stephen.'

'And that he had wanted to spend time with you; that he had wanted to ever since you had both been at school.'

'He was a complete dork at school. Every spare moment, there he would be sitting down reading a science fiction book or *Moby Dick* or *Treasure Island*, or something like them.

'But not you.'

'Now I thrive on reading and the documentaries on television, but back then, all I wanted was to be with my girlfriends making silly talk, and after I turned fourteen, it was the boys I went for.'

'You played the field?' Wendy asked.

'Harmless kissing around the back of the bike shed.'

'Harmless?'

'It wasn't even a bike shed, and there were plenty of places to disappear if you wanted. Many a young lad found out about the facts of life in that school.'

'Bob Palmer?'

'Not with me, he didn't. There was one girl, a plain-faced girl with horn-rimmed glasses who was after him. No idea what happened to her, no idea what happened to my girlfriends either.'

'Is this young woman important?' Larry asked.

'To Bob, she may be.'

'Palmer is distraught, his brother's in the ground, you're the closest person to Stephen other than him. What happened after the funeral?'

'I went to Bob's house after the funeral. Bec Johnson was there, as was the vicar. We had a few drinks, reminisced over his brother. Strange how agreeable those get-togethers can be.'

'And after that?'

'I stayed that night with him. Is that what you wanted me to say?'

'We want the truth,' Wendy said.

'Stephen was dead, and Bob was as upset as me. It seemed the right thing to do. I slept with Bob that night, and left him in the morning, a smile on his face. I never saw him after that.'

'Did the experience help you?'

'Not really. Stephen was fond of his brother, not that you'd know it. He would have approved of what I did.'

'Did you approve?'

'I believe that I left that house calm. I never shed a tear for Stephen again.'

To Wendy, the woman's action, even if a little extreme, seemed plausible.

How Bob Palmer would have accepted that the woman of his dreams had loved him and left him was not known. However, it didn't seem relevant; they were there to find what they could about Stephen's death, how to prove that Hamish McIntyre had killed him. They needed the reason, and Liz sleeping with Bob after his brother had been murdered was not a motive.

'At the funeral,' Larry said, taken aback by the woman's honesty, 'there was a third woman. She was dressed in black, a wide-brimmed hat, a veil, black stiletto heels.'

'It was a long time ago, and it's not a time and place that I choose to remember. But yes, I do remember her.'

'What can you tell us about her?'

'She was one of Stephen's playthings.'

'Any more?'

'She was married, about my age, maybe a little older.'

'How do you know she was married?'

'She was my rival, I instinctively knew. I knew he had another woman that he was keen on, keener than he was on me.'

'But why? You were free, attractive, and you wanted him,' Wendy asked. It was late in the afternoon, and in another hour it would be dark. She was glad that she had put a small overnight case in the back of the car. It was a five-hour drive back to London; she didn't relish the trip that late at night.

'Why do we love certain people and not others, why did he? After Stephen's disappearance, I met my first husband, a doctor. The man could make paint peel off the wall of any room he entered, yet I loved him for his decency and his love for me. It was refreshing after Stephen.'

'He sounds like Bob Palmer.'

'Bob was a dreamer; my husband was not. He gave our children and me a great life, and if sometimes I wished he could have been more romantic, there's something seductive about being comforted in the warmth of a loving family.'

'You were married when you slept with Bob Palmer.'

'It was once; no one ever knew, not my husband, certainly not my children. I couldn't see it as being unfaithful as there was no emotional connection with Bob, no intention to leave my husband or to deceive him. It was a necessary act of compassion in a moment of weakness. Maybe you don't understand, but it matters little now. My husband died, our eleventh year, and some were good, some were not, but I had no intention of leaving him, and I never looked at another man during that time.'

'You never answered the question as to why you knew she was married.'

'I think I did. He was with me, but he wanted her. But he couldn't have her, the reason was obvious. And there she was at the funeral, the woman that I had despised.'

'You didn't confront her?'

'What for? Time had moved on, I was married, and Stephen was dead. I didn't want to talk to her, but I couldn't hate her. To me, she didn't exist.'

'We need to find her.'

'I can't help you there, and I didn't study her that closely at the funeral. I'm afraid your trip here today has been wasted.'

Wendy would have said it hadn't, in that Bob Palmer had lied about him and Liz.

The verdict was out on whether Liz Spalding was a good or a bad person. Wendy would be willing to concede that she was the first of the two; Larry, if asked, would have reserved his judgement for later.

Chapter 12

Hamish McIntyre prided himself on his orchids, and he wanted nothing more than to spend his time with them, ensuring the pH of the soil was just right, the humidity and the temperature of the conservatory were at the optimum, and that he could focus on their colour and variety, and not on the past.

Five years ago he had decided that the aggravation, the stomach ulcer, the high blood pressure, weren't worth it any more and he'd passed on to a colleague the mantle of leadership of his criminal empire. The clubs, as well as the drug importation and distribution businesses, were no longer his.

McIntyre now preferred to forget his dubious past, but he could not, because it reared its ugly head too often. It had happened twice in the past five years, and now it was happening again.

Gareth Armstrong, the ever-loyal butler, and now confidant of the gangster, had entered the conservatory. 'Hamish, the word on the street is that the police are sniffing around.' Whenever there were visitors in the house, Armstrong would not address his boss by his first name, but when it was just the two of them, then a degree of informality ensued.

McIntyre put down the small trowel, removed his gardening gloves, and sat down on an old wooden folding chair.

'What is it?' he asked as he raised a glass of freshly-squeezed orange juice to his mouth.

'Does the name Stephen Palmer mean anything to you?'

McIntyre trusted Armstrong with his life, but he could not trust him with the truth, not this time. 'No, never heard of him.'

'It's just that the police have reopened the enquiry into his death; they've been asking questions, meeting up with his brother, old girlfriends.'

'How do you know this, and why should I be concerned?' McIntyre said nonchalantly.

'The word is that Palmer was a used car dealer who was murdered twenty years ago. They're trying to pin his death on you.'

'The police were always trying to stitch me up for one crime or another, never succeeded. Why bother now? I've retired.'

'Were you involved?'

'If I were, I'd tell you, but I wasn't, so that's that. Anything else?'

'I thought that if you were involved, I could help in any way I could,' Armstrong said, purposely ignoring his boss's denial.

'Thanks, Gareth, but I'm not. Where did you find this out?'

'The police have been around to where the man died, where he's buried, not that there'd be much to see. His death was violent, so they say.'

'Gareth, don't be obtuse. How much do you know? Who's feeding you this information?'

'I've a contact, works with the police, an informer, although he doesn't tell them anything they don't already know. Sometimes he feeds them nonsense, gets paid for doing it.'

'Whoever was involved, and it isn't me, what were you told, in detail?'

Armstrong pulled up a seat. He wanted to loosen his tie as the conservatory was too warm, but he did not. He enjoyed the respectability that the position of butler at the mansion afforded him. For too many years, he had struggled, wanting to be honest, unable to be so as the cost of living was too high, the life of crime too easy. He knew, even though he was not a smart man, that the mention of Stephen Palmer had hit a raw nerve with his master. He would help regardless.

'There are plain-clothes asking questions nearby to where this Stephen Palmer lived; who were his friends, who were his girlfriends. It seems the man used to put it about.'

'What else?'

'An Inspector Hill and a Sergeant Gladstone spoke to the man's brother, met with a woman in Oxford.'

'Sergeant Gladstone was here the other day.'

'I know. I didn't like her.'

'That's where you're wrong, Gareth. You broke the law, and you know that. You were caught, you served your time. Personally, I don't have anything against the police, bribed a few in my time, frightened a few others, helped a few out for favours received, but hate serves no purpose. Treat them with courtesy and respect; fight them when you have to.'

'I still don't like her.'

Gareth had read a few books while he'd been in prison; considered taking the opportunity to complete his schooling, most of which he had skipped, considering that it was basically a waste of time, and crime was easier. To him, breaking into a shop was better than working for a company that sold it the security alarm; selling drugs on the street was more sensible than becoming a chemist. And besides, at the age of fifteen, he was making more money than the headmaster of his school, a thriving business selling uppers and downers, cocaine and heroin. He had purchased them from a Trinidadian, dividing the drugs up into smaller quantities, more in the budget of his contemporaries. His places of choice for conducting his trade were at school or the local youth club, a barn-like warehouse fitted out with some chairs, a table tennis table, a few well-used bats and a shortage of ping pong balls, the place run by a zealous and overactive vicar who thought he was achieving something, but wasn't.

One of the books that he'd read in the prison library talked of the criminal mind, not that he could understand it, too technical for him, but he had gained something from it, the types of personalities that commit acts of violence.

He wondered as he sat with his boss, not that it would change his respect for the man, what type of personality was Hamish. Was he a sociopath or a psychopath? He vaguely remembered the definitions for both traits; a sociopath had superficial charm and good intelligence, attributes that Hamish displayed in abundance. Also, the antisocial behaviour, but Hamish wasn't like that, nor did he demonstrate poor judgement and a failure to learn by experience. Gareth ceased his evaluation of his boss; he hadn't read the book thoroughly, and besides, what did it matter. And as for Hamish's denial of involvement in the death of Stephen Palmer, he didn't believe it for one minute.

***

Charles Stanford, previously interviewed as he was the owner of the house where Marcus Matthews had died, had been mainly discounted from the investigation. It was not wise to do so, Isaac knew that, but the man had no black marks against him, and he had been well regarded as a judge before he had prematurely resigned from the position. A check of the cases he had presided over, a detailed look at who he had represented as a barrister, showed no correlation between him and Matthews. But there had to be, Isaac knew that, and if not with the dead man, then with someone on the investigation's periphery.

'We've not been able to make the connection between Marcus Matthews and Charles Stanford,' Isaac said as he sipped his coffee. It was early morning in the office, and outside on the street, the rain was pouring down and the temperature was unusually cold for the time of year. Wendy's body ached, Larry's stomach rumbled, but a lot less than it had a few days earlier. It was only Bridget and Isaac who had no reason to complain.

Life was good for Isaac. His marriage to Jenny went from strength to strength, and now their talk had got around to children, the time for the two of them to become three. He had to admit the idea excited him, and he knew his parents, retired back in Jamaica, would approve.

Bridget also felt that life was good, not that she had any intention of becoming a mother; that period in her life had come and gone.

Larry's shirt was not as tight as it had been a few days previously, his belt was in one notch, and most noticeably his breath was not smelling of stale alcohol, although his smoking had not reduced, and he had brought the smell with him into the office. Another issue to address with him, Isaac thought, but there were more pressing matters.

It was a phone call later that morning from Wally Vincent in Brighton that had raised further interest in Stanford. As Vincent had put it, Stanford was becoming a nuisance again, shouting at the neighbours, establishing a no-go area on the pavement at the front of the house. The police had been there a couple of times in the last couple of weeks to remove the makeshift barriers, but each time Stanford had put them back. The man showed all the signs of someone who should be locked up for his own safety, and if he wasn't going to desist, then they weren't sure what to do. Eccentricity, madness and paranoia were hardly crimes that justified a lengthy period in the cells, and the resultant publicity, hounding a respected judge, an old man, was not wanted.

Four hours later, Larry and Isaac were in Brighton. Vincent felt like making a comment about Larry's improved appearance but declined; he had sensed the tension between the two of them on their previous meeting.

'Stanford's become a damn nuisance,' Vincent said as he ate his lunch, steak and chips, at a restaurant close to the seafront, a blustery gale blowing off the sea, a few seagulls milling around, but no tourists to feed them. To add insult to injury, Larry could see that Vincent could eat a full plate of food and still keep off the weight. No doubt the man was a drinker, Larry thought, but felt no need to comment. For him, chicken with rice and salad, small portions. It satisfied the hunger, gave him the energy to do his job, but it wasn't a meal, never would be.

And now the latest ultimatum from his wife: stop smoking.

Still, he had to admit it wasn't all bad. With his reduced intake of food, his abstinence from alcohol, and a walk around the block every morning, he was fitter and had more stamina. His wife had responded in kind, so instead of his badgering her for affection, it was her who had initiated it on the last couple of occasions.

'What makes a man such as him act this way?' Isaac asked. He had ordered the same food as Larry, but to him, the meal was more than sufficient, even if the chicken was dry and the salad wasn't as fresh as it could have been. Still, it was Vincent's choice of restaurant, although Isaac would be paying.

'I've not given it much thought. All I know is that we have to deal with it if it gets out of hand. One day, he's calm, the next he's barking mad. The latest episode, he's out on the street screaming at the dog over the road, not that it had done anything. It's a little terrier, yaps on occasions, but we all learn to live with noise and irritation.'

The problem with Stanford, according to Wally Vincent, was that one word out of order, one attempt to cajole him into behaving better, and Stanford, mad as he was, still had influence. An ex-judge, a former barrister, Queen's Counsel – allowances were made for someone with those credentials.

To Isaac, it did not excuse him from further questioning. He had a murder enquiry to conduct, not that it was going that well at all. Marcus Matthews' body languished in a cold and sterile room, not being released to his nearest and dearest, not just yet. The autopsy had been conducted, Forensics had completed all their checks, the pathologist's report, long on detail, short on useable facts, was in the hands of those that needed it. Another couple of weeks and Samantha Matthews could dress in black and be the grieving widow, even if it was six years too late.

Chapter 13

Charles Stanford opened the door on the third knock.

'This is official,' Wally Vincent said. This time he showed his warrant card.

'If you've come about that dog, you're wasting your time,' Stanford said. He was dressed in an old dressing gown; it was clear that he had not shaved for several days.

'It's either here or down at the station,' Vincent said.

'I've got my rights; I've done nothing wrong.'

'We're not here about the dog,' Isaac said. 'We need to know of your association with Marcus Matthews, also Hamish McIntyre.'

'McIntyre, I know.'

'How?' Isaac thought the man had taken one step back when the name of the gangster was mentioned. He had only mentioned McIntyre on the spur of the moment. If the connection could not be made to Marcus Matthews, then Hamish McIntyre could be another direction to take the enquiry.

'I was a judge, you know that well enough,' Stanford said. 'He was before me once, disturbing the peace or something like that.'

Isaac knew that the man was evasive. There had never been any indication that Stanford had trouble remembering the past. A colleague of McIntyre's had been up before him on a case of grievous bodily harm, the death of a man in unusual circumstances, and the jury had recorded a verdict of not guilty after the evidence, supposedly cast iron, had been dismissed.

However, whatever the reason for the verdict of innocent, Stanford had conducted the trial correctly.

'Your house in Bedford Gardens has to have some relevance to Marcus Matthews, and by default Hamish McIntyre,' Isaac said. 'We must establish that connection today.'

Vincent could see that Isaac was determined, but he had been dealing with Stanford for a long time. He knew that the DCI was not going to get far.

'There's no connection I know of,' Stanford said. 'We've been through this, now, how many times? As far as I'm concerned, the house can fall down. I've not been in it for more years than I care to remember, and I have no intention of revisiting it. Now, if you and your colleagues could leave my premises, I'd be much obliged.'

Regardless of Stanford's protestations, Isaac had no intention of leaving. The man was a hostile witness, ex-judge or no ex-judge, and Isaac would not let him fob them off.

'Then, Mr Stanford, I will require you to accompany us to the police station,' he said.

The door finally opened fully to let the police officers enter the house.

'I'll be making a formal complaint to your superiors,' Stanford said.

Isaac had heard the 'formal complaint to your superiors' many times before. He dismissed it without consideration.

'Why would I be involved in the murder of a petty criminal, a person of little worth and less importance,' Stanford said.

'Mr Stanford, we are within our rights. However, we are willing on account of your past and illustrious career to allow our interview to be conducted at your house,' Isaac said, aware that flattery would probably have little impact.

Inside the house, the four men entered a room to the right of the hallway. It appeared to be the one room in the house that was in good condition; it was the man's library and study. On two of the walls, bookshelves reached to the ceiling. A cursory glance by Isaac showed that most of the books were legal references. He was impressed by the room, but not by the man who sat down in a voluminous armchair.

'Get on with it,' Stanford said. 'I've no time for messing around with this.'

'I don't think DCI Cook is here to waste your time,' Vincent said. He liked the DCI's style, but didn't think much of his inspector. Vincent was an ambitious man, he would admit that, and London was where he should be. He'd gone as far as he could in Brighton and dealing with the likes of Charles Stanford and the other troublesome people in the city no longer interested him. And as for murders, one or two a year, and most times a more senior officer would take the case. He, Wally Vincent, would be left with little to do, and the man who invariably took the case was not competent, and the man knew it.

'It seems like that to me,' Stanford said.

Isaac took no notice. 'Mr Stanford, you've made it clear you do not know Marcus Matthews. If we accept that premise…'

'Whether you accept what I said or whether you don't,' Stanford interjected, 'is not important. I've granted you access to my house, now make the best use of it.'

Larry had not said much up until now, due in part, in his opinion, to the overbearing attitude of Wally Vincent. He felt the need to make his mark.

'Mr Stanford, we've been to Bedford Gardens,' Larry said. 'There's no way that Marcus Matthews would have chosen that house at random. He and whoever killed him must have had advance knowledge of who owned the house and the fact that it would be empty.'

'I'm afraid that you, DI Hill, have a fanciful mind for the obscure,' Stanford said. Isaac could see the man was irritable, verging on anger, and anger was a great asset in the hands of a seasoned investigating officer.

Sensing the change, Isaac seized the opportunity and raised his voice to indicate a new level of seriousness. Stanford was playing them for fools. 'Inspector Hill is correct,' he said. He was sitting on the front of his chair, bolt upright, his eyes focused on Stanford.

'I don't think so.'

Wally Vincent, not used to the approach that Isaac was taking, sat back. It would be he, DI Wally Vincent, who would have to deal with the flak; it would be he who would be called in to see the chief superintendent to answer Stanford's complaints. Even if the man hadn't been an ex-judge, a formal complaint always required an internal investigation and a response to the person who had instigated the complaint.

'We checked you out,' Isaac said. 'We're aware of your record of achievement; we're also aware that you were involved in two controversial cases, a barrister in one and a judge in the other.'

'I acted correctly in both cases.'

'But they must give you cause for concern sometimes.'

'If you must know, and I don't see why I should tell you, then yes, the last case is never far from my mind. The woman, for reasons unknown, condemned herself.'

'What do you believe was the truth?'

'Her background, where she had come from, the trafficking of women from that country to England, she must have experienced it.'

'But you as a judge had no option but to sentence her to prison.'

'I was powerless to do otherwise. And then she committed suicide by throwing herself off the roof of the building. It continues to haunt me, the anguish in her mind, the despair of never seeing her children again. Mitigating circumstances could well have given her a much-reduced sentence, but I couldn't do it, the legal system would not allow it.'

'You defended a man against the charge of murder, he got acquitted. And then the man committed another murder. How did you feel about that?' Wally Vincent said. He didn't want to be left out of the investigation, although he felt they were badgering the old man.

'Inadmissible evidence, I'm afraid. The police must accept the blame for that, not me. But yes, another person dead. It must have happened to the three of you,' Stanford said as he raised himself from his chair, went over to a bookshelf and picked up a book.

'These continuing delays can do you no good,' Isaac said.

'I have no more to say on the matter,' Stanford said as he put the book back on the bookshelf. 'My conscience is clear as to what happened in one of my houses.'

'Then, Mr Stanford, by your attitude and your reluctance to speak the truth, we can only consider you as a hostile witness.'

***

The visit to Stanford's house, regardless of Isaac's determination, proved to be a waste of time. It was agreed that either the man was up to his neck in what had happened or he was just an eccentric old man.

With no more to go on, Isaac and Larry made the trip back to London; there would still be time for the evening wrap-up meeting. This time it would be Isaac who would have to admit that he had failed in his objective.

In the office at Challis Street, four key team members sat down. Wendy had some updates, and she was keen to tell them what she had found out. Even though she had been a police officer for many years, over thirty now, she still got a thrill from doing her job well.

'I've been working with Bridget on the cars that Stephen Palmer had sold from his used car lot,' Wendy said.

'It wasn't easy,' Bridget said. 'The records from that far back are not as good as they are today.'

'Bridget persisted, and with me doing some legwork, we made a connection to one of the persons of interest.'

'Okay, let's have it,' Isaac said. 'Who is this person?'

Wendy, a grin on her face, said, 'Samantha Matthews purchased a car from Stephen Palmer, a Jaguar.'

'Is she the woman at the funeral?' Larry asked.

'It's a possibility,' Isaac said. 'Liz Spalding said her rival was a married woman.'

'It makes sense,' Larry said.

With the updated information, and Isaac keen to strike while the iron was hot, he and Wendy made the trip out to Samantha Matthews' home. The woman was not pleased to see them.

Wendy instinctively knew why the woman was reluctant to let her and Isaac into the house; Isaac did not realise at first, but soon did. She was entertaining, and she did not want a disturbance while she had a man in the house.

'Mrs Matthews, we have disturbing information regarding you and Stephen Palmer,' Isaac said. Regardless of what the woman wanted and disregarding the probable reaction of her father, Isaac did not intend to stand on the front doorstep of the house for long.

'Tomorrow, early,' Samantha said. She was dressed casually in a loose-fitting blouse and a short skirt; she looked cheap and tarty, but then, Wendy thought, that was the effect that she wished to impart to her, as yet unidentified, lover.

'Mrs Matthews, we believe that you may have been involved with Stephen Palmer at the time of his death,' Isaac said. 'We can either stand here and debate this matter, or else we can come into the house, sit down in your front room, and listen to your response as to whether we are correct or not.'

'I can give you five minutes, but there is nothing to tell.'

Upstairs, in the house, the sound of someone moving around.

'Mrs Matthews, we know there was a third woman at Stephen Palmer's funeral. Were you that woman?' Wendy asked. She had taken the direct approach; no need to procrastinate. If the woman was keen to be back up the stairs and in the arms of her lover, she would be more ready to tell the truth. And besides, she had not killed Palmer.

'I met Stephen at a rough period in my life, my marriage to Marcus was not going well. He was increasingly involved with my father and his business enterprises. I was lonely, and Stephen was a charming man. In a moment of weakness, I allowed myself to be seduced by him.'

Wendy, not as naive as the woman probably thought she was, knew that she had not been weak. Samantha Matthews was a woman of passion, and Stephen Palmer, by all accounts, was a tall, good-looking individual who women yearned for, and who knew how to treat them well. Marcus Matthews had only ever been described as a good man, a kind man, disregarding the fact he was a criminal. Wendy could understand Samantha's weakness, as her husband had been more of a Marcus than a Stephen.

'This is a serious matter,' Isaac said. 'You decided to keep this information secret. Why?'

'It's not something a woman is proud of,' Samantha said.

'And now you have another man upstairs in your bed,' Wendy said. 'You must have had concerns when Palmer vanished.'

'I know what you're thinking, but I'll not believe it of Marcus or of my father.'

Wendy could see she was increasingly agitated to get her and Isaac out of the house. The previous good impression that the woman had given was rapidly being diminished.

'Why did you attend the funeral?' Isaac said. He had never been as enamoured of Samantha Matthews as Wendy was. She was the child of a vicious man, even if she was not vicious herself, and she must have known what the man was capable of, what he had done in the past.

'He helped me out in a difficult period of my life. I had to pay my respects,' Samantha said.

'For three years, you believed that he had vanished, but at the funeral you were under no illusion as to what had happened. He had been murdered.'

'Yes, I knew.'

'But you didn't suspect your father?' Isaac asked. His patience was rapidly wearing thin.

'Three years had passed, Stephen was dead, life was good.'

'It's hardly a reason not to believe that your father was responsible.'

'It was to me,' Samantha said flatly. She was a convincing liar, Isaac had to admit. She knew the truth, but why had she not confronted her father at the time of Palmer's disappearance, and then, why not when the man was found dead in a warehouse.

Isaac could only believe that Samantha Matthews, in spite of her education, her social standing, her affluence, and the fact that she had never been in trouble once in her life, was no different to her father. It was clear that the affection that Samantha and her father felt for each other was well-founded. Both of them sickened him down to his gut.

It was not possible to get any more from the woman; she had admitted to her affair with Stephen Palmer, but nothing else.

Isaac and Wendy left the house to Samantha Matthews and her fancy man.

Outside, Wendy took a phone from her handbag and dialled Challis Street Police Station. Surveillance would be placed on the house; they needed to know the name of the man in Samantha's bed.

Chapter 14

Dean Atherton, a small-time crook and part-time police informer, updated Armstrong on the police investigation. The two men met in a pub not far from McIntyre's mansion.

'How do you get all this information?' Armstrong said. He was dressed casually, his day off. The suit and tie were gone; in their place a pair of beige trousers and a blue shirt, open at the neck.

Atherton, an unusually thin man – he said it was something to do with his genes – drank his first pint in one gulp. Armstrong looked over at the barman and lifted his glass, an indication for two more pints.

'I keep my ear to the ground, that's all,' Atherton said. Armstrong liked the man; they had both shared a cell in Maidstone prison five years previously, and while it was luck who you shared with, he had struck lucky that time.

During the hours of darkness in the small cell, the two men had recounted the stories of their lives and how they turned to crime. Atherton had tried to avoid prison, but his family, including his mother and father, regarded crime as a vocation.

He had been a bright student, Atherton said in that small cell, but his parents had not encouraged him to continue his studies beyond the age of fifteen. And then, as he was taking stolen goods across the city in his backpack, the police had caught him, a conviction as a juvenile offender against him. After that, the opportunities to study, the enthusiasm to continue, were gone.

Three years later, one week before his nineteenth birthday, Atherton was convicted for the more severe crime of robbery, receiving a two-year sentence, out in one for good behaviour.

He had never been a master criminal, always skirting on the edge of the next major crime that would ensure his fortune. But it never came, and all the good hopes that he had had as a child had come to nought. Life for him now consisted of a small and dreary one-bedroomed flat, three floors up, no lift. Still, the man was philosophical about his fate, and as long as he had food in his belly and enough for the occasional flutter on the horses and an occasional beer, he wished for no more.

Armstrong identified with the man's outlook on life. However, he had Hamish McIntyre, a decent place to live, a weekly salary, the chance to drive Hamish's cars, and the best food to eat.

'What's the latest?' Armstrong asked.

'Chief Inspector Cook has a good reputation. He's not a man who gives in easy, and if he believes that Hamish McIntyre is involved in the death of either Matthews or Palmer, he'll not give up until he has the truth.'

'Hamish is not involved; he's given me his word.'

'And you believe him?' Atherton said, a look of disbelief on his face.

'We need to protect him, you and I.'

'I don't see what it's got to do with me.'

'Maybe you're right, but I don't intend to allow the man to be convicted of crimes he hasn't committed,' Armstrong said.

'If McIntyre is forced into a corner, he'll come out fighting, so will you. I hope he'll remember those who had helped him. Me, for instance.'

Armstrong knew what Atherton was referring to. Hamish McIntyre was a man who looked after his friends, but not his enemies.

'Did you know Samantha Matthews was screwing Stephen Palmer?' Atherton said.

'And if she was?'

'It's a motive for murder, don't you think?'

***

Wendy was angry that the two constables she had assigned to keep an eye on Samantha Matthews' house had missed the man who had been upstairs.

'He must have known we were there,' the ginger-haired Constable Gerry Hammond said. Wendy had seen him around the station, yet the first time she had given him an easy job, he had fluffed it.

Constable Nick Entwistle hadn't fared much better, but then she had never been impressed by him. Six years in the station, he had not yet made it to sergeant, and it looked as though he never would. For one thing, even though he was only in his twenties, his weight was starting to increase. The once fit and active man who used to run competitively at the weekends changed after he was shot in the leg while apprehending an armed man. He had received an award for bravery, but now that was forgotten, and the enthusiasm that he had once displayed was long gone.

'He must have gone out the back door,' Entwistle said. 'We were there all night. He must have left around two or three in the morning.'

'Where were you two? Asleep?' Wendy quizzed.

'There was a Volvo parked around the back, and it was there most of the night, but in the early morning it was gone.'

'We passed the registration number on to Bridget Halloran,' Hammond said.

'Let's hope you're right,' Wendy said.

The two constables' failure wasn't the only disappointment that day; Larry had failed to make the early-morning meeting, only walking in at 10 a.m.

'In my office, Larry,' Isaac shouted from his office.

'Sorry about the late arrival,' Larry, looking bedraggled, said as he sat down.

'Close the door. I don't want the whole department hearing what I have to say to you.'

'It was a rough night.'

'Another drunken night, and how many more of these do you intend to have?'

'I was trying to get leads, and you know how it is. I have to drink with them, my informers, the criminals, those who know something.'

'We've spoken about this before on too many occasions. I've been tolerant, but I can't continue to overlook what you keep doing, not even for the sake of the department. Your wife, what has she got to say?'

Larry shifted uneasily in his seat.

'Your wife? You never answered my question,' Isaac said.

'She wouldn't let me in the house. I tried to explain that it was a murder enquiry, and I was only doing my job.'

'I can't blame her,' Isaac said. 'No woman would tolerate what you're putting her through. Where did you sleep?'

'In the car, the only place.'

'Will she let you in the house now?'

'I hope so.'

'So do I. I need you fit and ready for service. You've got two hours to go home, have a shower and brush your teeth, and whatever you do use plenty of deodorant. We need to raise the pressure on Samantha Matthews, and probably Hamish McIntyre.'

***

Liz Spalding walked down the lane from her cottage to the village not far away. It was a pleasant day, and the sun was shining, although there was a cool breeze coming from the sea. The visit of the two police officers, the reopening of the investigation into the death of Stephen Palmer, had caused her to reflect on the past and query the present.

She had not altogether been truthful with the police. She had told them that she had been fond of Stephen, had even loved him, not that she had been obsessed with the man, desperate for him to marry her, but he had another. How she hated that woman, and yet at Stephen's funeral she could do nothing but stare at her, not able to say one word to her.

The new man in her life was coming that night; she wondered if she should continue with him. After

Stephen's death, she had married soon after, a good and decent man, but it had not been the same, not as it had been with Stephen.

'Good day for a stroll,' an old and arthritis-riddled woman who was passing said.

'It sure is, Mrs Venter,' Liz said warmly. The old woman, Liz knew, was the local busybody, but she was regarded as harmless by the local community.

Liz continued walking down the lane; it wasn't that far from the village, but it was downhill. On the way back, it would not be so easy, and she would be carrying supplies from the local supermarket.

She decided to sit down on a rock at the side of the lane, with a view out to sea; a sailing boat, its sails unfurled, could be seen in the distance. Closer inshore, two fishing boats were returning with their catches.

As she sat there, reflecting on the beauty of the place, another woman came and sat down by her side.

'It's beautiful down here,' the woman said. Liz could tell she was not a local; she assumed she was another person down from the city looking for a holiday home in the area.

'I'm thinking of staying here myself on a more permanent basis,' Liz said. There was a familiarity about the woman. It puzzled her.

'I've only come for one reason – to see you.'

It was then that Liz made the connection; it was the mysterious woman from the funeral, the woman who had kept her away from Stephen; it was her rival.

'It's been a long time; do we have anything to talk about?'

Liz wasn't sure what else to say or what to do.

'I loved him, the same as you,' Samantha Matthews said.

'It's been twenty years; the past is the past, and no amount of recriminations or sadness will bring him back.'

'I had to see you one time to explain what happened and why he had died.'

'Does it serve any purpose, our meeting like this?'

'My father found out I was having an affair with Stephen, you know that?'

'No, I didn't, why are you telling me this? Of what use is it to me?'

'My father killed him, and now the police want to know the truth, but I can't tell.'

'What do you intend to do?'

'I only know of one certainty at this time. What happens today will decide my actions hereafter.'

'I never knew your name,' Liz said. She felt calm sitting next to the woman, as if time had somehow transmuted the woman into a friend.

'Samantha. My father is Hamish McIntyre, have you heard of him?'

'I can't say that I have,' Liz said. She wasn't sure where the conversation was heading.

'My father is a criminal. I have always known what he is, and he has always treated me well.'

'But he killed Stephen. And now you have told me the truth. What do you expect me to do? Tell the police?'

'My father taught me well. Those we love, we love with an intensity; those we hate, we do not allow to live.'

Samantha stood up and snatched Liz roughly from where she was sitting. The woman wrapped her arms firmly around Liz's body from behind. Taken by surprise, Liz struggled to comprehend what was happening, her feet dragging on the rough ground. In the distance, the sailing boat continued to bob in the sea; closer inshore, the two fishing boats had entered the small harbour. Sheep grazed in the field, taking no notice of the two women, one attempting to scream but unable to.

'You're the first,' Samantha said. 'You may not be the last.'

With the last of her strength, Samantha lifted Liz off the ground and threw her off the cliff to the rocks below.

Chapter 15

Constables Hammond's and Entwistle's attempts at surveillance had proved to be a total disaster; they had also failed to identify the man's car correctly.

It was a soon-to-be irate man who had answered the door of the house in Hampstead, only to be told that his car had been parked in the road at the back of his business partner's home on the night in question. Not only that, he'd been on a business trip overseas and his wife, who clearly had been cheating on him, had the keys to the car while he'd been away.

Tricia Anders was the femme fatale who had spent the best part of the night in her lover's bed, only arriving home in time to welcome her husband back after his long trip, no doubt full of platitudes of how she had missed him.

Wendy had to chuckle to herself at the thought of the previous night's assignation. Tricia Anders was no spring chicken; she was in her sixties, although she looked good for her age. It gave Wendy hope that somewhere there was still someone for her.

'You've got this all wrong,' Tricia said. Her husband sat on the other side of the room, staring at her. When he had first learnt the truth, he had wanted to grab hold of her, but Larry, freshly groomed after the dressing down by his DCI, had positioned himself between the two.

'Whatever the reason for you being parked in that road last night is not our concern. What's important is if you saw anybody else in the street. Do you know the woman in the house to the left of where you were?' Wendy said.

Tricia Anders replied weakly, 'No.'

'The woman's husband was murdered. His body was discovered recently.'

'Is this important?' Harry Anders asked.

'Mr Anders, you will have to bear with us,' Wendy said.

Wendy focused on Tricia Anders and went over and sat close to her. 'You need to think back,' she said. 'Was there anything unusual that you can tell us?'

'Apart from her making a fool of herself,' her husband said.

'Mr Anders, we have a murder investigation. If it's not possible to undertake that in this house, then we will have no option but to reconvene at the police station.'

Harry Anders sat back on his chair. He averted his eyes from his wife and looked down at the floor.

'After we've finished, we'll talk to Brian Jameson,' Larry said.

'He'll not be able to tell you any more than I can,' Tricia said.

'Too busy screwing you,' Harry barked.

'I'm afraid we have to focus on our murder enquiry, Mr Anders.' Wendy said. 'The situation here is domestic, not criminal. Mrs Anders, coming back to you, what time did you leave Brian Jameson's house?'

'Just after two in the morning. Harry was due back in the country at five, and then he'd take a taxi to the house. I thought he would be here just after six in the morning, although his flight was delayed and he came in just after eight.'

'How often have you been in Brian Jameson's house at night? How long have you been involved with the man?'

'I was lonely, and Harry's overseas a lot.'

'That wasn't the question. How long?'

'Five, maybe six months.'

'Did you always meet at his house?'

'Not always, but I've been there a few times.'

'Have you at any time seen a man come out of the next house at unusual hours?'

'I've not been looking, and most nights, Brian comes with me to the car to check that I'm fine.'

'Why?'

'The guilt, I suppose. I always feel afterwards that I've wronged Harry. He's not done anything, only not been in the house when I've needed him.'

***

Brian Jameson did not appreciate the presence of two police officers on his doorstep. However, he opened the door and let them in.

Both Larry and Wendy had shown their warrant cards, although the man knew who they were, why they were there, and their names.

'You've made life difficult for Tricia,' Jameson said. He was an older man than Harry Anders, balding on top. He also carried more weight than he should, and he did not look healthy, his skin blotched.

'This is a murder investigation, and you and Mr and Mrs Anders have been caught in the middle of it. How you and they resolve this situation is not our concern. What is important is what you might be able to tell us about the house next door,' Larry said.

'I don't often speak to Samantha, but I do know her. I've always found her to be a pleasant woman, and her children have always been polite and courteous.'

'Are you aware of her history?'

'If you're referring to her father, then yes.'

'Marcus Matthews?'

'I knew Marcus, and sometimes we had a drink at the pub together. He wasn't a big drinker, neither am I, but I found his company pleasant.'

'Did you know that he had a criminal record and that Samantha's father is regarded by the police as a dangerous man?'

'I knew the history of both men. Now let's get to the crux of the matter. What is it you want from me?'

'How do you know so much about Samantha's husband and her father?' Wendy asked.

'You spoke to Harry; didn't you ask him what his business was?'

'Not specifically. We know he's involved with IT.'

'We're involved with data security. Harry gets the business, and I deal with the technical side. I researched Samantha and her family after Marcus gave me some insights.'

'Why would you want to know about your neighbours?' Larry asked.

'No persuasive reason, but when Marcus disappeared that time I checked further into the family. I already knew Marcus had a criminal record. He had told me that once down at the pub, and he'd let on that his father-in-law could cause trouble.'

'Did you ever meet Hamish McIntyre?'

'Once or twice, and on both occasions he was friendly. I can't say that I spent time with the man or indulged in any lengthy conversations.'

'Are you aware that Samantha Matthews has a boyfriend?'

'I've seen a man there on several occasions, but what's his importance? He's only been coming around for the last nine months or thereabouts.'

Wendy could see that Brian Jameson was a more astute man than Harry Anders, and if the man knew more than he was saying, it would not be easy to prise it from him.

'Do you know who he is?'

'I know his car. Why don't you ask Samantha? After all, Marcus disappeared six years ago. What's wrong with her having a man?'

Neither Larry nor Wendy wanted to state that the reason they had not questioned Samantha directly was that she could still be involved in the death of Marcus.

'Can you give us a detailed description of the man's car?' Wendy said.

'It's a late-model BMW. I take it you want the registration number.'

'If you could.'

'I was on the street taking a photo of my car. I was trying to sell it, and the boyfriend's car was parked in front. I'll send you the picture.'

***

True to his word, Jameson emailed the photo of his car, Samantha's boyfriend's car visible in front of it. Wendy forwarded the picture to Bridget, using her smartphone.

In the office, Isaac was waiting for Larry and Wendy on their return. 'I hope you've both packed an overnight bag,' he said.

'What is it?' Wendy asked.

'Liz Spalding. She's been found dead.'

'Murdered?'

'The crime scene investigators are checking, so are the local police, but yes, it's murder.'

'Any clues?'

'Not yet, but the crime was committed in an open space. There's a strong possibility that somebody might have seen something. I'll stay here in the office, deal with whatever comes in, with whatever you find. You'll be meeting with a Detective Inspector Greenwood. I've told him that you'll be there today. And if it's late, don't worry about waking him up, he's expecting you to call. He'll be taking the lead so update him on our investigation.'

Larry phoned home, met with a gruff response from his wife, told her that he was going to be away for a few days. He knew she wasn't a person to stay angry for long and by the time he came back, all would be well in the Hill household again. Wendy had no such issues to worry about, only an old cat that needed feeding; Bridget would care for it.

Twenty-five minutes later, as Larry and Wendy were preparing to leave, Bridget shouted out, 'I've found out who the car belongs to. Have a good trip.'

The trip down to Cornwall took just over five hours, Larry and Wendy taking turns at driving. It was late in the evening, close to midnight, before they drove into the village. Inspector Greenwood had arranged accommodation for the two of them at a local hotel, a bar downstairs. Larry was determined to avoid it.

Jim Greenwood met them as agreed, even though it was late. He was a lanky man, a long thin face with a pronounced nose, not an attractive combination, Wendy thought.

'A forager down at the bottom of the cliffs found her. Sometimes items of interest wash up on the shore, and we've a couple of people in the village who like to look for these items, not sure why, as most times they only find an old can or a flotation device of one sort or another, rarely anything worth keeping,' Greenwood said.

'How long had she been there?' Larry asked.

'We leave that up to the crime scene investigators, but I knew her. I saw her three days ago up near her cottage. It's a small community, you soon get to know everyone.'

'Any witnesses?' Wendy asked.

'We're not sure yet. We're still conducting our enquiries, but it wasn't a secluded area where she was pushed off the cliff. Any reason why someone would have wanted her dead?'

'She's been part of our investigation for some time. She was involved twenty years ago with a man who was murdered under unusual and violent circumstances. We believe we have a connection to another person of interest as to why he died.'

'We questioned Mrs Venter, local busybody, harmless, friendly with everyone. She appears to be the last person that spoke with Liz Spalding. According to Mrs Venter, she and Liz exchanged pleasantries before each going their separate ways. They met no more than fifty yards from where the woman was thrown off the cliff. That was two days ago.'

'Thrown or pushed? You've not been clear on that,' Larry said.

'There are clear signs of a scuffle, one woman dragging the other. Either the murderer was stronger than Liz or caught her by surprise. According to the investigators, Liz Spalding was lifted at the edge of the cliff and thrown off. It's a forty yard drop onto jagged rocks, and then there was high tide, the body wedged in the rocks. Even after only a couple of days, it's not a pretty sight. An attractive woman, as you both know.'

'We've both met her before, and yes, she was attractive. Was she alone at the cottage?'

'It's been checked, and there was no sign of another person. There was a message on her phone. She had left it at the cottage. A man had phoned to say he had been delayed for a couple of days. We've got a phone number and a name. He's been informed. He's not been here yet, although we expect him to appear at some time.'

'Do you have a name?'

'You'll have it in the morning, as well as an update from the chief crime scene investigator. We'll also meet up with Forensics, have a chat to the pathologist as to when he'll be conducting an autopsy. Crime is a rare occurrence here, or at least murder is. Sure, we have one or two drunken youths who think graffitiing the church wall is a great pastime, but apart from that not much happens here.'

'Where is the crime scene investigation team based?' Larry said.

'They came down from Plymouth. I'm stationed there, but I live in the village. It's my patch, unofficially that is, that's why I've been given the lead in this investigation,' Greenwood said.

Chapter 16

Jenny, Isaac's wife, was not surprised when he phoned from the office, late as usual, to say that he would be another couple of hours. It was only one of the things that he loved about her, the fact that she was always sympathetic when work took precedence over the home. She switched off the oven where his meal had been heating, turned down the light, and went into the other room, to bed.

It was Bridget who identified the man from the car registration. Isaac had to admit that the man lived well, but then, that was to be expected as he was not only Hamish McIntyre's lawyer, or one of them, he was Samantha's lover. Inside the mews house, Isaac sat on a comfortable chair, the lawyer sitting opposite. The man was dressed casually; it was late at night, almost eleven.

'What do you want, DCI?' Fergus Grantham said.

It wasn't the first time the two men had met, and Isaac knew that the lawyer specialised in defending the criminal echelon in London. They had sparred in the courtroom on a couple of occasions, Isaac giving his evidence, Grantham using all his skills and wiles to devalue it, succeeding on some occasions, failing on others. Even so, Isaac could not feel any animosity towards him; even the most despicable was entitled to a fair trial. He was forty-seven years of age, and with a suntan courtesy of holidays in the Caribbean, he looked younger. He was as tall as Isaac, over six feet, and fit.

Isaac had had to give up running in his youth. He had been a promising athlete until a knee injury, but Grantham suffered from no such ailments, and he ran every day for four to five miles.

'Samantha Matthews is your lover. Is this true?' Isaac said.

'What interest is that to you? Her husband disappeared six years ago. One more year and he can be declared legally dead. I've been dealing with the paperwork for her.'

'We are concerned that Samantha is, by default, implicated in her husband's death.'

'Inspector, be careful what you say. As a lawyer, I'm recording our conversation. It could go against you. I have a deep affection for the woman, and she is also my client. Samantha has never been involved in any criminal activity, regardless of what you or your police department wish to think.'

'Samantha was having an affair with Stephen Palmer. Marcus was alive at the time and living in the family home. Palmer disappeared without a trace, only to be discovered some years later hanging from a beam in a warehouse. His death had not been pleasant. No doubt you know this.'

'It's before I became a lawyer, but yes, I know, only because you have badgered Hamish McIntyre and Samantha. Neither of them has any knowledge of how Palmer died.'

Grantham continued after a pause of several seconds while he took a drink from the glass at his side. He did not offer one to Isaac. 'Samantha is blameless of any crime, and yes, I do know that you have been at next door's house.'

'How do you know this?

'It's my job to know; how is not the issue here, is it? What are you going to make of the fact that I was upstairs in Samantha's house when your people were downstairs interviewing her? Unless you have proof of involvement, then I suggest you desist from pestering her.'

Isaac had to agree with the man on one point. They had nothing against the woman, except the fact that she was the daughter of a vicious man, a man who through skilful management and expert legal advice had remained out of jail, and who now preferred to stay at his mansion in the country.

'If there is no more, Inspector, then I suggest you leave,' Grantham said. 'We will regard our conversation as just that, would you agree? I have no wish to destroy your career, and to save the police embarrassment we will not talk of this matter again. After Marcus is buried, Samantha and I intend to spend a lot more time together.'

'Does her father know of your and Samantha's plan? Your current relationship?' Isaac asked, needling for more information before being shown the door.

'He would have no issues with Samantha and me, and I would advise you not to mention it to him. I suggest that you leave my house now and don't come back unless you have a warrant or proof of malpractice or criminal intent. Let me make it clear, you will not find either of those to apply against me.'

Outside on the street, Isaac took a deep breath. Grantham had been right, but it had been necessary for him to meet the man. He was one more cog in the wheel, another piece of information which on the face of it seemed irrelevant. But down in Cornwall, a former rival for Stephen Palmer's affections lay dead, a victim of foul play. Someone had murdered her for reasons unknown, reasons that would be discovered. Isaac returned to the station even though it was close to one in the morning. Jenny would be fast asleep at home. Another forty minutes and he would be there with her.

***

Larry and Wendy met up with the senior crime scene investigator in Polperro. It was 9 a.m. before he arrived and, as he told them, he was just wrapping up. The man had little time for the London police to be angling in on what to him was a local issue. That was what Larry interpreted from the man's attitude, and the fact that he did not introduce himself, did not shake his or Wendy's hand. Compared to Gordon Windsor, the senior crime scene investigator that Homicide worked with in London, he was churlish.

'You can see where she was dragged,' the CSI said. 'Over here, closer to the edge, you can clearly see where she was lifted up and thrown over the cliff.'

Even to Larry and Wendy that much was obvious.

'It was a woman,' the CSI said, explaining what he had to and no more.

'Any idea as to her height? Would she have had to be strong?' Larry asked.

'Not necessarily. The murderer would have had the advantage of surprise, and the time from where the woman had been grabbed to where she had gone over the cliff would have been measured in seconds, probably no more than ten to fifteen. The evidence here doesn't allow us to give the precise height of the woman, only that judging by the prints in the soil, she was most likely of a similar height to the dead woman. My report will put forward the premise, not the certainty. We have scuff marks of footwear on the ground, some belonging to the dead woman, others belonging to the murderer. The murderer was wearing boots, leather, black in colour.'

'High heels?' Wendy asked.

'Not from what we can see. We're confident that the boots were of good quality, and we have an imprint. I suggest you talk to the pathologist if you want to know about the condition of the body, but he'll tell you no more than I can. It's a forty-yard drop; she bounced off some jagged rocks on the way down before landing on the rocks at the shoreline. Death would have been instantaneous.'

Palmer had died at the hand of a man or men, so had Marcus Matthews, but now a woman was involved in the latest death. They were looking for two, possibly three murderers. The investigation was becoming complicated.

Liz Spalding's body had been removed the night before. Larry and Wendy walked down the lane to the beach and then along to the rocks where she had ended up; there was little to see. Nobody, not even the police or the crime scene investigators, could stop the action of the sea washing further evidence away.

'I suggest we go into Plymouth,' Greenwood said. 'I've set up an appointment with Forensics, and we'll be meeting the pathologist this afternoon. He'll be conducting the autopsy once we arrive. I intend to be present.'

At the station, there was a warm welcome from the others in the station, a few jokes about officers coming down from London to be shown how to conduct an investigation.

Larry was not in a mood to enjoy it, though; his wife had been on the phone, and yes, he was forgiven, but there was another demand when he came home. The smoking ban had been reiterated; the eldest child had a dry cough, the result of the stale cigarette fumes that were in the house every morning. He knew she was right. He took three quick puffs of the cigarette in his hand and then threw it away, the packet in his pocket and the disposable lighter soon after.

In Forensics, the chief scientist, a man of Indian extraction, although he spoke with a broad West Country accent, explained what they had found, the tests they had conducted.

'The boots we believe are Gucci, judging by the pattern on the sole. We can't be more than ninety per cent certain, but if they are, that would mean they were expensive. Not too many shops, at least down here, would sell boots like that. In London, I presume there are plenty of places.'

'Are you able to give a type number or any more details? Wendy asked.

'We're checking. If we have any further information, we'll let you know.'

Gucci boots in London, even if expensive, were within the financial reach of most women, especially the fashion-conscious and those gainfully employed in the City of London. Finding who could have purchased those worn at the murder scene would not be easy, Wendy knew that.

'Any more you can tell us about the woman who committed the crime?'

'We found a trace of lipstick on the dead woman's clothing. It wasn't hers.'

'Cars rarely travel up the lane as it is narrow. The only vehicles are local tradesmen and residents who live up there,' Jim Greenwood said. 'We don't have the luxury of CCTV cameras on every street corner as you do in London.'

In Pathology, five minutes' drive away, the pathologist's assistant introduced herself and took the three police officers into the pathologist's office. His table littered with papers, a laptop in the centre, a monitor to one side. He looked up, put down the mouse he had been holding and put out his hand to shake the hand of all three officers in turn.

'My name's Felix Taylor,' he said. 'Pleased to meet you. We'll be starting in ten minutes. I suggest you get yourself prepared.'

Neither Larry nor Wendy felt the need to attend the autopsy, as they had seen enough in their time, but Jim Greenwood was excited at the prospect.

'I've had a cursory look at the body,' Taylor said.

'Is there anything you can tell us?' Wendy asked.

'I'm reluctant to comment before I have conducted a full examination. As the woman's injuries will probably show, she died as a result of impacting the rocks at the bottom of the cliff. Injuries consistent with suicide, an accident, or, as it has been determined in this case, murder.'

It was unusual, Larry thought. Back in London, the pathologist, not an affable man, would barely give you the time of day. And no comment before the autopsy.

Wendy thought there was a refreshing air of informality out of London. She remembered back to when she'd been a junior constable in Sheffield, many years in the past now, the ease of conversation in the station. Of course, there were a few idiots, one or two up themselves, and others who brown-nosed at the first opportunity. Even so, London was better, especially with Isaac Cook as her senior.

Leaving Jim Greenwood in Pathology, Larry and Wendy took the opportunity to find a small restaurant for lunch.

'It's my wife,' Larry said as they sat down, each eating a salad. Larry had to admit that it had been some time since he had tasted food unimpaired by cigarettes and beer. 'I've got to stop smoking now,' he said.

'Cold turkey is best,' Wendy said. She knew he would suffer for a few weeks, the same as she had. He'd also find it hard to know what to do with his hands, the need to fumble with the cigarettes in his pocket, the need to take one out to stick in his mouth and light up.

Ninety minutes later, Greenwood joined them from Pathology. He ordered steak and chips. For once, Larry did not envy him.

'Nothing to report,' Greenwood said after he had emptied half a bottle of tomato sauce onto his plate. 'He sliced the woman open from stem to stern.'

Both Larry and Wendy could tell that Jim Greenwood had not handled the sight of the blood and bone and the woman's internal organs as well as he tried to portray. They knew that the pathologist would have executed a Y-shaped incision from her shoulder joints, meeting at mid-chest, the stem of the Y ending at the pubic region. He would have then removed the critical organs, including the brain afterwards, and then sent them to be checked and catalogued.

'Apart from that,' Greenwood continued, taking time out from his meal, 'Taylor's only other comments were that the woman appeared to be in good physical condition for her age, that she showed no signs of drug abuse, and that she could have probably lived to a ripe old age apart from her premature death.'

With no more to do in Plymouth and no reason to go back to Polperro, Larry and Wendy headed back to London. Jim Greenwood would continue with the investigation, and even if he was squeamish, he was a competent police officer. He'd not let them down.

Chapter 17

Hamish McIntyre was concerned; the continuing focus on his daughter, Samantha, troubled him. Gareth Armstrong had alerted him to DCI Cook's visit to Fergus Grantham the night before. And now the death of Liz Spalding, Samantha's rival for Stephen Palmer's affection.

'An unexpected surprise,' Grantham said as he opened his door to find McIntyre standing there.

'It's not much of a surprise,' McIntyre replied. He was looking for answers, willing to take whatever actions were necessary to remove the focus from his daughter.

'What was Cook doing around your house last night?' McIntyre asked as he sat in the chair that Isaac had sat in the previous night.

'He was just fishing. He's got no evidence against anyone, and his investigation is floundering. No doubt he's under pressure from his superiors for a result. I was the last possibility, a stone unturned, a chance for him to nibble away at me to gain some information.'

'And what did you give him?'

'Nothing, just a brief reminder that he's a police officer, and I am an experienced lawyer, and we're not on a level playing field.'

McIntyre knew he was being fed a pack of lies by Grantham. 'You'd better level with me,' he said.

Grantham could see that he was being placed in an unenviable position. He wasn't sure what the man's reactions would be if he learnt of the strength of the relationship with Samantha. He assumed it would be

favourable, but McIntyre had an unequalled reputation
for dealing with those who interfered in his affairs.

'I told him nothing,' Grantham said.

McIntyre stood up, came close to Grantham.
Under normal circumstances, the lawyer would have held
his ground, used his intellect to belittle whoever was
attempting to win a point against him, but not this time.

He sat quietly assessing the situation, trying to
figure out what to say. For once, he was without words.

'Let me tell you, Fergus Grantham, my daughter is
innocent of any crimes levelled against her. If you and
she wish to maintain the subterfuge that both of you
seem to be at great pains to do, then so be it. She's old
enough, single, and I approve of you as a consort for my
daughter.'

'Thank you,' Grantham said. One hurdle over, he
thought.

'Now, let us get back to where we were. What did
DCI Cook want here last night?'

'He had proof that Samantha and I were
involved. I was in the house that night when the police
came to interview her. He wanted me to admit that I was
there. They could have asked Samantha, but as Isaac
Cook said from that chair where you're sitting, Samantha
is still a person of interest. They're not sure how she ties
in to the deaths of Marcus and Palmer.'

McIntyre sat down again, this time choosing
another seat. Outside, Gareth Armstrong sat in the car.

'I've not spoken to her yet,' Grantham continued.
'He did not accuse Samantha directly; he only mentioned
that she was a person of interest, and now another
woman has died, someone who had been involved with
Palmer.' Grantham wanted to say that he suspected

126

Samantha, a logical conclusion. He knew he needed to be careful in what he said.

McIntyre raised himself from the chair and walked around the room, looked at the pictures on the walls, checked the book Grantham was reading and sat down again. He looked Grantham straight in the eyes. 'The police will suspect Samantha,' he said. 'I want you to find out from her what is the truth.'

'Are you seriously stating that your daughter could be responsible?'

'I'm saying nothing. If, as I believe, you and she are serious, then we need to protect her.'

'Even if she's guilty?'

'I hope she's not. Let the police conduct their investigation; you conduct yours and don't try to conceal anything from me.'

'Did you kill Stephen Palmer?' Grantham said.

'Others have accused me of lesser crimes. None of them is in any position to give you advice on how you approach me and what you say. I suggest you take heed of that fact. I am giving you my confidence; use it wisely.'

With that, McIntyre opened the front door of the house and left. Grantham sat for five minutes pondering on what had just occurred. To him, it sounded as though the man had given a de facto confession to the murder of Stephen Palmer and an admission that he was convinced that his daughter had killed Liz Spalding. He would need to act soon, and without hesitation.

***

Larry spent the day after Wendy's and his return from Cornwall in a haze. As Wendy had predicted, he fumbled in his pocket for his cigarettes, continually holding two fingers up to his mouth in the act of simulation. In the end and in desperation, he had purchased chewing gum to distract him.

An update from Forensics in Plymouth: they had identified the lipstick that had been found on Liz Spalding's clothing. It was nothing special, just a lipstick that could be bought in most chemists' and most department stores.

Jim Greenwood phoned soon after. 'We've had a visitor down here.'

'Liz Spalding's delayed man?' Larry said.

'Not him, Bob Palmer. He said he hadn't seen Liz for a long time, not since his brother's funeral. The man was distraught, wanted to see where she died. I got the local doctor to give him a sedative. He's at the hotel where you stayed. He's not committed any crime, apart from being a damn nuisance. What do you want me to do with him?'

'Find out how he knew she was down there. We've not released the name yet, not all the next of kin have been informed,' Larry said. 'It's almost twenty years since his brother took her out. Time hasn't moved on for Bob, and it's obsessive people who commit murder.'

'He could have killed Liz if Forensics is wrong,' Wendy said.

'It's unlikely, but then again, all these years, he could have been stalking her, too scared to approach, unable to leave the past where it belonged. Spend some time with Palmer, push him, find out what you can,' Larry said. 'Ask him how he knew it was Liz and how he knew she was in the village. We don't suspect him of murder, not of her. We should regard him as harmless, but of concern. Check out where he intends to go and what he plans to do after he leaves the village.'

***

Fergus Grantham sat opposite Samantha Matthews in the front room of her house. After his encounter with her father, and what he sensed was a change in the man from polite to malevolent, he was curious to see if Samantha displayed the same.

He'd never given much thought to McIntyre's reputation before. He was the man's lawyer, that was all. He was concerned that the woman he cared for had inherited violent traits from her father; after all, genetic inheritance is stronger than any acquired skills or values.

'You told my father that we're involved,' Samantha said. She was dressed in a green dress with matching high heels. It was still early, and she had not finished putting her makeup on when Fergus knocked on the door.

'He knew already. He offered no opinion for or against, but he was clear on one matter, his concern for you.'

'I've done nothing, if that's what he believes. What about you?'

I believe that you would be justified in any action that you might take.'

'Are you implying I murdered that woman? How dare you imply such a thing.'

Fergus realised he had not mentioned the name of Liz Spalding or her death. He wasn't sure if the police had.

If Samantha had killed the woman, he thought, how could she be so calm? What dark depths were there in her psyche? What else was she capable of?

He decided a different approach was required to remove her from any possibility of being arrested and found guilty of the murder. He, like her father, didn't care whether she was guilty or not.

'Your father is concerned,' Fergus said. 'He will protect you, regardless. As your lawyer and as a person who loves you, so will I.'

'I know,' Samantha said. She poured herself a small sherry, poured one for Fergus. She wasn't sure what to say, as she had no compunction or guilt about what she had done to the woman who had blighted her life. She knew that she had left the village with a sense of elation. 'There is nothing for you to do, Fergus, and nothing for my father to be concerned about. As you're here and you've got time, I suggest we go upstairs. Is that acceptable for a lawyer to consider?'

Grantham followed her up the stairs. He knew the truth; the reason was not important, protecting her was.

Chapter 18

DCS Goddard met with Isaac. They were in Goddard's office, the large window behind him, the impressive desk, the leather-backed chair, the symbols of seniority on display.

'One murder of a minor villain, and where are we now?' Goddard said. 'What's the count, if you're including Liz Spalding?'

'Stephen Palmer's death is linked with the deaths of Liz Spalding and Marcus Matthews. McIntyre's daughter, the widow of Marcus Matthews, probably killed Liz Spalding.'

'The tie-in with Stephen Palmer?' Goddard asked, although he had been keeping up to date with the reports that Isaac was regularly submitting.

'Samantha Matthews was having an affair up to the disappearance and the now known murder of her lover, Stephen Palmer. At the same time, he was taking out Liz Spalding.'

'Does the neighbourhood where Samantha Matthews lives know of her family history?'

'According to her, nobody does, or else they're wise enough not to deal in idle gossip. Her next-door neighbour knew, but he was sleeping with his business partner's wife while the man was away drumming up business. The man had his own secrets, no gain in revealing someone else's. He has no connection with any of the murdered people, other than a neighbourly friendship with Samantha, a few occasions exchanging pleasantries with her father, and he used to have the occasional drink with Marcus Matthews.'

'Is there any way you can pin the murder of Stephen Palmer on Hamish McIntyre?'

'He was close to where Palmer died, before and after. It's conclusive to us, not provable in a court of law. A prosecution wouldn't hold up, not after twenty years. Marcus Matthews was there as well. Whether he committed the act – after all, it was his wife that Palmer seduced – or whether he was just a bystander, we don't know. The body had been too long in the warehouse; the vermin and the insects, the pigeons in the roof had destroyed any chance of forensic evidence.

'Our first case, the death of Marcus Matthews, is still at a standstill. McIntyre did not kill him. Liz Spalding was killed by a woman, ninety-nine per cent certainty on that. We now have an added complication in that we believe Palmer's brother, a nerdish and timid man, had also discovered where Liz Spalding lived. We've got our contact down in Cornwall, DI Jim Greenwood, following up for us. He'll be talking to Palmer as soon as possible to find out why he was there, how he knew she was there, and more importantly, whether he has been stalking her all these years.'

'Could he be her murderer?'

'She slept with Bob Palmer that one night after the funeral. If Palmer is guilty of any crime, why hasn't he acted before? And if he believes that Samantha Matthews' family were guilty of crimes against his brother, then who knows what the man could be capable of.'

'How long before a result?' Goddard asked. 'Questions are starting to be asked on high. Why is it,

Isaac, that every time there's a murder case, and you're the SIO, the body count starts rising?'

'Nothing to do with me.'

'How's Jenny?' Goddard asked, aiming to change the subject. He had total confidence in his DCI. He knew the man would not give in until the case or cases were solved.

'Jenny's fine, life couldn't be better.'

'Make sure it stays that way. Keep me updated, phone at any time. Give me something to pass on. I have people to report to, the same as you.'

***

Bob Palmer woke from his sleep, splashed some water on his face, looked out of the window, not quite sure where he was. He opened the door of his room only to see a police officer sitting on a chair opposite.

'Detective Inspector Greenwood would like to have a word with you when you're ready,' the young constable said.

Palmer finally realised why he was there. The sedatives had been potent, and he was sad. He closed the door, put on a shirt to go with the trousers he was already wearing and walked down the stairs to the small bar. Jim Greenwood, already alerted that Palmer was awake, was waiting for him at a small table. On it was a plate of sandwiches and two coffees.

'I ordered for us,' Greenwood said.

'Why the policeman outside my door?'

'Why are you here?'

'I had to come.'

'That's as maybe, but how did you know she was here? We're not holding you responsible for her death, not at this time, but you had a fixation about the woman, is that true?'

'She was my brother's girlfriend. She should have been mine.'

'Life doesn't always work out the way you want,' Greenwood said. 'I wanted to be a superintendent, not a detective inspector, but that's how it is. Your brother died twenty years ago, yet you still pined for this woman.'

'You wouldn't understand it.'

'I wouldn't. I'm on my second marriage, and that's not going too well either. One door closes, another one opens. That's how I see it, but you, Mr Palmer, don't. Now, what's the truth? How long have you been stalking the woman?'

'I've never stalked her. I've kept an eye on her over the years through the internet, and sometimes by sitting in a car at the end of her road. I've seen the men she married, the men she went out with. I've always regretted that it wasn't me, but I never approached her, and I would never have harmed her.'

'Let us come back to your brother. He died, as I understand, as a result of an affair with a married woman. Do you know this?'

'I can't say that I know too much, and after twenty years, the memory tends to alter the facts.'

'It didn't alter your fixation on the woman, did it?' Greenwood could see that the man was still visibly upset. He called over to the bar and ordered two stiff whiskies, one for him and one for Palmer.

'I don't normally drink.' Palmer said.

'A stiff drink is the best thing. What are you going to do after you leave here? Are you going to go back to your house and mind your own business? Or are you intending to cause trouble?'

'I'm not sure. I want to react, but I don't know how to. Liz may have been promiscuous, judging by the number of men she has been with since Stephen died, but I always forgave her.'

'Don't you mean since the night she slept with you after the funeral. I've been given a complete rundown on who you are, the death of your brother and the suspects. Let me repeat the question, what do you intend to do?'

'I can't give you an answer. I've committed no crime. After this interview, I will leave and go back to my house, or I may go away on a trip. I'll attend her funeral; nobody cared for her as much as I did.'

Greenwood felt like grabbing the man and giving him a good shake, telling him to snap out of it, to be a man and get on with it, but he knew it would serve no purpose. And as Larry had said, the man was strange.

***

Samantha Matthews had not appreciated being questioned by Fergus. Sure, he was her lover, but she had nothing to answer for. She already knew that her father would protect her at any cost. And she had always suspected that her father had somehow been involved directly or indirectly in the death of Stephen, her first great love.

She had married Marcus two years before her affair with Stephen, a belief that with her husband that it was love eternal, but it wasn't. It was the need to have someone in her life apart from her father who cared for her, but it was Stephen who had shown her the depth of passion, a passion that would never be resurrected, not even by Fergus.

She sat in the back garden of her house. It was a warm day, and she appreciated the heat on her body. If asked, she could not give a reason why she had killed the woman, she only knew that it had been necessary.

It was after Marcus's body had been discovered that she found out where the woman could be found. Revenge seemed illogical to her, but then her father's actions at times had been irrational, driven by hatred and anger.

Liz Spalding had blighted her life, a life which could have been so different. If Stephen had lived, if Liz had not existed, she would have divorced Marcus and married him. However, she had just been another notch on the man's belt, she knew that now, seducing the daughter of a man who had a reputation for revenge against those who got in his way.

She knew more than she let her father know; she had listened at the keyhole of his study when she was younger, hearing him arranging crimes, discussing individuals who were getting in the way of his criminal empire. She remembered the night the gentlemen's club had burnt down, the joy her father had felt, the way he had lifted her up off the ground and given her a big hug. He had told her that life was good, and it was only going to get better, and then another man had died. A man who had been associated with the club. She had only been young, but she understood.

As her father aged, his empire was unravelling, given to others less capable. She went back inside the house, picked up the keys to her car and left by the front door.

She found her father in his conservatory; he looked older each time she saw him.

'You asked Fergus to check me out,' Samantha said.

'Do you need protecting?' Hamish said.

'The situation has changed. It's time for me to take control.'

'It's a lonely road if you choose to go down it.' Hamish wasn't sure what to say. Samantha was right: she had committed a heinous crime, and only the criminal world could protect her.

'Why did you kill Stephen? Samantha asked.

'Palmer was not genuine in his affections for you.'

'I couldn't resist the man, but you had no right to harm him.'

'I had to for you and your child's sake, you must understand.'

'For a while, I hated you.'

'If you intend to become involved in my business interests, I need to know if what happened to Liz Spalding applies to me.'

'Not you, father. I could never harm you,' Samantha said.

The man looked at his daughter, unsure if she had told him the truth.

Chapter 19

Tricia Anders was in the hospital with a broken arm and severe bruising on her body and face, given to her by her husband.

Harry Anders sat forlornly in the cell at the police station. He was contrite. 'I couldn't help myself,' he said. 'It came as such a shock. I never expected it. Not of my wife and not of Brian. I've always known he had an eye for her, but then that was the man's nature, flirtatious, preferring to spend time chatting up the women than drinking with the men.'

'You'll have to answer for your crime,' Larry said.

'I'm not sure that it matters any more. Our business has obviously been destroyed. It had done us well over the years, and Tricia had no reason to complain about the lifestyle, but then who knows what goes through the minds of people. Loneliness, and I'm responsible for that, too busy chasing the next deal. Tricia felt neglected.'

'What do you intend to do now?' Larry asked. 'They'll release you soon enough. You'll have to answer for what you did, but it'll probably only be community duty, anger management classes, a fine.'

Larry wondered how he would have reacted under the circumstances. Tricia Anders had been a decent woman, still was, but she had erred in a moment of weakness.

'What about Brian Jameson?' Larry asked. 'What are you going to do about him?'

'He's been to see Tricia, I know that, and he's been down here to the police station. They've not let him in to see me, not yet, but if he wants to talk, that's fine. We were business partners for a long time, friends for longer. Hopefully, I can repair it with Tricia, but if she's keen on Brian, there's not much I can do.'

Larry left the man to his sorrows. Outside, he had a chat with the arresting officer and put in a word for Harry Anders, explained the situation.

'My wife took off, found someone else,' the officer said.

'What did you do?' Larry asked.

'What any hot-blooded male would do.'

'You struck him.'

'Not that it helped. She moved in with him the next week, took the dog as well. All I got for it were bruised knuckles and a trashed kitchen. Still, it could be worse. I found myself another woman, causes me no trouble.'

***

It was two in the afternoon before Bob Palmer left his hotel. Jim Greenwood had seen him drive away, concerned that the man was about to do something foolish, and he'd given him a lecture about taking care, not taking the law into his own hands. The fact that he was grievously upset would be of no consideration if he caused trouble. Greenwood was sure he had wasted his breath.

Bob Palmer had been irrational, barely able to restrain the tears. 'Maybe it's for the better,' he had said.

'Liz has troubled me for many years. I can't wish ill of the dead, but who knows, maybe I'll get on with my life now.'

Greenwood phoned Larry and Wendy to update them on the situation. He had done as much as he could. The missing male friend had finally appeared; he had been at a seminar in the north of England, and although he was sorry that Liz had died, he seemed to take it in his stride.

'I'll send you a printout of who she phoned, who phoned her, messages received and sent,' Greenwood's final words before ending the phone call.

Pathology had submitted their final report. The cause of death consistent with falling from the top of the cliff onto the rocks below. Forensics had no more, other than a strand of hair from another person on the dead woman's clothes.

'Any idea where the hair came from?' Larry asked.

'I'll send you the report,' the forensic scientist said. 'She could have picked it up anywhere. It could belong to the murderer, but then again, it might not.'

'What else can you tell us about it?'

'Blonde, but it's been dyed. We've analysed the dye that had been used and an approximate time when it had been applied. DNA could prove crucial.'

***

Bob Palmer drove away from the village and from Liz. She had been his life for so many years. He knew that people did not understand him, but what did he care. His life had slipped by, his chance at happiness gone forever. He remembered that night so long ago, the love that she had shown him, the kindness, the warmth of her, and then before he had woken up, she was gone. He had not left the house for four days after that, not washed, not shaved, barely ate.

Without knowing where he was going after leaving Polperro, he found himself at his brother's graveside. It was clear that no one had tended it for a long time. No flowers, weeds growing around the headstone, even birds sitting on it and defecating. He set to work to clean around the area. Liz had loved his brother, he knew that. And whereas Stephen had loved her in his own way, there was another woman, and she had been at the funeral. He was convinced it had been her in the village. He didn't know why, intuition he supposed, but whoever she was, he would confront her.

He had had brotherly love for Stephen, but he had not been a friend. It had been subtle, Stephen's putting him down, but its effects were long-reaching, even today. The thought of Stephen standing there, laughing at him filled him with rage.

The church vicar came over to where Bob was tidying the grave. It had been nine years since he had visited it, yet the vicar, a short man with a healthy mop of hair and a squeaky voice, still remembered him.

'Mr Palmer, you've come to see your brother,' he said.

'I thought it was about time.'

'It's always good to see when one of my flock returns.'

Palmer remembered the man's enthusiasm from before. He wasn't religious, no strong convictions either way, but in the quiet moments in the house when it had all seemed too much, he had knelt by the side of the bed and prayed. He had prayed for Liz, he had prayed for him to forget her, but his prayers had never been answered.

'Do you remember the funeral?'

'There weren't many mourners.'

'It was what Stephen would have wanted.' Bob Palmer knew that wasn't true; it had been what he had decided. No speeches at the local pub afterwards, one after the other holding up a glass and telling the others what a good person Stephen had been, no hoorahs for him. The man had caused him enough aggravation in life; he had had no intention of allowing him the luxury of continuing the degradation.

'What about those at the funeral?' the vicar said.

'Bec Johnson, you know of. She still lives in the area. I see her from time to time. The other women. One was Liz Spalding, a girlfriend of his. She's dead now.'

'I'm sorry to hear that. A long time ago?'

'Three days, according to the police. She was murdered, thrown off a cliff.'

'How tragic. Were you close to her?'

'I hadn't seen her since the funeral. She was Stephen's girlfriend. She was a friend of mine, even though we had lost contact.'

'I'll pray for her,' the vicar said. 'Have they found the person responsible?'

'Not yet. Tell me, Vicar. Do you remember another woman, dressed in black, wide-brimmed hat flopping down over her eyes?'

'Vaguely. I'm not certain that I spoke to her. Or maybe I did out of courtesy.'

'What can you remember of her?'

'Ah, yes, now I remember. I did speak to her. She didn't have much to say, and she was clearly upset. I could see that her eyes were red, so she had obviously been crying.'

'What else? How did she speak? Educated, an accent, anything that could identify her?'

'Let me see,' the vicar said, resting his chin on one hand. 'I see so many people, and it was so long ago. She spoke well, polite, educated, certainly not working class, probably came from money. Why do you need to know?'

'It seems important to tell those who were at the funeral that Liz is dead. I can phone Bec, but the other woman was, I believe, a rival girlfriend. I'm afraid my brother played the field.'

'He'd not be the first in this graveyard. We're not here to judge, only to give comfort to those who remain, to bury those who have passed on.'

'Anything else about this woman? No matter how minor you might think it is.'

'I shook her hand. I remember that her sleeve moved up her arm a little and on her inside arm, just above the wrist, there was a small tattoo. I didn't have long to look, but I think it was a small butterfly, the sort of thing people after a few drinks are inclined to do. Not that she looked like a person who drank and she wore a wedding ring.'

'Stephen was one of your sinners.'

'He's forgiven now.'

Palmer knew he did not have the generous nature of the vicar. He would not forgive. Not until he had dealt with the person who had killed Liz.

***

Ten o'clock in the evening, the meeting had just concluded, and the team in Homicide were preparing to leave for the night. Jenny had said she would wait up, and Isaac and she would have a meal together and share a bottle of wine. Larry's wife was equally agreeable, and she would be waiting for him as well. Bridget and Wendy were back off to the house they shared; both would have more drinks than they should. It had been a long murder investigation, and still nobody had been arrested.

It was Isaac who took the phone call. 'Wally Vincent here, I've got an update for you.'

Isaac could tell that the man was pleased with himself. Also, that he had left work earlier than they had, and he was clearly on the way to being drunk.

'What is it?' Isaac said.

'I suggest you get your team on a conference line. It could well have a bearing on the case.'

Isaac phoned Jenny; told her he was delayed. She took it well, didn't offer any comment, only to say that she'd see him when she saw him. Larry didn't phone his wife; he was hopeful that he would only be delayed for a few minutes. Bridget didn't care either way. Wendy was tired, but she had eaten a cream bun twenty minutes earlier. Whatever time she got home was fine by her; the wine could wait, although the cat would be starving by the time they arrived.

Isaac's desk phone was on speaker. 'It's all yours, Wally,' he said.

'I hope you don't mind, but I've been following up on Charles Stanford. I've been to the house in Bedford Gardens. Spoke to a few people, met up with the two kids who found Matthews's body.'

'No problems from us, glad of the assistance,' Larry said.

'We appreciate the help,' Isaac said. He was perturbed that Vincent hadn't had the courtesy to phone him, but it was a minor issue.

'It was one of the children, Billy Dempsey,' Vincent said. 'According to his mother, he can spin a tale, been in trouble a few times for telling lies. But this time I reckon he was telling the truth. He's a smart kid, remembers a lot. The other boy didn't help at all. But let me get back to Billy. He said he was out on the street. It was eleven months ago. He said he was skateboarding, not sure if they do that anymore. More likely he was up to mischief.'

'What did he say?'

'He said he saw an old man enter the house where Matthews was found.'

'Are you certain he was telling the truth?'

'I do. I could tell whoppers when I was younger. I knew what to look for.'

'Did you show him any photos?' Isaac asked.

'I showed him one. I don't think he was looking at the old man that carefully in Bedford Gardens, but he was certain the man in the photo was the person he'd seen.'

'Stanford?' Isaac said.

'Spot on, Charles Stanford. There are no cameras in the street, so we can't prove it one way or the other, but I reckon it's him.'

'If that's the case, I suggest that Larry and Wendy get down to Brighton at the earliest opportunity,' Isaac said. 'The three of you can bring Stanford in and give him the third-degree.'

'What time in the morning,' Larry said.

'I've got someone keeping a watch on Stanford's house. He's going nowhere, and I don't want to conduct an interview at this time of night, harassment if it goes pear-shaped. Be down here by seven in the morning, and we'll compare notes in my office. You can update me on the case, and we can discuss how we intend to conduct the interview. Not sure if he'll bring a lawyer with him,'

'Thanks. Larry and Wendy will be down there tomorrow,' Isaac said. 'I'll leave it up to you three. If what we have is proven, it brings the focus back on Marcus Matthews.'

Vincent ended the phone conversation. Isaac knew that the man had some drinking to catch up on.

Isaac phoned Jenny, the meal and a bottle of wine were still on. Larry, even though he would be late, knew his wife would be there for him. Wendy realised that she could only have one drink that night. She needed a clear head for the next day.

Chapter 20

Charles Stanford did not react well to the three police officers on his doorstep at eight twenty in the morning. Wally Vincent had taken responsibility for informing him that his presence was required at the police station; a marked police car with two uniforms was parked on the road.

'We've received disturbing information about you and your house in Bedford Gardens. We can't conduct an interview here.'

'You're making an error of judgement,' Stanford said. He was dressed, as usual, in old clothes.

Only fit for a bin, Wendy thought.

'Give me ten minutes,' he said as he closed the door.

'If he's not out by then, we're going in,' Vincent said.

Stanford reappeared within eight. He had changed into a suit, and it was clear that he had washed his face and combed his hair.

'You'll rue the day,' he said.

Vincent knew that he probably would. He'd be in the superintendent's office later in the day, explaining what he was doing hassling an old man. This time he would have a satisfactory answer. He had enjoyed investigating Stanford, travelling up to Bedford Gardens, interviewing key people and finding out facts that had been missed by DCI Cook's crack team.

Stanford did not need the marked police car. He sat in the back of Vincent's car, alongside Wendy. He said little, looking out of the window during the journey. Vincent opened his passenger door on arrival. He even said thank you.

In a suit and at the police station, Stanford seemed to change. No longer the downtrodden antisocial eccentric, but a man of importance. Several of the other officers made his acquaintance.

Wendy gave Stanford a cup of tea, offered him a sandwich or something else to eat, which he declined.

'Get on with this,' he said.

'Mr Stanford, you're allowed to have legal representation,' Larry said.

'I know the law better than you do. Time is precious, and it's ticking away. Let's get this fiasco over and done with.'

Wendy left the interview room. It would be Wally and Larry on the police side of the desk, Stanford on the other. Vincent went through the mandatory procedures, informed Stanford of what was to occur, his rights. The man opposite him sat back, his arms folded, taking no notice of what was being said. When asked his name, he answered clearly, concisely, and without hesitation.

'Mr Stanford,' Vincent said, 'further investigation confirms that you visited 11 Bedford Gardens on or about the third day of June of last year.'

'How do you know this?'

'People have been interviewed. A man fitting your description was seen entering the property.'

'I've not been there for a long time. I suggest you re-examine your evidence.'

The evidence of a young boy known as a habitual liar, a mischief-maker, was not solid, but if it was proven that Stanford had been at the house, then why was he concealing that fact? After all, visiting a three-storey home did not mean that Stanford had climbed up to the top floor. Even when he had climbed it, Larry had felt the strain, and the last flight was particularly narrow and steep.

'We can provide proof,' Vincent said.

'If someone has been in there in the last nine or ten months, it wasn't me.'

'It's eleven,' Larry said.

'Eleven, have it your way,' Stanford said, a disinterested look on his face. 'If you care to check you'll find no record of my travelling to London. No train ticket or taxi and I don't own a car.'

'Very well, let us for the purposes of this interview agree that you were not in that house. We still believe there must be a reason for Marcus Matthews to have been on the top floor. It is not a coincidence. There is a connection between you and Matthews and without doubt Hamish McIntyre.'

'Did he kill Matthews?'

'We have proof he did not. It could have been you.'

'I'm an old man. It's a long way up those stairs. Have you tried it?'

'I have, it's a tough climb' Larry said, or it had been, he thought. He was certainly more active than in the past; out in the park with his wife at the weekend he had managed to run for some of the distance, even putting on his shorts and his trainers too.

'Mr Stanford, we're getting nowhere,' Vincent said. He was concerned that nothing would be said or gained to justify his actions. If that were the case, the superintendent with an almost certain letter of complaint would haul him over the coals. He did not relish that possibility.

'Mr Stanford, let us go back to the reason for your retirement. You were a barrister, Queen's Counsel and a judge, you must know the importance of us being able to do our job unhindered by people who do not reveal the truth. What would happen if someone had appeared before you, reluctant to say all that they knew, especially in a murder investigation?'

'I'm not a judge here. I'm a private citizen, and I have my rights. I regard this as a severe intrusion, and now you want to ask why I retired. I believe that I spoke of that the other day in my house. I revealed my disappointment over the death of Yanna White. It affected me greatly. I've told you this. Why am I telling you this again?'

'If any other illegal activities have occurred in that house, in addition to the murder, of course, then you may well bear responsibility.'

'Verbiage, utter rubbish,' Stanford said in frustration. 'You've got nothing, yet you persevere with this nonsense. I suggest we wrap this up. You can give me a lift back to my house, or else I'll catch a taxi and send the bill to you.'

'I suggest we break for ten minutes,' Vincent said. 'Mr Stanford, you're welcome to sit outside and make yourself more comfortable.'

'I'd be more comfortable at home. What do you want ten minutes for?'

150

'We need to make a phone call to London.'

***

Isaac regretted agreeing to Wendy going to Brighton.
Larry could have gone on his own. After all, Wally
Vincent was down there. Wendy could have helped him
out on the street and checking around the murder scene.

It had been decided during the previous night, at
one in the morning, when Isaac had phoned Larry, who
had been fast asleep, that he would follow up on
Vincent's good work, seeing if anything else could be
found.

The three police officers sat around Vincent's
desk, his phone on speaker, Isaac up in London.

'What do you have?' Larry asked.

'I'll let you three go first.'

'We've interviewed Stanford. He's saying little, and
unless we give him something that he can't deny, he's
going to walk out of the station soon enough.'

'Inspector Vincent, Wally, regardless that he didn't
inform us that he was in Bedford Gardens, has done a
sterling job. I've met with Billy Dempsey and his parents,
the young boy's sure of what he saw. I'm with Gordon
Windsor and two of his team. They were thorough in
their investigation before, but I've asked them to focus on
the front of the house, especially around the door, and to
see if they can find anything under the dirt and grime. It
seems certain that Stanford has been in the house at some
stage.'

'How long ago?' Vincent asked.

'The condition of the prints is bad, but they're
more recent than twenty years. Windsor believes they

151

could have been placed there within the last three years. He can't be any more precise, but we can prove that Charles Stanford has been into 11 Bedford Gardens.'

'Anything else?' Wendy said.

'Windsor's got two of his people checking, and the area at the top of the house, including the last flight of stairs, was vigorously checked the first time. One thing is clear. Stanford has not been up in that room, not in the previous few years and definitely not in the last eleven months.'

'Could he have killed Matthews?' Vincent asked.

'There were fingerprints on the bottle of wine that was found, two men, and none belong to Stanford.'

Stanford had asked for a pizza. He looked up at Wally and Larry on their return.

'I've always heard that the condemned man has a pizza,' he said.

Larry and Wally sat down, then Wally restarted the interview, reiterating the conversation so far.

Stanford said nothing as he ate his last slice of pizza. 'Not bad,' he said. 'It'll save me cooking later.'

'Detective Chief Inspector Isaac Cook is at Bedford Gardens, at your house, with a crime scene investigation team,' Vincent said. 'They've found your fingerprints on the door handle of the front door of your house.'

'Twenty years ago, maybe.'

'The condition of the prints is not good, but they are proof that you have been in the house recently. What were you doing at 11 Bedford Gardens in the last year?'

'Nothing can be proved.'

'We're trying to solve a murder,' Larry said. 'You must understand that our actions are not personal. It's the truth we want.'

'I'm a private man,' Stanford said.

'Yes, we understand all this,' Vincent said, with a sigh of frustration.

'One year ago, give or take a few days, I received a phone call. It was anonymous.'

'What was it about?'

'I was told that my house was being used for criminal activity.'

'What sort of activity?'

'The voice told me drugs were being stored in the basement.'

'What did you find?'

'Nothing.'

'Then why do you think you received that phone call?'

'Someone wanted me to find the body, but they couldn't have known that I wouldn't climb those stairs, not at my age and in my condition.'

'Do you have any idea why they wanted you to find the body?' Larry asked.

'I've no idea, and as to why they chose my house, I don't know.'

'You could have told us this before and saved yourself a lot of trouble,' Vincent said.

'All I want is to be left alone.'

'We need to trace that phone call,' Larry said. 'Any idea of the date, other than a few days either way?'

'I keep a diary. I can give you the day and the time, as well as the date that I visited Bedford Gardens, and yes, eleven months is probably correct. Now if there is no more, I will leave you at this police station while I go back to my house and my life.'

'Is there any more you can tell us? Larry asked.

'I will send a message to your phone with the date and the time of the phone call. If you can trace that, then so be it. But quite frankly, I'm not concerned either way.'

Wally Vincent concluded the interview.

Stanford left, this time shaking the hands of the two men, and Wendy's.

Chapter 21

It wasn't as though he hadn't wanted Tricia, Brian Jameson thought. It was just that he was comfortable on his own in the house, with the occasional lady friend if he wanted one, but most times he didn't.

It had been Tricia who had instigated the romance. Harry had trusted his partner implicitly, and if Tricia and Brian had wanted to meet occasionally, that was fine by him.

Then one evening, over a bottle of wine, she had lent over and placed her hand on top of his and told him that Harry was neglecting his duty. She had said that he, as his partner and friend, should help out.

But now Tricia was in the hospital, recovering. If her husband wanted to take his anger out on him, he would not resist.

'Harry,' Jameson said as he opened the door after someone had rung the bell.

'That wasn't very neighbourly of you, was it?' Samantha Matthews said.

'Come in, come in. I'll fetch us both a drink.'

'You told the police about Fergus, don't deny it.'

'I only said that I had a photo of his car. I never knew his name, and I've always minded my own business.'

'It didn't stop you seducing your business partner's wife.'

'How do you know about that?'

'I make it my business to know. Now, what should I do with you after you've put me front and centre into the murder investigation of my husband?'

'You never killed him.'

'Who said I did?'

'I liked Marcus, a good man. I'm sorry he died.'

'So am I, but it was a long time ago. What else do you know about me that the police don't?'

'I know who and what your father is. I care little on either matter.'

'Good.'

'Why?'

'Because we're going to work together. You're a hotshot man with a computer, and you're good at hacking them.'

'I test the security of computers and databases, put programs in place to make them safe from attack, strictly legal. There are contracts in place to allow me to do this.'

'And if it wasn't strictly legal?'

'I've never been asked before.'

'What if I asked you?'

'I'd say no.'

'Is that because you're frightened of being caught or because you regard it as unethical?'

'The first concerns me more. I've seen what these companies get up to, the taxation fiddles.'

'Then, Brian, you and I can work together.'

'If I say no?'

'You won't. The thought of it excites you, more so than the money.'

'If I'm pressured by the police to reveal more about you?'

'You know my father's reputation. You don't need to ask that question.'

'What about Fergus?'

'He doesn't need to know about what we're discussing. He will manage my legal affairs, and I might still marry him.'

'You're not sure?'

'He might not want to be involved, but you're a greedy man who wants to live well.'

'White-collar crime, no violence,' Jameson said.

'No more than necessary,' Samantha said. 'Don't underestimate me.'

'I won't.'

'And don't hack me. If I find out…'

'The same as happened to Marcus?'

Samantha did not reply. She only smiled as she closed the door behind her.

***

Hamish McIntyre reflected on the conversation with his daughter. Most men would have wanted a son to take over the family business, but there had only been a daughter.

He had given her the best of educations, the best of opportunities, and she wanted for nothing. Yet, since the admission that she had killed Liz Spalding, Samantha had changed. The thought of her killing the other woman sickened him. Not because of the act – after all, he had committed such acts himself – but because his daughter was no longer an innocent. He had seen the look on her face when she had visited him. It was hard and dangerous.

And she had known that he had killed Stephen Palmer. But she seemed to have forgiven him, and back then, twenty years in the past, she had been just a child, even though she was married to Marcus, with one child already, another soon to be on the way.

Gareth Armstrong could see the look of consternation on his boss's face. 'What is it?' he said.

'Samantha wants to take control of my business empire, or at least, what's left of it.'

'Do you want that?' Armstrong asked.

'I would have preferred to have left it the way it was.'

McIntyre reflected on his own mortality, the aches and pains that he felt of a morning, or when he'd been leaning over his plants in the conservatory. Another five to ten years and he'd not be able to control those who still reported to him, those he still frightened.

'Does she realise what she's getting into?' Armstrong said.

'I don't think she's thought it through, but she'll not be stopped.'

'Then what option do you have?'

'None.'

'You need to decide. Do you say no to her?'

'I've no choice.' He had no intention of telling Armstrong the details of the conversation he had had with his daughter. That she had murdered and she frightened him. There was a savagery about her he did not recognise. And if he was frightened, then what of others? Maybe a son hadn't been necessary. Samantha could have his business and his blessing. He took the phone out of his pocket and called her.

***

Brian Jameson felt elated after Samantha had left. The woman was right, he was interested in her offer. He had always known how easy it was to hack a company's database, to find out what secrets they had hidden, to check the payroll. With care and attention to detail, he could set up a bogus employee or a petty cash fund, and then siphon off small amounts of money regularly. In time, those small amounts would amount to a fortune.

In Samantha Matthews, he could see a strong and resilient woman, a woman more to his style. Tricia had always been a whimperer, wracked with guilt, worried that Harry would find out.

He fantasised that it had been Samantha in his bed and not Tricia the night Harry had returned home. After all, he was fit for his age and even though she was fifteen or sixteen years younger than him, she was a more attractive proposition than the wife of another man.

'I've not seen Harry,' Tricia said when Jameson phoned. 'He's probably at our place in the country. There's a suitcase missing in the house, and some of his clothes are gone.'

'Will you testify against him?'

'No. He was my husband for a long time, and besides, we can't blame him, can we?'

'I half-expected him to turn up here at my door.'

'That's Harry, not the bravest of men. He wouldn't have known what to say, probably felt that he was to blame.'

'Will you stay with him?'

'I don't know. It depends.'

'On what?'

'On us.'

'We should consider Harry. You would be better off with him.'

'It's not what I want.'

'We should do the right thing, don't you think?'

'It was only a fling, after all,' Tricia said.

'It was good while it lasted.'

'I'll make my peace with Harry.' The phone conversation ended. Tricia sat down and cried. She knew that Brian was right. She would go and see Harry, ask his forgiveness. The only fly in the ointment was that she loved Brian, not her husband.

***

Bob Palmer sat in the small kitchen of his drab house. It had been six days since he had stood at the graveside of his long-dead brother, six days since he had visited where Liz had died. He was confused, not sure what to do. His mind fluctuated between the bedroom of his house and that one night with Liz, and where she had died. He remembered what the vicar had said: a small tattoo shaped like a butterfly.

No matter how much he tried to remember the funeral, he couldn't; his mind fixated on Liz. The realisation that she would no longer be his, nor anybody else's, not any of the men she had married, none of the other men she had slept with.

The one definite factor in the whole saga was that someone had killed her, the same as someone had murdered his brother. And now the police were following up on his brother's death, interviewing people, checking facts, re-evaluating forensic evidence. If they knew something, or they had suspicions, he would need to know. It was clear the answers were not in his house. He needed to be in London.

'I've been a damn fool,' he said out loud. Not that anyone heard, as in that house there was no other life, just gloom. Taking stock of himself, he stood up, shook his shoulders, jumped on the spot, smacked himself around the face a couple of times. 'Snap out of it,' he shouted. 'Be a man, get on with your life. Find out who killed Liz. Do what is necessary.'

He had a shower and shaved, brushed his teeth and put on clean clothes. He then left the house, slamming the door. He was more determined than he had been for many years. With a look over his shoulder as he drove down the street, one last look at his house, he headed to the motorway and London. He talked to himself, he remonstrated, he switched the radio on and off.

On arriving in London, he found a cheap hotel close to where Stephen's car yard had been, although it was long gone. Not sure what to do next he walked into a pub on the corner. He wasn't a drinker, but drink makes people talk. And that was what he wanted, people to talk.

He propped himself up at the bar, ordered a pint of beer, indulged in idle conversation with the barman, and looked around.

'Does anybody in here remember Stephen Palmer?' he asked the barman.

'Not me.'

'He had a used car yard just down the road. There's a supermarket there now.'

'How long ago?'

'Twenty years.'

'I moved into the area four years back. No doubt a few of the regulars would remember back to then. Why the interest?'

'He was my brother, and I got to thinking about him after his old girlfriend died recently.'

'It's always sad when that happens.'

'Memories, that's all. I feel I need closure on her death. I fancied her back then, but she only wanted my brother.'

'Hey, Jacob,' the barman shouted out across the bar. 'Do you remember a Stephen Palmer? More your time than mine.'

'He's one of the regulars, been coming in here forever,' the barman said, turning back to Bob. Who's asking?'

'Gentleman at the bar. Says he's his brother.'

'Good man, your brother,' Jacob said after he had come over to where Bob Palmer was standing. 'I remember him well, always good for a laugh, never shirked on his round of beer.' The man stuck out his empty glass, a clear hint to Palmer that if he wanted to talk, he needed to supply the drinks.

Taking the hint, Palmer looked over at the barman. 'A pint for my friend, one for me. Pour one for yourself.'

'Don't mind if I do. Anything to eat?'

'I'd love one of your steak and kidney pies,' Jacob said.

'I'll have one for myself, as well,' Bob said. The man was worth a few drinks and a bite to eat.

'What do you want to know?' Jacob asked. Prematurely balding, his hair combed over, he looked mildly comical. 'He was a lad, your brother, used to put it about something shocking.'

'A mutual friend of Stephen and mine died recently. You might have known her, Liz Spalding.'

'Good sort, keen on Stephen. A lot of the lads fancied her, kept trying it on, but no success, not while Stephen was around. He could attract women to him like no one else.'

'He had other women, one of them was married.'

'Why the interest?'

'It just seems important to talk to people who knew him and Liz. She died suddenly, not so long ago. Her death brought back to me the time when Stephen was alive, our childhood together.'

'Married women bring trouble. I can understand you being upset, but I suggest you don't go asking too many questions.'

'Why? What's the problem?'

'Stephen, he upset some of the other men, took some of their girlfriends, especially the good-looking ones.'

'I still need to talk to people who knew him and Liz.' Palmer was aware that he was telling a good story, putting on a great act, almost enjoying himself, but never forgetting.

'I remember one girlfriend, she had a small tattoo close to her wrist,' Palmer said. 'He was keen on her, I know that, but he never introduced me to her. I'd like to talk to her about Stephen.'

'I suggest you leave it there.' Jacob said, picking up his steak and kidney pie and his beer and moving to the other side of the small room.

'What's up with him?' the barman said.

'I must've hit a raw nerve. I was asking him about one of Stephen's women. She had a small butterfly tattooed on her inside arm, near to her wrist.'

'Jacob knows his way around these parts. If he tells you to leave well alone, I'd suggest you do that. If you value your life, that is.'

But that was the issue: Bob Palmer didn't, not any more. He was on a mission of vengeance, and he would not be swayed. He needed to know what Jacob and the barman knew.

Chapter 22

Fergus Grantham sensed the change. The last time they had made love, the day when he had questioned Samantha about the events in Cornwall, their lovemaking had been mutual, a bonding of two souls. But now, three days later, as he lay back on her bed, he looked at her sleeping. Exhaustion, he thought. It had been a blood sport, a gladiatorial contest with Samantha initiating congress, demanding more of him. No mention of love, no sweetness, just animal passion.

And if Samantha had taken another person's life, she would be capable of doing it again.

He had been on his own ever since his wife had died suddenly. And now with Samantha's husband confirmed dead and soon to be buried, there was no impediment to the two of them getting married. But he wasn't sure if he wanted that any more.

Samantha turned over. 'Still awake?' she said.

'Yes, just thinking about things. Nothing important.'

Samantha studied him, uncertain where their relationship was heading. She had told Brian Jameson that it was white-collar crime that interested her. But she knew, as Jameson must have, violence is never far away. She had seen the man eye her up and down before, even on the day when she'd made the offer to him. He was older than Fergus by a few years. He wouldn't have the stamina to keep up, but sex is a potent drug. It makes men pliable in the hands of a skilful woman.

'Fergus, stop worrying. I'm not about to do anything stupid. I know that things are moving fast.'

'You need to be careful. The police are keeping a watch on you, attempting to tie you in with Cornwall.'

Samantha didn't reply to his advice, only said, 'I'm going to work with my father.'

'Are you sure? That's a dangerous road to travel.'

'I am, but I'm smarter than my father. I have the benefit of a good education, social skills.'

'We could be together on a more permanent basis.' Grantham wasn't sure why he had brought up the subject.

Samantha sensed the man wanted out. Not that she could blame him, but she still wanted him on her terms.

Fergus, she knew, could walk away from her and her father, his reputation as a defence lawyer intact.

She got out of bed, took a shower, dressed and left the house. She needed time to think. She needed to consider how to handle him, and if he were a risk, then she would need to consider the options.

***

Charles Stanford, now back in his house, reflected on the events at the police station. He had not handled it as well as he thought he should have. In the past, he would not have allowed the police to break through what he preferred to keep hidden; the problem was that the anonymous voice had sounded familiar.

But now, back in his house, he wondered what he should do. Should he confront the person whom he suspected?

But then, the voice had wanted the body to be found. The reason why eluded him.

He had considered going up to the top of the house at Bedford Gardens, but after the first floor, with the pain in his right leg, the soreness he felt in one shoulder as he held the bannister for support, he never ventured further.

Outside in the street, the yapping dog again.

His mind turned away from the police station and back to his house, the yapping dog, the nosy neighbours, and the general malaise in the area. He knew that Vincent, who may well be a good police inspector, had a soft heart. He could never believe that the man would enforce his removal from the house and into a care home.

He walked to the kitchen at the back of the house and put on the kettle, made himself a cup of tea and sat down. He opened the refrigerator, found little in there except for spoiled milk, a couple of eggs, a pizza which had remained unopened for some months and looked inedible. After the one he had consumed at the police station he felt a hankering for another.

Still dressed in his suit he opened the front door and left the house. It was the first time, apart from the visit to the police station, that he had looked and acted normal. He was confused by his anguish over the Yanna White case. What he should have done, not that he could have, but he had seen the woman standing there in the court, her head down, continually fiddling with her hands, the scratches on her arm, her frustration and her inability to talk of matters that remained deep and hidden.

A competent defence lawyer would have dealt with the case better, he would have done better, but the lawyer that had been provided – she had refused to accept her family's offer to give her a highly competent lawyer – proved to be young, ineffective, and quite silly.

He knew that if it had been him, he would have put forward a more robust defence; he would have provided background information on where she came from, regardless of what she wanted.

The day he was told of her death was a sad day, and yet, years later, he reflected on it on an almost daily basis. He walked down the street; his head held up high. He knew of a pizza shop not far away, not that he'd ever been in, but today he would. As he rounded the corner, he stopped mid-stride. He turned around and walked back to his house. Once inside, he closed the door, changed his clothes, hung his suit up on a hanger in the wardrobe, and sat down.

'It's no use,' he murmured to himself.

Outside the yapping dog. He opened the door, picked up a rock and hurled it, catching the dog mid-body, the dog yelping and running away, the owner nearby.

Stanford closed his door. He knew there'd be trouble, but he didn't care.

He stood up, went to the wardrobe and put on his suit again, this time taking money from a safe hidden under the floorboards. He then walked out of the house. If his life was forfeit, then so be it. Stale milk and two eggs in his refrigerator were not worth living for.

And as for the yapping dog, he'd had enough of it, enough of the nosy neighbours, the life he led. If he could, he would turn back the clock and declare Yanna White innocent of all crimes, subject to psychiatric evaluation. She had been the victim of sex trafficking he knew, so had the defence and so had the prosecution, but everyone had let her down.

***

Liz Spalding's body was eventually released for burial. While Stephen Palmer's funeral had been attended by very few, this time there was a full turnout. Of the three husbands, two were present.

Jim Greenwood had come, not to take an active part, but to observe who attended: if anybody was unknown; if anyone was there out of guilt or to see the result of their handiwork.

Bob Palmer was dressed in a dark suit and wore a hat, although he removed it in the church. It was not as concealing as the mysterious woman's hat at Stephen's funeral, he knew that.

Greenwood knew the man well enough, and Palmer had clearly recognised him, the reason he kept attempting to move away from him. But the police inspector was not a man to be easily deterred. He needed to know his mood, what he'd been doing, what he planned to do. As Palmer attempted to move one way around the outside of the church, Greenwood walked the other. They met midway.

'How are you?' Greenwood said. He didn't like funerals, having buried his parents a couple of years previously, and although he would have preferred to stay in his car and observe it, this was his first murder investigation and he was determined on securing a conviction. And if he were successful, it would mean a promotion, possibly the chance to move to London to work with the Homicide department at Challis Street.

That's what he really wanted, and Palmer, who could not be the murderer, was definitely on the hunt for that person.

The police officer knew that Palmer would not be confined to one area. He would have the freedom to move around the country, to spy on people, to check what they were doing, where they were from, who they were.

'I'm fine,' Palmer said.

Greenwood looked at him, looked under the hat, saw a man with sullen eyes, his mouth turned down. 'You were upset when we met in the village. Have you had time to reflect, to compartmentalise her death, to move on with your life?'

'I believe so.'

Jim Greenwood did not believe a word the man said.

'We've not found the woman who murdered her.'

'I know.'

'How about you?' Greenwood said sternly.

'How do you expect me to be? It's a funeral; people are sad at funerals.'

'Let's be honest, Mr Palmer, you've not got over Liz Spalding. You're the type of man who doesn't forget easily. You're obsessive, nothing wrong in that, but when it leads to criminal actions, then I can't ignore it.'

'I will mourn Liz in my own way. I don't intend to do anything criminal.'

'I don't believe a word of what you're saying. You're not going to let this lie, and why are you here? Why are you staying at the back, instead of meeting and mingling with the other people, talking about the woman, the normal sort of stuff?'

170

'I have no interest in talking to any of them.'

'You don't want to hear from her ex-husbands, do you?'

'No.'

'Then, Mr Palmer, stop beating around the bush. You're here to see if there's someone unknown. Isn't that the truth?'

'I'm waiting for you to do your job, but that doesn't look like happening soon, does it?'

'Someone, somewhere, will slip up. It may even be you; you may show us where to look.'

'I don't see how. I spend my time at home. I do have a business still, even if it's the quiet time of the year.'

'Is this the end of it?' Greenwood asked.

'It is for me. I will go back to my little place, probably drink a bottle of whisky and aim to forget.'

Greenwood, with no more to say, moved away. He took his phone from his pocket and made a call. It was Larry that answered. He was in the office at Challis Street, two notches down on his belt, a healthier glow in his face, a nicotine patch on his arm. He had even got over fumbling in his pocket for the cigarette packet. He felt better, more so than he had in a long time, but it had not come easy.

'I just met our friend Bob Palmer,' Greenwood said. 'He's at Liz Spalding's funeral, keeping to the back. I don't trust him. He may do something stupid.'

'Or he could find the guilty woman,' Larry said.' If he does, he's dead.'

'If you arrest her, you can get a DNA sample.'

'She's broken no laws, none that we can prove.'

'It just goes to show,' Greenwood said. 'If you've got money, then you can get away with anything.'

171

'Palmer's just a bit player in this.'

'I don't trust the man, likely to do something stupid. I suggest you keep very close tabs on him. If he's seen out and about, then check on him, give me a call,' Greenwood said.

'Any more you want from us?' Larry asked.

'My name on the charge sheet.'

'If we have proof, you can come up to London and make the arrest.'

'Palmer might attempt to kill her.'

'If he succeeds, then I will arrest him.'

'If he doesn't?'

'What I said before, the man is dead if he fails. Hamish McIntyre is protective of his daughter.'

'I'll take to you later. I've got to check out Palmer, find out where he's gone and what he's up to.' Greenwood put his phone back in his pocket.

He went over to where Liz Spalding had been buried. At the side of the grave, only one person stood: Bob Palmer. Tears were streaming down his face, he was shaking, speaking to the body. Jim Greenwood stood back, but he couldn't hear what the man was saying, as though he was mouthing the words silently.

Greenwood walked over and stood next to him.

Palmer looked at him. 'She was so beautiful. Why did she have to die?' he said.

'It's not the dead that suffer, it's the living,' Greenwood said as he walked away to leave the man to mourn on his own.

Chapter 23

Gareth Armstrong neither approved of Samantha Matthews becoming involved in her father's business nor did he like her. Not that he would have dared make either of those views known to her father.

He had come to understand how the man thought and acted, and not a stupid man – after all, he had read a lot of books in the prison library – he thought that Hamish would be better handing over to him. After all, he knew the criminal mind, whereas his daughter didn't.

It was Gareth's day off. He met with Dean Atherton.

'What is it, Gareth?' Dean asked. He could see the worried look on his friend's face.

'You know Samantha Matthews.'

'Not personally. I keep you updated, but apart from that I keep my distance from her and her family.'

The father and daughter had been spending increasing amounts of time together, going over the legitimate real estate, the offshore bank accounts, the procedure where Hamish received a percentage from what he had farmed out to others to run. Gareth had to admit that he had never seen Hamish as content as when he was with Samantha.

But Hamish was not totally comfortable with exposing her to the villains he had dealt with; he confided that to Gareth on a couple of occasions.

'Maybe it's best this way,' Hamish had said more than once, taking a philosophical approach to the matter. 'Samantha is a smart woman, better educated than I am.'

'What about the times when people act against her interests?' Gareth said. 'Will she be capable of doing what you did in the past?'

'I did those out of necessity.'

Gareth knew that wasn't altogether true. Hamish had a vindictive streak, the need to inflict pain occasionally. He had never been there when Hamish had dealt out violence and death, but he could imagine the scene: the gore, the blood-curdling screams, the anguish, and Hamish, detached from emotion, enjoying the experience.

And now Hamish preferred to be at his mansion, meeting with the locals and discussing community affairs, the church fête. Gareth knew that none of them knew who he really was. Most would have said he was an aggressive businessman who had succeeded in the city, and they were right, of course. But none knew the real truth, and almost certainly wouldn't be perturbed by it, or not enough to isolate the man. People weren't interested unless it impacted them personally and Hamish had been generous and accommodating, even inviting the vicar around on several occasions, the two of them sitting in the conservatory discussing what was needed for the area.

Hamish had put his hand in his pocket on one occasion, given over thirty thousand pounds, his name on a plaque in the church, proudly displayed, naming him as the benefactor whose generous donation had allowed the roof to be repaired.

'What did you mean when you said you wouldn't be interested in what Hamish got up to?' Gareth asked, returning to his conversation with Atherton.

'Be careful, Gareth, if you're thinking of becoming involved in his business. You know what he's capable of. He's a great friend, a fearsome enemy.'

Gareth changed tack. He called over to the barman for two more pints of beer.

Dean put his knife and fork down and rubbed his stomach, wiped the gravy off his chin. 'That was great.'

'Any time.'

'Gareth, why are you asking these questions? You've got a great deal going where you are, no need for crime, no reason to live in a small and damp flat the same as I do.'

'Idle conversation, that's all,' Gareth said, but he wasn't sure if it was.

***

Bridget had gone through Charles Stanford's phone records. On the day that he mentioned, he had received two telephone calls, one of no importance, the other from the anonymous caller.

'It's a pay-as-you-go phone,' Bridget said. She was in Isaac's office, updating him on the information that Stanford had, for whatever reason, given them. 'It's no help to us, I'm afraid.'

Isaac sat back on his chair, uncertain of how to proceed. They had two murderers in their hands, but they were powerless.

Hamish McIntyre had no need to provide an alibi. After all, twenty years in the past, and anybody who could have confirmed guilt or innocence would have probably forgotten or could even be dead. And with Samantha Matthews, the fact that she had been at her house on the day when Liz Spalding had died meant little. It was, after all, a five-hour journey each way. She could have driven at night, thrown the woman off the cliff, and been back in London before two in the afternoon the next day. Checks on her car registration number had proven unsuccessful up until now. Bridget was coordinating that activity but once out of London, the chance of using automatic number plate recognition was reduced. But Isaac knew she would not give in.

'Do you have Samantha Matthews' mobile number?' Isaac asked.

'I've already checked. She could have a pay-as-you-go as well. A lot of people do.'

'Let's come back to this anonymous call,' Isaac said. 'Are we able to get any clue from it as to whether it was a man or a woman? Stanford said it was a man, but that doesn't mean it was.'

'I can't help you. Nothing more to go on.'

Bridget left the office and returned to her desk. She had plenty of work to keep her occupied for the rest of the day. Larry was out of the office, meeting with one of his informers. Wendy was also out, but she was back in Bedford Gardens.

It was not only Isaac who had been perturbed by Wally Vincent's visit there. Larry and Wendy had as well, their professional pride damaged. He had found out something they hadn't.

Wendy met with Billy Dempsey and Andrew Conlon. Neither had been able to add anything more although Billy had been cheeky, tried to get smart with

Wendy. Not that it did him any good because Wendy, used to dealing with tearaway children when she was a junior officer in Sheffield, more years in the past than she cared to remember, had put him in his place quick smart.

Leaving the two young boys, she knocked on a couple of doors in the street. At the first house, an elderly woman invited her in, said she had something, but over a cup of tea Wendy realised the woman was just lonely and glad of a chat. She excused herself, knocked on another door. A young man in his twenties answered. He was high on recreational drugs.

'What do you want?' he said.

It was a beautiful house, no doubt plenty of money, but that never guaranteed that the children would grow up sensible, Wendy thought. Her sons had grown up a credit to her and her husband. No free cars for them, and if they wanted money to go out of a night, they had had to earn it. Both were married now with good wives and children, and they came to see her regularly.

But the man at the door knew nothing of the murder house, not much of anything. Wendy thanked him and left him to whatever he was doing. She walked past 11 Bedford Gardens, looked up at the house. Something didn't seem right. She walked around to the back, found an open door. She knew enough not to walk in. If there were people inside, it could be dangerous.

She took out her phone and called Larry, keeping her voice low. 'Get out to 11 Bedford Gardens immediately, park down the end of the road. There's someone inside the house.'

'Where shall we meet?'

'I'm around the back. I suggest you wait at the front. If someone comes out the front, you'll see whoever it is. I don't want to move from where I am, not now. How long will you be?'

'Fifteen minutes, twenty maximum. Can you stay there for that long?'

'I'll have to.'

***

Bob Palmer looked out of the hotel window. He could see very little; the only view he had was a brick wall no more than twenty feet away. If he looked up, a glimpse of the sky; down revealed only a narrow pathway cluttered with rubbish. Inside the room, a television mounted on the wall, a bed in one corner, a wardrobe that consisted of half-a-dozen metal hangers and a curtain instead of a door. He had chosen the place because it was depressing and dirty. He had no need for luxury, only penance for not protecting her as he should have.

In the pub, the barman had known something, he knew that, but Jacob, a man who had known both Stephen and Liz, knew more. But the regular had clearly been too frightened to say anything. Even after he'd wandered over to him, sat at his table, attempted to engage him in further conversation, the man had said little.

'Don't get involved,' he'd said. 'Leave now, go back to where you belong.'

After two minutes of Palmer's increasingly agitated conversation, the man got up from his seat, downed his drink in one gulp, and walked out of the door. His parting comment: 'You'll get yourself killed.'

When he returned to the counter, the barman ignored Palmer, gave him a drink when it was ordered, took the money and walked away. Eventually, tiring of the cold shoulder, he had walked back to the hotel, switched on the TV, a mind-numbing quiz programme followed by a reality show where couples paired off before being married, only then to find another, be unfaithful, fall in love again. He knew it was errant nonsense, carefully scripted, but in his confused state he could admit to having laughed a couple of times.

He spent two days in that room, not leaving it except to buy a drink or eat a meal. In the end, he took the rattling lift to the ground floor, paid with a credit card and walked out. He got into his car and drove around the area. He drove past Stephen's former car yard, one more time past the pub where the information he wanted was, and then past where Liz had lived. He turned the radio on loud in the car, remonstrated with himself for his stupidity, for not being willing to let go. He parked the car, locked the door and walked back to the pub, two streets away.

Inside the barman was dispensing drinks.

'I'll have a pint,' Palmer said.

'I'll be with you in two minutes.'

'Jacob not coming in today?'

'He usually comes in later for a meal and a couple of pints. If you intend asking more questions, I suggest you don't. People are sensitive around here. A few rogues come in here, some you don't want to get on the wrong side of.'

'What if I did?'

'Then you're a bloody fool. Don't get me involved.'

179

Outside the pub, Bob took stock of the situation. It was clear that no one was going to speak voluntarily. He walked away, heading back to his car. Coming down the street, Jacob, a jaunty swagger about him. The man tried to avoid him, but Bob was not going to be deterred. He grabbed the man by the collar and dragged him into a narrow alley.

'Now tell me, who are you frightened of?' he said.

'You'll get yourself killed.'

'The woman with the tattoo, who is she?'

'She comes from a dangerous family.'

'The woman killed someone that I was fond of. I need answers.'

'You need your head seeing to. Thump me if you want to, kick me in the groin and smash my face, but I'll not talk.'

'Tell me, I want to know.' Palmer knew his grip was weakening. He had never hit anyone before, not even at school when he was being bullied. Not because he had been the smallest or the weakest; only because he had been a coward.

'You may have little value for your life, but I do for mine,' Jacob said.

Palmer released his hand from the man's collar. 'If you won't tell me, someone else will.'

'Not around here, they won't.'

Free of the crazed man, Jacob scuttled down the road and entered the pub; he needed a stiff drink. He made a phone call. He wasn't going to forfeit his life due to a misunderstanding.

Chapter 24

It took Larry almost twenty-five minutes to get to
Bedford Gardens, not that it mattered because twelve
minutes after Wendy had spoken to him, a man came out
of the back door of the house. He was dressed in a heavy
coat, a scarf around his neck.

Mr Stanford,' Wendy said, 'it's good to see you.
What are you doing here?'

'A man has got a right to check his assets.'

'Maybe he has, but this is a murder scene.
Different rules apply.'

Stanford appeared nervous. 'I went up to the top
floor,' he said. 'Not much to see and it's a long time since
I've been up there. Your people made a bit of a mess,
damaged the paint. I'll expect recompense.'

'I don't see why,' Wendy said. 'You were quite
happy to let the place be pulled down before. What's
changed your mind? Not many people would want to buy
a house that a murder had been committed in.'

'It's my decision if I do, not yours.'

It was a brave act of defiance, Wendy knew. The
man had crossed the crime scene tape. It was enough to
take him into Challis Street and to question him further.

After Stanford had closed the back door and
locked it, the two of them went and sat in Wendy's car.
Stanford enjoyed the warmth of the vehicle.

'Mr Stanford, this makes no sense,' Wendy said,
'First you deny any knowledge of the house and the
murder, and then we find out that you were in the house

some months ago, and on top of that there's a phone call. Why don't you tell us the truth so you can go home, mind your own business, and we'll leave you alone?'

'I have no more to add. I gave you all that I knew. I was intrigued, and I had to visit the house; it was essential to understand what was so special about it. Why not somewhere else?'

'And why did someone phone you up, assuming that you would go and discover the body and tell the police.'

'It's a mystery to me.'

'There has to be a connection between you and the dead body, possibly the murderer, and definitely the anonymous voice.'

'Not that I know of.'

'Maybe you do, or perhaps you haven't made the connection. Think back over the years to those you've met and those you sentenced to prison. Men inside dwell on the reason that they're there. They don't consider that they had committed a crime and had been caught. To some of them, it was the person who caught them, but mainly it's the person who sat in front of them, a wig on his head, a gavel in his hand.'

'Yes, I know all this. I've had one or two threaten me as they were led out of the court. One or two, after they had been released, thought they could hang around where I lived, sometimes making phone calls, spraying graffiti on the fence.'

'In Brighton?'

'Not Brighton. And not here either. I had a place in Bayswater, but I've sold it now. No need to live in London.'

Wendy turned down the heater in the car; it was getting too hot.

A tap on the car window. It was Larry.

'Anything more to say?' he said, looking at Stanford.

'I've done nothing wrong, Inspector Hill.'

'That's as maybe, but you were in the house again. No doubt you're aware how bad this looks.'

'Not at all. Two and two make four, not five, or don't you know that.'

'I know it well enough. You keep coming up with hidden snippets. You were looking for something, a clue, an idea, anything.'

'Mr Stanford admitted that much to me,' Wendy said. 'He's interested in putting his old skills to work again.'

Wally Vincent had come up trumps. Stanford could as well, Larry knew that, especially if he was hiding something from the police.

Larry, feeling the chill outside, got into the back of Wendy's car.

'I've been speaking to your sergeant, explaining my interest, trying to make some connection to this house and to the murder,' Stanford said.

'I've spoken to Mr Stanford about this,' Wendy said. 'He's the key, even if he doesn't realise it.'

'Why don't you cooperate with us, Mr Stanford?' Larry said. 'You're not going to cover the ground, not as quickly as we can, and you're not that agile, are you?'

'The brain's still active even if the body is failing.'

'And that's it, isn't it? We've reawakened your analytical mind, your ability to see through people to evaluate situations. You had a distinguished record as a judge; there's no doubt given the opportunity you could apply your expertise more successfully than we could. We're just plodding policeman, but you're an intellectual with the capacity to conduct deep thought and analysis.'

'I might be able to, but I'm dumbfounded about this house.'

'Do we need to go back to Challis Street, Mr Stanford?' Larry said.

'I don't see what for.'

'What will you do after here?' Wendy asked.

'I'll go back to my house in Brighton.'

It was strange, Stanford thought as he sat in the sergeant's car. Each time, I reveal a little more. Why do I do that? Why don't I keep my mouth shut or tell them everything I know?

'Level with us, Mr Stanford,' Larry said. 'Give us all that you know and leave the investigation to us. We're dealing with very violent people here, people who have no hesitation in killing and maiming. Do you understand that?'

'I think I recognised the voice,' Stanford said. 'And believe me, I wasn't trying to hide that from you. Not immediately at least. When I received a call, there was something familiar about it, but then I had met so many people over the years, some good, some bad, some psychopathic and evil.'

'We're listening,' Wendy said.

'When I received the call, I was frightened. It had a sense of malevolence about it.'

'But you came to the house?

'A compulsion. I had to.'

'Yet you still chose not to tell us.'

'I told you, I didn't want to become involved. There's nothing wrong with that. A body upstairs that I had nothing to do with. Questions would be asked, aspersions made, guilt by association. My reputation would have been compromised.'

'We can accept that,' Larry said. 'Tell us about the voice. Who do you think it sounded like?'

'I can't prove it. I don't want my name mentioned as the source.'

'In a trial, we might have to, but for now, I'll give you my word.'

'I don't know why this person spoke of crime in the house. It would have been easier to tell me to look on the third floor.'

'Eventually, the reason will be known,' Wendy said.

'It was an old man, a firm voice. A man used to leadership.'

'A criminal?'

'It was Hamish McIntyre who phoned me. I'm sure of it.'

'Which means,' Larry said, 'that he knew his son-in-law was dead at the top of your house.'

'I can't tell you any more. I intended to check this house out and then to confront the man. He's older now, not as dynamic as he was, and besides, I would have left notification as to where I had gone and who I was seeing.'

'How?'

'I would have detailed my thoughts and my actions, put them in an envelope and mailed them to Bedford Gardens.'

'Assuming that if we couldn't find you, we would have come looking?'

'You would have checked this house, found the letter and followed up on what I had written.'

'And if you survived an encounter with McIntyre, you would have come here, picked up the letter, gone back to Brighton and we'd never know.'

'If he'd admitted to knowledge of Matthews' body in this house, then I'm not sure what I would have done or said.'

You would have done nothing,' Larry said.

'Marcus Matthews was of no value, nor is Hamish McIntyre. Either of them dead and buried is fine by me. As a judge, I maintained neutrality. As a private citizen, I do not. The scum of the earth, the two of them, all of their cohorts as well.'

'Can we trust you to go home,' Larry said. 'Shout at the neighbour's dog if you want to, throw rocks, but otherwise, stay put in that house. Neither Sergeant Gladstone nor myself want to be peeling your body off a wall somewhere, is that clear?'

'It's clear. Please keep me informed as to what goes on.'

'Is there any connection between Yanna White and Hamish McIntyre?' Wendy asked.

'I can't prove it. Hamish McIntyre is an amoral man. To him, Yanna White and the other women would be nothing.'

'Do you believe that?'

'She was trafficked by men such as McIntyre. If it weren't McIntyre, it would have been someone else; the man had his fingers in many pies.'

'Thank you, Mr Stanford.' Larry said. 'People have died, and the chains are being rattled. Other people could well die, and we don't want it to be you.'

Larry got out of the car, opened the door for Stanford, shook his hand and wished him well. Before leaving, Stanford walked around to Wendy's side of the car, opened her door and thanked her.

As he shuffled down the street, Larry and Wendy could only see a tired old man.

***

Jacob had attempted to make the phone call, but with his hands shaking so much it was impossible until he had drunk two whiskies to calm him down. He had not only known Stephen Palmer and Liz Spalding; he had also known Hamish McIntyre in the past when he'd lived in the area at the start of his career. He had been just a local hoodlum then, but Jacob knew him well enough to occasionally have a chat and a drink in the pub with him.

Outside the pub, Jacob lit a cigarette. He punched in the number; at the other end of the line, a phone rang. It was answered by a man Jacob didn't know.

'Can I talk to Mr McIntyre?' Jacob said. 'It's a matter of some importance.'

'You can tell me.'

'I prefer to talk to Mr McIntyre. Someone's been nosing around, asking questions. I thought he should know.'

'Are you looking for money?'

'Money for information, no way. All I want is a quiet life.'

'Smart man,' Armstrong said. 'I'll get him for you.'

Armstrong walked through the house, found Hamish watching the news on the television. He handed over the phone. 'It's for you,' he said. 'Someone sticking their nose in.'

Hamish took the phone and put it to his ear. 'What is it?'

'Hamish, long time,' Jacob said.

'Get to the point.'

'Jacob Wolfenden. We used to get together years ago, down the pub, have a chat.'

'Oh, yes, I remember. How are you?'

'All the better for talking to you. Someone's been asking questions, and I don't want to be involved.'

'Trouble for me?'

'There's a man who says he's related to someone who died a long time ago.'

'Give me the facts and don't worry, Jacob.'

'He's asking about a woman with a butterfly tattoo, just above her wrist on the inside of her arm.'

Hamish remembered when Samantha had come home drunk one night, the tattoo proof that she had made a fool of herself.

'Why does he want to know?' Hamish asked. He had been sitting down before, but now he was up and walking around. Jacob, he knew, was a man who never asked questions, and had never committed an illegal activity in his life.

'He believes that the woman…' Jacob said, unwilling to mention the name.

'We know who we're talking about here, don't we?' McIntyre said.

'I didn't want to say her name.'

'Fair enough, Jacob. You're safe with me. Nothing will happen to you. Now tell me the full story.'

'Palmer believes this woman is involved in the death of another woman.'

'The other woman?'

'Liz Spalding.'

'I see. Where can we find him?'

'He's been in the pub a couple of times, a damn nuisance. Kept asking me questions, not that I gave him any answers. Sure, I mentioned that I knew his brother, Stephen; Liz as well. When he started asking piercing questions, I backed off and went and sat on my own.'

Wolfenden decided it was best not to tell McIntyre that he had warned Palmer to back off.

'The next day, he grabbed me in the street,' Jacob continued. 'Dragged me into an alley. I was scared, but I wasn't going to talk. In the end, I got away. What should I do?'

'Where can I find this *individual?*' McIntyre said, the emphasis making it clear to Jacob that Palmer had trouble coming his way.

'I haven't seen him since, but it was only an hour or so ago. I tried to phone before, but I needed to calm my nerves.'

'You had my number?'

'I've had it for many years.'

McIntyre thought that was possible. He hadn't changed the number on his phone for a long time. And Jacob, an insignificant man, he trusted.

'Go back to the pub, go back to your drink. Let me know if you see this man or you have any idea where he is.'

Hamish put the phone down and called to Gareth. 'There's a man asking questions. I want you to find out who he is and grab him.'

189

'Where do I find him?

'Get down to the Stag Hotel, find Jacob Wolfenden. Don't threaten him, he's okay with me. He'll update you.'

'Do you trust him?'

'The man knows who I am and what I can do. Find out who the other man is, put out feelers, ask around. But don't be too obvious.'

'And when I find him?'

'Keep tabs on him. The police are not far behind. He may have spoken to them and told them things he shouldn't have.'

'And then?'

'I'll need to consider the options, but don't let on that you know anything that can help him. Is that clear?'

'Yes,' Gareth said.

Chapter 25

Down in Cornwall, Jim Greenwood was keeping the team updated, questioning the locals, trying to find out if there had been a car in the area at the time of the woman's death that didn't belong to a local. But that was a needle in a haystack approach, Greenwood knew. The village was scenic; it attracted more than its fair share of tourists, some staying at the local hotel or a campsite up the road, others walking down by the harbour, taking a few pictures, and then driving on to the next tourist attraction.

'I believe Charles Stanford,' Wendy said in the office at Challis Street. 'He was telling the truth this time.'

'If he was,' Isaac said, 'what can we do with this information? We can't go asking McIntyre directly if he made a phone call on a specific date to an individual about a crime at Bedford Gardens, can we?'

'We have to somehow,' Larry said.

Isaac was pleased that the man had turned the corner. He hadn't been sure that Larry would succeed, as alcohol is seductive to some, but so far, he had. It was in large part due to his wife's encouragement and that of his colleagues in the department. The danger was when everyone became complacent.

'We can speculate,' Isaac said. 'Why would McIntyre be interested in Marcus Matthews' body being discovered? If he hadn't killed him, which we know he hadn't, then why did he want the body found? And how long had he known that it was there?'

'It had been six years,' Larry said. 'Did he know that it had been there for all that time? And if he did, why hadn't he told his daughter? We've got more questions than answers.'

'Is there a question?' Bridget said. 'I couldn't find out who made the phone call to Stanford. If Hamish McIntyre knew the body was there, then he knows the murderer. Do you have knowledge of his associates, the sort of person who could commit murder?'

'McIntyre's associates wouldn't have gone through such a convoluted exercise. And they wouldn't have entered into any sort of agreement with Matthews,' Isaac said. 'We've discussed this before, we're looking for an ethical man, a man of strong morals.'

'A criminal with a conscience,' Larry said.

'Not necessarily a criminal. We know that Matthews, apart from his criminal activities, had a strong social bent, an underlying ethic.'

'Doesn't help,' Larry said. He couldn't see their conversation going anywhere. If McIntyre was important, then he needed to be pressured.

'Hassle McIntyre, is that what you're thinking, Larry?' Isaac said. They had worked together for some years now. He knew instinctively what Larry would be thinking. He was a bull in a china shop type of police officer, the sort that goes in guns blazing, although Isaac knew that wasn't the best analogy, as no police officer was armed unless they had the authority. They'd had a case a couple years back when the need to carry weapons had been agreed to. Larry had taken one for a while, so had Isaac, but he had never been comfortable with the idea. Wendy had refused. In the end, the man who had killed four came meekly, and no weapons had been necessary.

'How else do you expect us to get to the bottom of this?'

'Where is Stanford now? Back in his home?'

'We've got Wally Vincent keeping tabs on him. He went around to check the other day, even got an invite in for a cup of tea. Stanford's turned over a new leaf, although Wally's not confident it will last.'

'A clear conscience?' Wendy said.

'Stanford thought that McIntyre may be involved with the trafficking of women.' Isaac said.

'It will be almost impossible to prove,' Larry said. 'And besides, what would he have done? It's usually the gangsters back in the country of origin who are responsible.'

'He could have financed the transportation, ensured that the lorries they were coming in on had been modified for the transportation of human cargo. He could have dealt with the drivers, bribed them as necessary, threatened others. And once the women were in the country, he could have arranged the safe houses. Any sign of occupation at Bedford Gardens?'

'We've all seen the report from the crime scene investigation team,' Larry said. 'No one has lived in that house for a long time.'

'Before that?'

'Dust accumulates over the years, and everyone would have been looking at the period pertinent to the crime.'

'Who owned it before him? Check it out, talk to them. See if there's anything untoward.'

'The locals might have seen something,' Bridget said.

'People mind their own business, you know that,' Larry said. 'If they had been slipping women in late at night, one or two at a time, and confining them to a room, keeping them quiet, nobody would have noticed anything. Nobody had seen Charles Stanford go in there eleven months ago.'

'Larry's right,' Isaac said. 'People are blind, and if it doesn't affect them directly, they don't get involved. What happens if people see something that makes them feel uncomfortable? Do they report it to the police, or do they walk on by?'

'Walk on by most of the time,' Wendy said. She had had a car stolen from outside her house one night. A man walking his dog later admitted that he had seen the felon, thought nothing of it, even though the man had a crowbar on the door handle. It was human nature, she knew that. Mind your own business, look out for yourself, and endeavour to have a peaceful life.

'I'll find out what I can about the house,' Bridget said. 'Give me a couple of hours, and I should have something for you.'

'In the meantime,' Isaac said, 'McIntyre. We need to revisit him, but we need to be very careful.'

***

Armstrong followed Hamish McIntyre's instructions, up to a point. He wasn't going to harm Jacob, Hamish had been clear on that, but there was no reason why he could not scare the man. Too many years in prison had made him distrustful of anyone until proven to the contrary.

194

He had drawn up alongside Jacob. Hamish had described how he had remembered him, skinny, looked like a weasel.

Armstrong leant out the window of the Mercedes. 'Jacob, over here,' he said.

'What for?'

'We spoke on the phone.'

'Hamish?'

'The name's Gareth, Gareth Armstrong. I work for the man. He told me you're a good person. Someone I should talk to.'

'I don't want any trouble.'

'There's no trouble getting into the car, is there?'

Jacob knew he didn't want to, but the man had influence with Hamish McIntyre. To not get into the car would be pure folly, he thought.

Pulling away from the kerb, Armstrong accelerated into the traffic and headed away from the area.

'We could talk over a pint,' Jacob said, making small talk. He regretted phoning Hamish. 'But if you fancy a cup of coffee. I'm easy either way.'

Armstrong could see that the man wasn't comfortable. It was the effect he wanted.

'It won't take long. We need somewhere private. I need to know more details of what you said to Hamish.'

'I told him all I could. Just that this Palmer was looking for a woman, nothing more.'

'So, what's the connection?'

'What did Hamish tell you to do?'

'He told me to find Palmer, find out what he was talking about, why he was interested.'

The car was moving fast; soon, they would be in the country. Jacob knew this was not a friendly little chat. This wasn't what Hamish McIntyre had said would happen.

The car came to a halt outside an old barn. Gareth got out of the car, went around to the other side, grabbed the man by his collar and pulled him roughly into the barn.

'You may have told Hamish a story, but I'm looking out for him. I need to know more,' Armstrong said.

'There is no more,' Jacob bleated as he was roughly thrown to the ground. The place smelled of animals and hay, and he suffered from allergies. 'There's no more to say. I told Hamish all I knew.'

'Okay, let's get back to where we were. Palmer, what does he look like?'

'Nothing special, nothing like his brother. An irritating whine to his voice. Mr McIntyre won't like you holding me here. He promised me that I would be safe.'

'I needed to know you were telling the truth. Mr McIntyre looks after me well. I'm not going to let anyone, not you, not even Palmer, get in the way of that. You met Palmer in the pub, I know that much.'

'In the pub, yes. He was interested in his brother and Liz Spalding. The barman called me over. He knew that I'd lived in the area for a long time and that I probably knew them.'

'Did you?'

'Yes, I did. Stephen was a good guy. Liz was the sort of woman men lusted over, but she was keen on Stephen. Only he was a player; he had other women on the side, couldn't help himself.'

196

'The other women?'

'Palmer thought one of them was involved in the death of Liz Spalding. I told Mr McIntyre this much. I never mentioned her name.'

'For your own protection?'

'What else could I do? I remember Hamish when he used to live in the area. Back then, he was on the way up. He had a few girls turning tricks in an old hotel up the road, buying and selling whatever, making a name for himself.'

'Do you believe this woman murdered Liz Spalding?'

The situation was calmer. Jacob got up off the ground and sat on a bale of hay. Armstrong sat across from him on another bale.

'I don't get involved. Palmer thought there was a connection and he wanted to find the woman. I wouldn't talk to him. He knows that I know who she is.'

'Who is it then?'

'Did Mr McIntyre ask you to find the name of the woman?'

'Not directly.'

'He knows who it is. If I tell you and it gets back to Mr McIntyre, he'll not be pleased.'

'And if you don't tell me, I'll make sure to tell him that you were difficult.'

Armstrong sat for a moment. He looked around at their surroundings, realised that the countryside and he did not agree. Even so, he had managed to wangle himself an easy job at the last prison, out on the prison farm.

'This is not what Mr McIntyre agreed to, is it?' Jacob said.

'Not entirely, but he wants me to find Palmer. And if Palmer is looking for this woman and he makes the connection, that's where I'll find him. And if the woman is important to Hamish, he won't thank me if she comes to any harm.'

'I thought he'd be in the pub again. He was angry and wanted to hit me, but he couldn't.'

'Why not?'

'As I said, Stephen was a dynamic sort of person, a person you could look up to, but his brother had nothing going for him. He said he was fond of Liz, but I reckon it was more than that. He was the sort of man who would have been pining after his brother's girlfriends, never getting one, feeling the frustration.'

'Jacob, work with me, and we'll find Palmer.'

'Nothing criminal. Maybe I've been a fool all my life, but I've not done anything. It's probably the reason why I never amounted to much in life, but it suits me fine now. As long as I can afford a drink and lunch out occasionally, then I'm content.'

'I'm content as well,' Armstrong said. 'Hamish has treated me well, given me somewhere to live, a nice motor to drive, money in my pocket. I want for nothing, and I'm not going to let him down. Anything that helps me to find this Palmer, I need to know. Now, who is this mysterious woman?'

'It's his daughter,' Jacob said reluctantly.

'Samantha?'

'He's only got the one.'

'Let's go, Jacob. Do you know where he was staying?'

'No idea. Each time I met him, it was either in the pub or on the street. He's not a local, I know that.'

Armstrong helped Jacob up from his seat, and the two men drove away. Half a mile down the road, a pub. A couple of pints later, a good feed, and all had been forgotten. Jacob was still frightened. A misinterpretation, a wrong word, and Hamish McIntyre would be after him.

Chapter 26

The pieces in the puzzle were coming together, Isaac could see that. Down in Cornwall, Jim Greenwood was performing well, as was Wally Vincent in Brighton. Soon enough, somebody, somewhere, would make the connection, or else one of the murderers would make a mistake.

Hamish McIntyre was out in his mansion, Samantha at his side; Gareth Armstrong not far away.

Gareth updated Hamish on his conversation with Jacob Wolfenden, omitting that he had roughed the man up.

Bridget set up a phone conference, dialled in Greenwood and Vincent. The team were in the conference room at Challis Street.

'I've not given up down here,' Greenwood said. 'I've still got some ground to cover although nobody in Polperro seems to know very much. Mrs Venter, the last person to see Liz Spalding alive, believes she did see another woman.'

'Did you follow Palmer after he left the village?' Larry asked.

'As best I could. He revisited his brother's grave, spoke to the vicar.'

'Did you speak to him?'

'Not directly. I spoke to the man's wife. He was at a seminary for a couple of days.'

'Then it may be a good idea to go back,' Isaac said. 'Have a chat with the man, see what Palmer told him.'

'I wouldn't write him off,' Greenwood said. 'He's not going to leave this alone.'

'We've got another one down in Brighton. Wally Vincent is looking after him.'

'Since his return, the man's been a model citizen,' Vincent said. 'Almost affable.'

'What do you reckon, Wally?' Wendy said. 'Is he holding something in reserve?'

'You'd never know with Stanford, a smart man, deep, thinks things through.'

'If Hamish McIntyre hears of these two, their lives won't be worth living,' Larry said.

'We still need to go visit the man,' Isaac said. 'How do you confront a man and accuse him of making a phone call to Stanford when we have no proof?'

'A dangerous customer,' Greenwood said, 'from what Larry was telling me.'

'He is. We're Palmer's best protection. If he knows something that we don't, he'd better tell us, leave it to us.'

'Coming back to Stanford,' Larry said. 'He told us that he believed that McIntyre was the person who phoned him. Wally, any reason to think he knows more?'

'I don't think so. The man's talkative enough at the present moment. I don't want him to clam up, just keeping it friendly for now.'

'No complaints to your superintendent about harassing him? Wendy asked.

'None at all, and the superintendent even patted me on the back the other day, told me what a good job I was doing and to keep him updated.'

'Promotion in the offing?' Larry said.

'Who knows?'

'Let's get back to a plan of action,' Isaac said. 'We need to find Palmer and fast. Jim, stay with Stanford, maintain a cordial relationship with him. Although he did manage to get up to the third floor in Bedford Gardens on his last visit.'

'You don't suspect him, do you?'

'Not at this time. Jim, get back to the vicar, find out what Palmer may have told him.'

'I'll make a trip up to Oxford, meet with Palmer again,' Larry said.

'Normally I would agree with you,' Isaac said. 'But this time you'd better focus on Palmer, see if he's in the area.'

'I'll check out Palmer's house,' Wendy said.

'I could do with a few hours out of the office,' Isaac said. 'I'll go with you.'

***

Jim Greenwood was the first to act. Even though it was midday and it was a long drive, he was in the car and out to where Stephen Palmer was buried. He found the vicar tending to his vegetables in the small garden at the back of the vicarage. The vicar's wife was in the kitchen.

'How can I help you, Inspector?' the vicar said.

Greenwood had not met the man before. 'I spoke to your wife the last time. She said that Bob Palmer had been up here.'

'I found him by the grave, trying to tidy up around it. It's dreadful how people neglect their loved ones after a few years. I try to do my best, pick up the occasional weed here and there, but I can't do it all, not any more.'

'I'm sure those in your care understand,' Greenwood said. He wasn't much of a churchgoer, and when his time came, it would be a cremation, his ashes thrown into the river and those mourning him down to the pub, a few drinks on him.

'I like to think they do,' the vicar said. 'But how can I help you? What more can I tell you that my wife hasn't?'

'The minor details can be crucial. The man may have said something, asked you something seemingly obscure; but to us, it may be significant.'

The two men sat down on garden chairs.

The vicar's wife, a comely woman, round and short with rosy cheeks and a pleasant smile, put a couple of cups of tea on the table, a plate of home-made scones with jam and cream. 'They're freshly baked,' she said. 'As good as you get anywhere in the West Country.'

Greenwood, partial to a scone, applied the jam and cream generously; so did the vicar. The two men sat quietly for a couple of minutes. A robin flew by, a thrush gave its melodious song.

'We get deer at the bottom of the garden in winter,' the vicar said. 'They've got used to us now, and we always try to give them something to eat. Never get too close to them, though, no chance of hand feeding.'

Greenwood felt at ease. The vicarage, a two-storey building, more than three hundred years old, had a certain charm about it. He looked at the vicar and his wife, comfortable in each other's company. He realised that was what he would have liked with his first wife, but she was gone and the second was giving trouble. It wouldn't be long before he'd be on his own again.

'How long did you speak to Palmer?' Greenwood said.

'Ten minutes, no more. I had to get back to the house, prepare for Sunday's sermon, not that many turn up these days. Are you a religious man?'

'I'm afraid not.'

'Not many are, but I think they're missing something good in their lives. It's not only about money and power, is it?'

'I try to live a good life,' Greenwood said. 'Sometimes a few too many drinks, and maybe my language is a bit colourful. But I'm a police officer, and sometimes we see things we'd rather not. Shakes your faith, the inhumanity.'

'Sin, the work of the devil.'

'That's not why I'm here, is it?'

'No, I suppose it isn't. You want to talk about Mr Palmer. You want to find out who killed that poor woman and to punish the person for their crime.'

'My job is to find and arrest the person.'

'What goes through the minds of people who do such things?' the vicar said.

Jim Greenwood thought the man should get out and about a bit more. Naivety, a belief in the meek inheriting the earth, the good ensured of a place in heaven, was alright in the church, an admirable sentiment. But he knew that evil abounded in the most unlikely of places. It had even come to a small village by the sea.

'That's not my concern. And as to the woman's punishment, that's up to a judge and a jury to decide, not me.'

'Mr Palmer told me about the dead woman. He spoke about his brother, but not as much as he did about her.'

'I spoke to him the next day after the murder. Told him to leave well alone, but I don't trust him. I'm convinced he's going to do something.'

'You spoke to him out of a feeling of goodness in your heart?'

'I think you're putting too fine a point to it, Vicar,' Greenwood said. 'I don't want another dead body, and I don't want to have to arrest the man. Quite frankly, he's plain stupid.'

'He spoke about the other two women at the funeral. He said he knew one, Bec Johnson.'

'I've heard that name mentioned before.'

'It was the other one he was more concerned about, the woman with the hat.'

'We know who the woman is, but we can't prove she committed the murder. Palmer, who hasn't found out who she is yet, believed she was Liz Spalding's rival for Stephen's affections.'

'A married woman, he believed.'

'He was unable to give us much in the way of information, only that she wore a wedding ring.'

'He questioned me about her. He didn't know about the tattoo.'

'What tattoo? It's not been mentioned before.'

'I shook the woman's hand, offered a few words of consolation. She thanked me, made a few remarks about what a sad occasion it was, the usual stuff.'

'*The tattoo?*' Greenwood asked again.

'On her right hand, just above the wrist on the inside, a small butterfly was tattooed there. Is it important?'

'I'd say so, Vicar.'

Jim Greenwood knew what he had was dynamite. 'Thank your wife for the tea and scones, they were delicious. I have to make a phone call.'

'I can't think of anything else. If I do, I'll give you a call,' the vicar said.

Greenwood walked around the house, opened the garden gate and moved over to near his car. He took out a cigarette and lit up. His phone, last year's model, was in his inside jacket pocket. He took it out and made a call.

***

Armstrong considered his options. If he were intent on seizing Hamish's criminal empire, it would mean the man's daughter had to be out of the way.

So far, he had been honest with his boss, telling him what Wolfenden had said. He had even looked around the area, visiting the pub in question, checking out the alley where Palmer had accosted Wolfenden.

Armstrong knew that he did not have the innate street cunning of Hamish, nor the intellect of his daughter. But what he had was a lot of time in prison, contacts, people who owed him a favour, or would do anything if the money was right.

In the mansion, Samantha was nowhere to be seen. Hamish, freed from discussing business-related matters with his daughter, was back in the conservatory tending to his orchids.

'I've got feelers out,' Armstrong said. 'I need to take off for a few days, check out a couple of addresses. The man doesn't appear to be in London at this time.'

'Four days, no more. I want to know where this man is. See if Wolfenden has been discreet. I don't want my daughter open to ridicule and innuendo.'

'Wolfenden?'

'What does he know?'

'He knows the reason Palmer's asking questions. He knows your daughter.'

'I gave my word that he was safe,' Hamish said. 'If the police talk to him?'

'Who knows with people like him? Decent, honest, credit to his neighbourhood.'

'Naive and stupid, you're right, Gareth. If his freedom is on the line, he'll talk. And once the police make the connection…'

'There's still no proof.'

'It may be best to nip it in the bud. Are you up to it?'

Armstrong knew what McIntyre was intimating. He'd held up a few places in his time, threatened people with guns, but the man was suggesting murder. He wasn't sure how to reply. He took a couple of minutes to think it over.

'I'll do it,' Armstrong said. If he did this for Hamish, he knew that his position would be more secure. He would be the natural successor if Samantha were either killed or incarcerated.

Samantha returned as he was leaving.

Although he wanted to be rid of her, Armstrong had to admit that she was a attractive woman; the sort of woman, if he were a few years younger, who would have suited him just fine.

Chapter 27

Bob Palmer left the area soon after dragging Wolfenden into the alley. He was confused, unsure where to go. In the end, he found himself back at his house. He peered through the curtains in the front room, saw his neighbours, washing the car or taking the dog for a walk or playing with the children. None of it interested him.

The best he could do was to go back to London, possibly revisit the Stag Hotel, not that he had enjoyed the ambience of the place, nor the recalcitrant attitude of the barman. And if Jacob – he never knew his surname – had made an official complaint, there was the possibility that the police would be interested.

He spent the night in the house, not sleeping, increasingly agitated, before leaving in the early hours of the morning before the sun had risen.

In London, he checked into a hotel ten miles away from where Stephen had conducted his business. He had thought in his confused mind to start enquiring at the local tattoo shops, but he decided against that. He made a few phone calls, old acquaintances of Stephen's that he had known, but most of them had moved on; a few answered the phone, none expressed any interest in meeting the dead man's dull brother.

Palmer turned on the television in the room, an old black and white movie, *Sherlock Holmes* he thought it was, but he wasn't focusing. Inside him, the constant welling up of emotion, thinking back to that night with Liz.

Nobody cared about her, only him. He had seen the other mourners at the funeral, sad faces for sure, but a few weeks and they would get on with their lives.

He walked out of the hotel and took a bus back to where he had met Jacob. He walked into the bar, even though he had said he would not.

'A pint of beer, he said to the barman.

'If you're looking for Jacob, he's not here.'

'Jacob, not this time. I've no questions, not any more. And if I did, you wouldn't tell me, would you?'

'If you're aiming to drag me into an alleyway, the same as you did Jacob, don't expect to come out of there in one piece. People like you sicken me. Nerdy, clinging, unable to deal with life.'

'You're right, I suppose. They're both dead, Stephen and Liz; get on with life, that's what I say.'

The barman, experienced as he was with dealing with people down on their luck, people with a sad story to tell, knew that the man did not intend to get on with his life.

He hadn't liked the look of him the first time, and as to why he had ventured into the pub again... God only knows, he thought. And if they ever find out that he's looking for her, then it's his funeral, not mine.

'I'll give you a word of advice,' the barman said. 'Get out of here before someone sees you.'

'Who?'

'I'm giving advice, not details. It's up to you to make your own decision. I can supply you with beer for as long as you keep paying, but I don't want blood in here; not yours, not mine.'

'Then give me a name,' Palmer said.

'Not a chance.'

In the bar, Bob Palmer could see very few people. It wasn't an attractive place to be, not trendy, out of tune with the modern customer.

To one side of the bar, an elderly couple sat holding hands, probably reflecting on their lives, he thought. Near to the open fire at the rear of the bar, an old woman sat, a small glass in front of her. She was knitting. He remembered his mother used to knit, but that was a long time ago. Nowadays, nobody had the time. Three young people sat along the far wall. He was sure they were underage, but the barman obviously didn't care, and neither did he.

'Give me a hint, and I'll go,' Palmer said.

'I've given you my advice. That's all you're going to get from me.'

'Jacob, what time do you expect him in?'

'He's a free agent, comes and goes as he likes. Wish I could. I'm stuck here with two children at home, a wife who needs more money. Are you single?'

'I'm single, always have been,' Palmer replied.

Nothing like it. I can remember when I was on my own, plenty of good nights down the pub, not this dive, mind you. No shortage of women, ready and able.'

'Why did you get married?'

'She told me she was on the pill, but you can't trust them, never can. She wanted a kid, but she wanted the ring on the finger as well. I was done for.'

'Jacob? Where can I find him?'

'Look here, Palmer, I've been civil to you, but get out of here, please. It's good advice I'm giving you. If you don't go, I'll have to make a phone call, not that I want to. I don't want to tell these people where you are. You're probably a decent enough guy, mind your own

211

business as a rule. You're educated, I can see that. This place is for losers.'

Not sure what to do, Palmer downed his drink and left. Outside, on the other side of the road, keeping out of sight, Jacob Wolfenden. He made a phone call.

***

The team in Challis Street realised the importance of what Jim Greenwood had found out from the vicar. Isaac and Wendy were in the car heading to Palmer's house in Oxford.

Isaac was on hands-free, Larry and Greenwood on the conference call. 'Palmer hasn't made the connection yet?' Isaac said.

'Not according to my contacts,' Larry said.

'He soon will. Is the tattoo correct?'

'I've seen it,' Wendy said. 'Not that I thought much of it. There's more than one woman in London with tattoos on her arm.'

'Palmer is not looking for those women,' Greenwood said. 'If he talks to the right people, he'll find out the name.'

'And when he does? What do you reckon?' Isaac said.

'Barely able to blow the skin off a rice pudding, but if the man's aggrieved, sees himself as the dead woman's avenger, then who knows.'

'He's capable,' Wendy said. 'Men like him keep to themselves all their lives, but once riled, they're unstoppable. If he finds Samantha Matthews, he'll do something stupid, regardless. Probably thinks there's a place for him in heaven, Liz at his side.'

'I don't think he's religious,' Greenwood said.

'He doesn't have to be,' Isaac said.

'What do we do?' Larry asked.

'We're not going to give Samantha Matthews protection, that's for sure. And if we let her know about Palmer, then we know what will happen.'

'Her father will act.'

'Catch-22,' Isaac said. 'Palmer's heading into areas that he doesn't understand or know.'

'Or cares about,' Wendy said.

'What's Wally Vincent got to say for himself?' Greenwood said. 'He's got the judge down there. He may know more, possibly find another clue from Stanford.'

'Not sure he can,' Isaac said. 'We can get him on the line. Give me two minutes to bring him in.'

'We're not far from Palmer's place,' Wendy said.

'Stay back, keep an eye on the house from a distance; see if anyone's there.'

The phone rang in Brighton, Wally Vincent answered.

'We've got Jim Greenwood on the line down in Cornwall,' Isaac said. 'Palmer has a important clue to this mysterious woman that we didn't know about previously.'

'McIntyre's daughter?'

'That's it. And the man doesn't need proof, not like we do.'

'I don't think there's much I can do,' Vincent said. 'Charles Stanford, from what we can see, hasn't got anything to do with this.'

'Talk to the man, explain the situation. He hates McIntyre. We need to know if there's anything else that he may have missed, something that will give an insight into McIntyre; a reason to meet with the man again.'

'I thought you were going to do that anyway.'

'We're looking for Palmer at the present time. The man's been hanging around in London, nearby to where his brother lived, but now he's disappeared, and we're worried.'

'We're not the only ones in this street keeping a watch on Palmer's house,' Wendy said. 'Do you see the Mercedes over there?'

'I see it,' Isaac said. 'I even know whose car it is.'

'McIntyre's?' Larry said.

'It's the same registration number. We can't see the driver from here.'

'You know what that means?' Wendy said.

'Bob Palmer is in serious trouble. McIntyre's out to get the man.'

'He'll protect her at all costs,' Larry said. 'Bob Palmer is a dead man if we don't get to him first.'

'Samantha is at greater risk. McIntyre, or whoever is in that car, will value their own life, Palmer won't.'

'Do we have anyone keeping a watch on her?' Isaac said.

'Not round the clock,' Larry said.

***

Wendy saw the Mercedes pull out from the kerb. Quickly, she started her car and drove into the driveway of a nearby house.

'It's a cul-de-sac; he'll have to come back this way. I don't want us to be seen,' she said.

'Keep a watch on him in your rear-view mirror,' Isaac said. 'See if you can see who the driver is.'

Inside the house where Wendy had parked, a face peered out. The front door opened soon after. 'You can't park there,' the occupant of the house said.

Isaac wanted to get out of the car and show his warrant card, but he didn't want the driver of the Mercedes to see him.

Wendy waved to the woman, tried to let her know to hold on for one minute, but she wouldn't be quietened.

Isaac smiled at the woman, said nothing.

The Mercedes drove by, both Wendy and Isaac looking in the rear-view mirror. Wendy glanced around, trying to get a better view. There was only one thing they were sure of through the tinted windows of the other vehicle: Gareth Armstrong was driving.

Isaac got out of the car and laid on the charm.

'Sorry about my outburst' the woman said. 'We get a few hooligans around here, blaring music, causing trouble. Only the other week, they had a massive party up the road, the police came. We didn't get much sleep that night.'

'How long have you lived here?' Wendy said.

'Twelve, going on thirteen years. It was a good place back then, but it's gone to the dogs now.'

'The house at the end of the street, the one with the yellow front door. What can you tell us about it?'

'Not a lot. Keeps to himself. My husband uses him to do his tax returns every year. He's self-employed. Bob does a decent job, doesn't charge too much. There's always some money to come back to us. Apart from that, there's not much I can tell you about him. He doesn't talk a lot, polite when you see him, which is not that often.'

'Anything else?'

'Not really. We know he had a brother, but he died some years ago. He mentioned it to my husband once when they were over at his house.'

'Have you seen him lately?'

'He was here the other day. I could see the light on in his house, but I didn't see him. His car was out on the street, not sure why, as he's got a garage to one side; but as I said, he minds his own business, we mind ours. The ideal neighbour if you ask me. It won't take long to put the kettle on.'

'We'll take you up on your offer,' Isaac said. Wendy was surprised, as she thought he would be keen to get back to London, to follow up on the Mercedes. But then a local woman with local knowledge might know something useful.

Inside, the house was neat and tidy, nothing out of place, but otherwise not a lot of charm. On a sunny windowsill in the kitchen, a cat was curled up. A dog, initially excited to see visitors, sat in an old cane basket.

My husband is out and about a lot, busy, doing well for himself,' Sheila Godfrey said.

'We're concerned about Mr Palmer,' Isaac said. 'He received tragic news recently, someone he was fond of.'

Wendy wasn't sure how much Isaac was going to reveal. She imagined it wouldn't be too much as the woman was an unknown. Although she seemed trustworthy, gossip was gossip. The street reminded her of where she lived, and Wendy knew that behind the curtains, people with keen noses and even better eyesight were watching and waiting.

She had had trouble once with a nosy neighbour complaining about her sons. She had given the woman a piece of her mind, not that the sons didn't need a good talking to afterwards. Sneaking girlfriends in through the back window was definitely not on, although later on, when both of them were married, they had had a good laugh about that night, over a few drinks.

There seemed to be no reason to stay longer. Wendy backed the car out of the driveway and drove up to Palmer's house. She knocked on the door, went around to the back, saw nothing untoward.

'No need to enter,' she said on her return. Isaac had stayed in the car, making phone calls.

'I don't give Palmer much for his chances,' Isaac said.

Chapter 28

'If I get this straight,' Richard Goddard said, 'someone's going to die.'

Isaac was in his chief superintendent's office following his return from Oxford, updating him on progress. 'It's almost inevitable. If McIntyre's got Armstrong hanging around Palmer's house, it can only mean one thing, the game's up. And McIntyre, if he believes his daughter murdered Liz Spalding, or even if he doesn't, doesn't take kindly to people getting involved in his business, and definitely not his daughter's.'

'A family affair, is that it?' Goddard said. 'Two brothers for the price of one.'

'Either we give Palmer protection, or McIntyre will pick him up at some stage.'

'Where's this fool now?'

'We've checked his house, he's not there. He must be back in London somewhere, close to where his brother used to live.'

'Larry Hill, out on the street?'

'He's in the area checking with a few of his contacts.'

'The best you can do, if you see this Palmer character, is to bring him into the station, put him in a cell for a few hours, let him cool his heels.'

'What charge?'

'Wasting police time is as good as any.'

Goddard understood the dilemma. Hamish McIntyre had no crimes outstanding against his name, none that could be proved. And now the man was, to all intents and purposes, retired.

'We're confident that McIntyre knew that Matthews was dead in that house,' Isaac said. 'Not that we can prove it.'

'Any suppositions as to why he would have known the body was there?'

'None that we can think of. If he didn't kill the man, which we know he didn't, he must know who did.'

'A pointless exercise on his part?' Goddard said.

'McIntyre doesn't do anything without thinking it through first. He knows the connection and the reason why. He must think we're absolute dullards, unable to find the proof.'

"He wants someone convicted for the crime, is that it?'

'It has to be.'

'Can you bring him to the station?'

'He won't come voluntarily. And his lawyer will be protecting him.'

'Grantham?'

'The man's got his feet under the table. On the one hand, he's involved with the daughter; on the other, McIntyre relies on him for legal expertise.'

'Any chance of proving the case against the daughter?'

'Greenwood's probably gone as far as he can in Cornwall.'

Isaac's phone rang.

'A coincidence. It's Jim Greenwood,' Isaac said to Goddard. 'I need to talk to him.'

'Here is as good as anywhere else.'

'What is it, Jim?' Isaac said.

'I've been following up on this car angle, trying to make sense of it. I phoned up a colleague in St Austell. It's a thirty-minute drive from the village. Asked him to look around.'

'Any luck?'

'I reckon so. Samantha Matthews' car was there on the date of the murder. CCTV camera at the railway station.'

'We're getting closer. That proves we can place her in the vicinity. Can we tighten it even further?'

'We're working on it. We're not sure how she would have got to the village if her car was parked some distance away. There's a bus service, but it's not very regular, and she would have been visible. A taxi we'd rule out for the same reason.'

'How else would she have got there?'

'Too far to walk.'

'If she hadn't taken public transport or a taxi it can only mean one thing, she drove,' Isaac said.

'No cars were reported stolen during the period,' Greenwood said.

'How long would she have needed to get to the village, commit the murder and get back to where her car was?'

'Two hours, maximum of three.'

'Any chance she could have stolen a car, committed the crime, and brought it back before it had been missed?'

'People daily commute from St Austell, leave their car at the station. It's possible.'

'If you find the car she took and prove that it was in the village, we might have a case against her.'

Isaac ended the call and looked over to Goddard.
'The case against Samantha Matthews is looking stronger.'
'Conclusive?'
'Not yet, but give us time. We'll get the woman yet.'

***

After the phone call from Wolfenden, McIntyre knew he needed to act. Palmer was causing trouble, ruffling feathers, getting closer to Samantha.

Wolfenden, not comfortable to be involved in something he knew was dangerous, followed instructions. He kept back from Bob Palmer as he walked down the street, followed him as far as the train station, and got on two carriages behind him. At each station, he got off, looking for Palmer, getting back on if he couldn't see him. Uncomfortable as he was, given the precarious situation he was in, he had to admit to a sense of excitement, a sleuth stalking his man.

At the third station, Palmer got off, Wolfenden in pursuit. He saw him enter a rundown, flea-bitten hotel two minutes from the station. He phoned McIntyre who phoned Armstrong.

'Stay where you are,' McIntyre said. 'Keep a watch on that place and if Palmer comes out, follow him. And don't lose him, not this time.'

'I didn't want to be involved,' Wolfenden said.

'You're not. Gareth will be there soon enough, leave it to him.'

'Once he's here?'

'Make yourself scarce. I'll see you right, mark my words. I look after my friends, you know that.'

Jacob Wolfenden knew that well enough but was he a friend or a threat. Bob Palmer had been a nuisance, but he had had to tell McIntyre about him. Even now he wasn't sure of the truth. Had Samantha been responsible for the death of this other woman? He supposed he could check, but ignorance was safer.

Armstrong arrived an hour later. 'Is he still inside?' he said.

'No one's come out, not yet.'

'You've not been in?'

'Hamish told me to stay outside. What do you intend to do?'

'That's not your problem.'

'I don't want to be involved.'

'You're involved whether you like it or not. Either you're with me on this, or you're not. Which is it?'

'I just want to go back to the pub, have a drink, mind my own business.'

'Don't we all. Sometimes a man has got to stand up for what's right.'

'Not me,' Wolfenden said. He no longer felt the excitement that he had experienced earlier. He knew now that he was inexorably involved and he didn't like it. A lifetime of minding his own business down the drain, purely because he had tried to protect his own skin.

'Wait here,' Armstrong said.

'What are you going to do?'

'What needs to be done. Here are the keys to the car. When I come out the front door of the hotel, make sure you're there with it.'

'I have no option, have I?'

'None at all.'

Armstrong crossed the road and went into the hotel. At the reception, a downcast woman in her fifties, a cigarette drooping out of her mouth, the ash about to fall on to the desk. She looked up. 'You want a room?' she said.

'One of your best,' Armstrong said.

'Best, we don't have. It's either a view of the street, not that there's much to see, or else a building site out the back.'

'Whatever.'

'Out the back, it is,' the woman said. She continued to look at the television raised high in one corner. Not looking up again, only seeing the hand pass across the money for the room.

'One flight up, second on the left. Room 14,' she said. 'You'll find the light switch just inside on the right. One other thing, no women.'

Armstrong knew that didn't ring true. It was the sort of place where men brought women. The only issue was how much you slipped her to look the other way.

'I've got a friend staying here, the name of Palmer. What room's he in?'

'Room 23, up one flight from you. He went for the deluxe.'

'Deluxe, what's the difference?'

'The same as yours, only the sheets are cleaned more regularly.'

'Cheaper?'

'They're all the same price. And remember, no women.'

Bypassing the first floor and the room he had just paid for, Armstrong continued up one flight. Outside

Palmer's room he paused, put his ear to the door. It was quiet. He knocked on the door.

A voice from inside. 'What is it?'

'Room service.'

'You didn't see the sign on the door?'

'I saw it, but it's my job that's at stake here. If I don't check the minibar, I'm paying for the contents.'

'Give me one minute.'

The door opened; the two men stood looking at one another.

'You're not room service,' Palmer said. 'Not dressed in a suit.'

'You and I need to have a little chat.'

'About what?'

'You've been asking questions.'

'How do you know?'

'I've got the answers.'

Armstrong hesitated for a moment. Entering the hotel had been simple enough, so had finding Palmer. But now, with the man in front of him, he needed to make decisions. The man could remove the threat of Samantha, or else he could dispose of him that day.

'What kind of answers?'

'You've been looking for a woman.'

'She was a friend of my brother's.'

'Liz Spalding?' Armstrong said.

'She was my brother's girlfriend, a friend of mine.'

'Do you believe the other woman murdered her?'

'I need to talk to her. Maybe I'm wrong, I don't know,' Palmer said. The man who stood in his room looked hard and cruel. He wanted to trust him, to give him money for information in return, but why was the man standing there at his door?

Since he had set out from the village, he had felt empowered. But now the nervousness and the fear returned. One wrong word and this man would be violent. He knew that he wanted to get away, maybe to go back to his house, to forget everything.

'I can give you her name, but I'm not sure how it's going to help you,' Armstrong said. 'She comes from an influential family who don't like people interfering. You'd be better advised to leave well alone.'

'That's what Jacob said, so did the barman. Liz didn't deserve to die. It's up to me to make it right.'

'I thought we had a police force in this country.'

'If she's as influential as you say, there'll be no proof, will there?'

'You don't need proof. But are you capable of action?'

In that room, two men who had never killed discussed the possibility. Of the two of them, Armstrong knew that he was the one most likely to do so.

'Why are you here?' Palmer asked again.

'I need to consider the options. Either I help you, or I let this woman's family deal with you. What's it to me?'

'I don't need help, just a name.'

'You can't stay here. Come with me, and we'll find somewhere quiet and out of the way. You need protection; for now, that's all I know.'

'I can't trust you," Palmer said.

'I can't blame you. I'll make it easier for you.' Armstrong took out a heavy stick that had been in his pocket and smashed it down on Bob Palmer's head. The man collapsed onto his bed.

Armstrong looked out of the window, saw the Mercedes down below. 'Come up here, the second floor,' he said to Wolfenden on his phone.

Wolfenden freaked out at the sight of Palmer slowly regaining consciousness on the bed, blood on his face.

'Clean him up. We don't want blood in Mr McIntyre's car, do we?'

'I don't like this,' Wolfenden said.

'The man's had an accident. We need to get him to the hospital.'

Wolfenden was almost wetting himself with fear. He did what he was told.

As the two men, one on either side of Palmer, helped him down the stairs and out past reception, the woman looked up.

'He's not feeling well,' Armstrong said as he passed across four fifty-pound notes. 'Keep the room for him.'

'I hope he gets better,' she said.

Armstrong knew he had been right. It was the sort of place where you took women, where you hit men, where anything was possible for a price.

'You're driving,' Armstrong said.

In the back seat, Gareth Armstrong and Bob Palmer. Palmer's belongings were still up in the room, as were his car keys.

Chapter 29

Diane Connolly was shocked when two police inspectors presented themselves at the hospital out on Porthpean Road in St Austell.

'I don't usually leave my car down at the station in their car park. Well, actually never. It's not far from where I live, and it's expensive, but it was my friend Gale. We keep in touch, friends at school, but she's gone her way, I've gone mine. I'm on nights at the hospital most of the time, but I reorganised my shifts. We said we'd meet up in London for the day. She's off overseas, and I hadn't seen her for a few years, so we agreed to meet up, have a few drinks, hit the shops in Oxford Street.'

'It's a long way to go just for a day,' Inspector Mike Doherty said.

Jim Greenwood and Doherty had known each other for a few years, occasionally meeting up for a drink, the chance to talk about crime and policing. Doherty had to admit that he was slightly envious of his friend. The man had a murder investigation, something he had hankered after for quite some time. In St Austell, nothing much happened. Just the tourists coming through, heading out to the Eden Project eco domes, three miles out of the town. A few drugs now and then, the occasional burglary.

'I took the early-morning train up, first class. I thought I'd treat myself, and I was running late. I hopped on it at the last moment, left my keys in the ignition, the door unlocked. Stupid thing to do, wasn't it?'

'We've all done it one time or another,' Greenwood said.

'When I got back, I was surprised the parking fee wasn't as much as I thought it would be. But now we know, don't we?'

'We sure do,' Doherty said. At 10.05 a.m., your car was driven out of the car park. It returned at 2.16 p.m. that afternoon.'

'Whoever took it had a lot of nerve,' Diane Connolly said.

'We'd agree with you on that. How was the woman to know that you wouldn't be back until late at night?'

'I was on the last train back, didn't get in till around nine thirty in the evening. We had a good time, the two of us. Gale and I hit the shops, spent more money than we should have, a few drinks. By the time I got on the train I was tipsy, I can tell you that. Slept most of the way back, got off the train, went home, a shower, a bite to eat and back to work. By the time I hit my bed fourteen hours later, I was out for it.'

'When you left the car,' Greenwood said, 'did you speak to anyone or see anyone?'

'I was rushing, I know that. There was a car parked next to me, red, I think it was. I said hello to the woman, she nodded back.'

'We can confirm that it was the woman who took your car. Did she know that you wouldn't be back till late?'

'I might have mentioned it to her. I was excited, a day out, first-class, meeting up with an old friend. You know how it is. I could have said to her that I was off to London, coming back late.'

'Would you recognise her again if you saw her?'
Doherty asked.

'I doubt it. I wasn't looking that closely and it was
still dark, a bit chilly. I was wrapped up, so was she.'

'It's important.' Greenwood said.

'Why would someone take my car? What's the
point?'

'The woman drove it to a village not far from
here, committed a murder and then drove back to the
station.'

'My car! I can't believe it.' Diane Connolly sat
down. She was visibly upset. 'We see people dying here,'
she said after a couple of minutes, 'but you get used to
that. But now you're telling me that my car was used in a
murder.'

'Unfortunately, Miss Connolly,' Greenwood said,
'that's the truth. It is evidence I'm afraid. Have you
cleaned it since you came back?'

'I meant to, but I don't get much time off, so the
answer is no.'

'It will need to be impounded. Our forensics
people will go over it.'

'It's not as if it's much of a car, probably only
worth a few hundred pounds. I don't think I could ever
drive it again, not now, knowing what happened. Is it that
murder down in Polperro?'

'Yes, that's the one.'

Diane Connolly handed over the keys to her car.
'Please take it. I've got a few things in the boot, a jacket
inside the car, not much else. Let me have them when you
can, but otherwise, you keep the car.'

'I'll see to it,' Doherty said. 'The forensics people
will be down within a couple of hours. They'll truck it out

from here. If you don't want to see the car again, I'll make sure you don't.'

Jim Greenwood phoned the team in Challis Street, to tell them that he was returning to Polperro. Mike Doherty was staying in St Austell, waiting for Forensics to arrive.

Ten years younger than Jim Greenwood, Doherty had to admit that Diane Connolly was pleasantly attractive. If she was free, the same as him, he intended to ask her out.

***

Bob Palmer came to, uncertain where he was and what was happening. He tried to stand up, unsure why he couldn't. He could see that it was dark, a shaft of light entering through a crack in the roof up above.

He shouted, but no one was listening.

Armstrong entered the barn, the old wooden door creaking as it opened. Palmer was sitting on a bale of hay, the same one that Jacob Wolfenden had sat on not so long before.

Outside the barn, Wolfenden waited. He had not wanted to drive to the place, but he had followed instructions.

Palmer looked up when he saw Armstrong. 'Why?' he said.

'You keep asking questions. I'm not sure what to do about you.'

'I've done nothing wrong.'

'Not yet.'

'I'm hungry, I need to relieve myself.'

'I'll make sure you're fed, don't worry. But for now, you can stay there while I consider the options.'

'What options?'

'It's simple, really. Do I kill you now or do I let you kill someone else? It's a dilemma. I don't know which choice to make.'

'Let me go. I won't tell anybody about this. I won't tell anyone about you.'

'I'm afraid, Palmer, you will.'

'I wanted to kill that woman, I'll admit to that, but not now. Believe me, please let me go.'

'You'd better get used to this place. You'll be here for a few days.'

Outside, Wolfenden could hear the conversation. He was ready to run, but where. They were in the country, a muddy track leading up to the barn, trees on either side.

He took out his phone, no signal. He couldn't even phone Hamish McIntyre to tell the man to leave him alone.

Armstrong came out of the barn. 'Sorry about that,' he said. 'He's trouble, that one.'

'I'm not. Hamish said I'd be safe.'

'You were before you found Palmer.'

'And now?'

'What do you reckon? You could cause me serious trouble, get me locked up again. And believe me, I enjoy my freedom.'

'What about him inside?'

'I've not decided yet. It depends.'

'On what?'

'I'll tell you, Jacob. Someone's going to die. It's either Bob Palmer or Hamish's daughter. One of the other. Which one do you think I should choose?'

'I don't want to know.'

'Do you ever watch old gangster movies, James Cagney?'

'Sometimes.'

You know what happens when people like me tell the hapless victim the truth? A confession, except there's no priest involved, no Hail Marys.'

'I can't remember.'

'You couldn't have been watching.'

As Wolfenden stood there, frozen to the spot, Armstrong pulled open the door of the Mercedes, took a gun out of the glove compartment and shot him in the head.

As he stood over the body, Armstrong said, 'They never have a chance to tell anyone what they had been told. That's the truth, isn't it?'

With that, Armstrong stripped the man down, put his clothes and his shoes in a pile some distance from the barn, threw diesel fuel over them and set them alight. He then dragged the body, heavier than he had expected, over to a 44-gallon drum. He removed the lid and heaved the man inside. He then filled it with acid which he had purchased two days earlier. It was good to have contacts, no questions asked, he knew that.

He had killed his first man; the second wouldn't be so difficult.

***

Mike Doherty had been impressed by Diane Connolly. He couldn't say the same about her car. With Jim Greenwood on the way back to the scene of the crime, he stood alongside the old Subaru.

Even if she didn't want the car again, it was, given that the tax was due to be renewed in one month, at the end of its useable life. The rust under the wheel arches, the bald tyres at the back, and the crumpled appearance would deem it fit only for the scrapheap.

He peered through the car window but didn't touch the vehicle, even though he was wearing gloves. On the back seat, magazines, the old jacket that had been mentioned. On the passenger seat at the front, a used train ticket, a fine for illegal parking and a notebook.

He walked around the car, making sure that no one else came near. It was parked in the hospital car park, vehicles on either side. One of them, a late-model Range Rover, the other, a Toyota Camry. Neither of the cars was of any importance.

The team arrived from Plymouth. Doherty showed them the car. Photos were taken from every angle. The driver of the Range Rover returned, Doherty asking him to be careful as he backed out from his parking space. The driver of the Toyota was a visitor to the hospital; his child in for appendicitis. He moved it soon enough. With the area clear around the car, the forensics team commenced some checks.

'We'll be more thorough once we get back to Plymouth,' the senior forensic scientist said. 'We've been told how important this vehicle is. We'll check for fingerprints here on the outside, anything else we can find.'

Phillip Strang

The activity around the vehicle soon attracted a few onlookers. Doherty found a couple of uniforms to come and keep people at a distance. Just over two hours later the vehicle was loaded up onto the flatbed of a truck. It was chained, and a plastic cover put over it.

Doherty knew it was going to be a long night. He wanted to be there in Plymouth when it was checked. Before leaving, he went back into the hospital to tell Diane Connolly what was going to happen.

'I don't want to see it', she said. 'If what you say is true, the thought of it upsets me.'

'It's had a rough life,' he said.

'It got me from here to there. Always started, even on a frosty night.'

'Are you single?' Doherty asked. He thought he was a little premature but what the heck. Life was too short.

'I'm too busy for relationships.'

'Next week, I'd like to ask you out as you've been helpful.'

'Is that normal police practice, taking out everyone who helps?'

'Is that a yes or no?'

'It's maybe. Depends on whether I'm busy or not.'

'I'll take that as a yes.'

'You're sure of yourself.'

'No time like the present.'

'As you said,' she agreed.

***

Armstrong found Hamish in the garden at the rear of the mansion. He was sitting down on a chair next to the pool.

234

'You've dealt with it?' Hamish said.

'Easier than I thought.'

'Take a seat, help yourself to a drink. Any problems?'

'Nothing that I couldn't handle.'

'Good man. The other matter?'

'Your friend at the Stag?'

'That's the one.'

'He and his inquisitive friend won't be causing any more distress.'

'Samantha intends to move out here on a more regular basis,' Hamish said. 'I like the way she thinks. She wants to make everything legitimate, get out of crime altogether.'

'The retainers you're being paid by the others?'

She wants to come to an agreement with them. A one-off payment.'

'Isn't that what the Mafia did in America, go legit?'

'You can't fight the law forever. They're like the Inland Revenue; one day they'll catch up with you for the tax you haven't paid. And no matter how smart you are, one day you'll slip up, and it'll be the police at the door, handcuffs at the ready.'

Armstrong thought that maybe he had slipped up. Palmer was back in that barn. He'd need to go out there every so often to make sure the man was fed, to make sure his bindings were tight. Too tight or too loose, both had an inherent risk.

The man could squirm, tighten the bindings, stop the circulation to his legs or his arms, even kill himself. Or there was a risk that the ropes would loosen.

'If Samantha's here, what's my position?'
Armstrong asked.

'Nothing changes. She'll be here three days a week
and then go back to her house. She's still got Fergus
Grantham. It appears she's lining up someone else to take
on as a partner in one of her business ventures.'

'New lover?'

'Probably not. Samantha's smart, she knows what
she's doing. More capable than I was, I'll have to admit to
that. I'm more brawn than brain.'

Armstrong left the man on his chair and went
back up to his place above the garage. He sat down,
considered the options, wished he had Samantha's brain
capacity.

He thought it through. On the one hand, if he
freed Palmer, the man might be able to kill Samantha, but
on the other, if the man were caught, he'd talk.

And if he succeeded in killing Samantha, he'd be
free. Even Palmer wouldn't have the sense to hang around
for long; or would he? The man could end up back in his
old house in Oxford and then what? The police would
have him in the interview room.

Armstrong went downstairs, got into the
Mercedes and backed out of the garage. Hamish wouldn't
miss him for a few hours.

Chapter 30

It was good that Diane Connolly didn't want her old Subaru back, Mike Doherty thought. Due to the seriousness of the crime and the lack of evidence, the forensics team were putting in a special effort. The outside of the car had been checked in detail, nothing found other than Diane Connolly's fingerprints on the driver's side. That wasn't unexpected, as it had been a chilly morning and Samantha Matthews was likely to have been wearing gloves. Inside was checked as well; yet again, no fingerprints. The seats were carefully removed, as were the carpets.

Jim Greenwood had asked the forensics team to look out for stray hairs.

'We know what we're doing,' a gruff reply. Greenwood had come across this before: degree-educated, thought themselves better than a police officer with a couple of GCEs to his credit. 'There are hairs in the car, we know that, but they appear to be the car owner's.'

'You got a sample from her?'

'DNA and some hair before we left the hospital. She must have taken people in her car at one stage or another.'

'I'll find her and check,' Doherty said. Jim Greenwood, he knew, would have shown more deference to the forensics, but it didn't matter. And besides, now he had a reason to contact Diane again. He found a quiet spot and phoned.

'Who else has been in your car?' he said.

'It's not the sort of car that people like to get into, is it?'

'Not now, it isn't,' Doherty said. 'Who else has been in the car in the last month?'

'I only use it for work and the shops of a weekend. And it definitely doesn't get serviced.'

'How many people?'

'Two, it's definitely only two people.'

'Do you have names for them?'

'Blossom James is one of them. She's from the Caribbean.'

'Black?'

'I'm not sure we should mention a person's colour any more, but yes. She's definitely black, short curly hair.'

'Easy to isolate. Anyone else?'

'Yasmin Chand. Her heritage's Indian, although she speaks with a West Country accent. She gets upset if you call her anything other than English.'

'Even so, her DNA will be Asian. If that's the only two, then we probably don't need to trouble them, not yet.' Then Doherty said, 'I thought Tuesday.'

'What for? Your next phone call?'

'You and I, a restaurant in town.'

'I'm working the night shift on Tuesday.'

'Wednesday, then.'

'Wednesday, 7 p.m.'

Doherty ended the call, a beaming smile on his face.

'We found someone else's hair in the driver's seat,' the forensic scientist said. 'What about the car's owner? What did she have to say?'

'Next Wednesday,' Doherty replied.

'What does that mean?'

'Sorry, miles away. The only two people who've been in the car in the last month were a black woman from the Caribbean and an English-born Indian, Asian DNA, I suppose.'

'It's neither of them. We found a few blonde hairs. We'll check it out, but it looks Caucasian.'

'You've got the results from the blonde hair found at the murder site?'

'We do. We'll compare, let you know. The results won't be through today, though.'

***

Palmer couldn't loosen the bindings that held him tight. He was parched, his throat was sore, his wrists were red raw. Time had lost all meaning, and his thoughts no longer dwelt on Liz, only on his dire situation.

He heard the sound of a car outside, the slamming of a door, the creaking of the barn door.

'I see you're still here.' Armstrong said.

'Why are you doing this?'

'We spoke about this before.' A grin spread across the man's face. 'I've solved my dilemma,' he said. 'You don't want to know what it is, do you?'

'Not now,' Palmer said.

'I thought I could use you, but you'd only cause me trouble later on.'

'I'll do what you want.'

'Jacob hadn't done anything, not really. My boss told him that he was safe. But then he changed his mind, the same as me.'

'Untie my hands.'

239

'I will in a minute, but you know what they say, your first kill is always the hardest. Jacob Wolfenden's outside.'

'I heard a gunshot before.'

'It would be good if you understood,' Armstrong said, realising that he was baiting the man, enjoying the power he exerted over a fellow human being. In prison, it had been him who had been subservient, always licking the boots of the prison officers, sucking up to the prisoners who ran the place.

Armstrong left the man and walked out of the barn. He lifted the lid of the drum. All he could see was a revolting mass of acid, flesh and fat. The smell was horrendous; he slammed the lid shut. A 44-gallon drum wouldn't take two men, even though Wolfenden had been underweight.

'I could leave you here,' Armstrong said on his return. 'You might be discovered one day, or I could set the barn on fire, but that would draw attention. There wouldn't be much of you left, just a burnt cinder. My boss owns this place, and he'd not appreciate anyone knocking on his door. They're bound to if they find a barbequed man. He's getting old now, wants a quiet life.'

Armstrong looked at the man in front of him, sitting with his head down, not moving. 'There's a compost heap outside. I'll make sure you're well covered. Think of it: in death, you'll be giving life back to the soil. An admirable end to a worthless life. How are you with a shovel?'

No answer.

Armstrong raised himself from the bale of hay, feeling the pain in his back; the reality that he wasn't as young as he once was. He lifted Palmer's head, looked the man in the face, saw his eyes closed, his mouth slightly open. 'You're still with me,' he said.

A gasping sound from the other man.

'It seems a waste of a bullet.'

He looked around the barn, found some fencing wire. He wrapped it around Palmer's neck and twisted.

Afterwards, he realised that it had been too easy; and not only that, he had enjoyed it.

Outside, the compost heap, a legacy from when the farm had been viable. He took the shovel and started digging a hole in it, big enough for a body. Returning to the barn, he dragged Palmer outside, stripped him as he had Jacob Wolfenden,

Changing out of his suit, he put on a pair of overalls and a face mask, and changed his shoes for workman's boots.

In the boot of the car, a chainsaw. Decomposition is faster if the bones are reduced in mass, the body sectioned up into more digestible pieces, he knew.

Twenty minutes later, exhausted, he removed the blood-soaked clothing and the boots, and put them where he had burnt Wolfenden's and Palmer's clothes. A dosing of diesel fuel and all evidence was destroyed. The chainsaw was also doused in fuel and set on fire. The bellowing soot-laden smoke rose into the air. He enjoyed the sight of it, hoped that no one saw it above the trees. He knew that Hamish had enjoyed occasionally slaying a man. He hadn't believed that he would have as well.

***

The barman at the Stag Hotel knew two things very clearly. One, he hadn't seen Jacob Wolfenden for a couple of days, which was unusual. And, more importantly, you did not say more than you needed to, especially to police officers.

The last time he'd seen Jacob in the pub was before Palmer had reappeared, although he had seen him briefly on the other side of the road. Jacob hadn't seen him and had moved away, following Palmer, or at least that's what it seemed to be.

He wasn't sure what to do. If he told Inspector Hill, a man who clearly liked a pint of beer, that he suspected that Jacob Wolfenden had come to some harm, he'd be forced to explain why. He'd have to say what Palmer had wanted and why Jacob wouldn't tell him. How he had told the inquisitive man to leave well alone and to mind his own business. He was a barman, and he had heard the rumours about McIntyre; who hadn't.

'Sorry can't help you there,' he said, as Larry passed over a photo of Bob Palmer.

Larry looked around the bar, formed an opinion. It wasn't his sort of place, although it sold one of his favourite beers. It had been some time since he had tasted alcohol, and the smell of it still raised an emotion in him. He wanted to grab hold of the barman, to down a pint.

'Why are you sweating?' Larry said.

'It's hot in here. I just brought up a barrel; it's hard work.'

'I've been around the area, asked a few questions here and there, spoken to one or two friends.'

'Informers?'

'People who keep their ear to the ground. Those that understand that a friendly policeman comes in handy, especially when they're serving underage drinkers.'

'I can't help you.'

'Even if you knew something, you wouldn't tell me either. Is that about the sum of it?'

'Sometimes I hear things, barmen always do. I've learnt not to take it in, to let it pass through from one ear to the next.'

'I can understand people not wanting to talk. It's not that simple, though.'

An old man walked into the pub and over to the bar. 'A pint of your best,' he said. He looked over at Larry. 'One for you?'

'Thanks, but not today.'

'You've got it wrong,' the old man said. 'Alcoholic? I'm Fred Wilkinson, by the way.'

'Yes, I am.' It was the first time Larry had openly admitted the fact.

'What is it? Stress at work, the wife giving you aggravation, the children answering you back. We've all gone through it, turned to the drink, tried to forget, just another one for the road. It doesn't help. All you get is more aggravation, end up losing your home, the respect you once had.'

'The wife and the children are fine,' Larry said.

'What are you? Accountant, engineer?'

'I'm a police inspector, Challis Street.'

'Fair enough. Plenty of stress, villains you'd rather not have to deal with, sights you'd rather not see.'

Larry pushed the photo across to the old man. The barman looked on anxiously.

'It won't do you any good. One or two pints of a night does no harm. You're a police officer, used to self-control.'

'Give me a half-pint,' Larry said. Maybe the old man's right, he thought.

'He's familiar. I've seen him in here.'

'We need to find him. Any help would be appreciated.'

Larry put the glass to his mouth, took a sip. He put it back down on the bar.

'You've got to learn how to control yourself.'

'In the meantime, the photo.'

'He upset Jacob; I know that. I could hear him tell the photo to leave well alone. Stormed out of the place, did Jacob. Usually he sits at the bar or on his own, drinks a few pints and leaves.'

'What happened after that?'

'The photo came back up to the bar, sat on the chair you're sitting on,' Fred said. 'Just about the only excitement that night.'

Fred looked over at the barman. 'You must remember what the man said.'

'Withholding evidence is a crime,' Larry said. 'I'm from Homicide. A couple of murders so far. We don't need another one.'

'He was a nuisance. I told him to get out. I had customers to serve, and he's getting in the way. I said to him that if Jacob tells you to leave well alone, then do just that. Jacob's lived here for a long time. He knows everyone; I don't.'

'He's right,' Fred said. 'That's why everyone likes Jacob. Too many people these days sticking their noses in.'

'We're getting somewhere,' Larry said. 'Bob Palmer, that's the name you identified, is warned off, but he doesn't take any notice. Is that it?'

'That's it,' the barman said. 'The second day, this Palmer character grabs Jacob in the street, threatens to hit him, not that he did. Jacob's soon in here, downs a couple of whiskies, a pint of beer. and then he's outside making a phone call.'

'To whom?'

'I didn't ask. As I said, I mind my own business.'

'Where is Jacob?'

'Jacob Wolfenden, that's his full name. I've not seen him for a couple of days, unusual as he doesn't miss his daily imbibe, not often, that is. You get used to seeing the regular faces, get to know something about them. But Jacob doesn't say much. Not about himself anyway.'

'We know that Palmer's looking for someone.'

'There's only one person around here who scares everyone,' Fred said.

The barman looked at him. 'You shouldn't go there, Fred.'

'Why's that?' Larry said.

'I'll tell you,' Fred said. 'The man doesn't frighten me, not any more. And besides, what can he do? I'm getting old, so is my wife. The man might be a vicious gangster, but I've known him all my life.'

'How do you know him?'

'He's my cousin, younger than me by a few years.'

'It won't stop him,' the barman said.

'Family is all-important to him. We're related on our mothers' side. As children, we had time for each other, played in the street sometimes, went to the cinema together.'

'What's your background, Fred?' Larry asked.

'The same as Jacob's. Kept my nose clean, did an honest job for a fair salary. I'm not ambitious, not like my cousin.'

'Your cousin's name?'

'I thought we'd dealt with that. Don't you know the villains around here?'

'I know the name of one.'

'Hamish McIntyre, that's who you want. If Jacob isn't around, talk to him. Don't mention my name, that's all.'

'I thought you weren't frightened of him.'

'He wouldn't harm me, not seriously. He could put me in hospital for a few days, though. I prefer to keep away from those places.'

'It's over to you,' Larry said, looking at the barman. 'Fred's in the firing line. Whatever I learn here will reflect back on him. Now, what was Palmer asking?'

'He was looking for a woman.'

'And?'

'A woman with a butterfly tattooed on her right arm, on the inside near the wrist. Leave me out of this and let me go back to selling drinks. Jacob didn't want to be involved, neither do I.'

Larry left the pub; his beer remained untouched.

Chapter 31

Wendy found out where Wolfenden lived, a remarkably pleasant house. Even though he had led a quiet life, never rising to any significant seniority in the factory where he had worked, he had obviously been a frugal man: never spending a lot of money, saving it where he could.

'It doesn't bode well,' Isaac said. It was the regular early-morning meeting. As they were integral to the investigation, Jim Greenwood and Wally Vincent were dialled in.

'So where is Palmer?' Larry said.

'What do we have on Hamish McIntyre? Has the man been up to his old tricks?'

'We've had no reports of him leaving his place, and we know that his daughter's there a lot of the time. Thick as thieves, those two.'

'An apt term,' Wendy said.

'If Palmer had gotten too close, McIntyre would have acted, which appears to be the case,' Larry said.

I'd agree with you on that,' Isaac said.' And Jacob Wolfenden's missing as well.'

'Which means the body count is no longer three; it's five. Does Chief Superintendent Goddard know yet?'

'He's been updated. He's not happy about it, but there's not much he can do, other than pressuring us to do better.'

'Better? We're doing all we can.'

What did the barman say, Larry?'

'He thought that Wolfenden was keeping a watch on Palmer.'

'His car has been found but not the man.'

Where is it now?'

'It's been impounded,' Wendy said.

'The hotel?'

'The man was helped out of the hotel by two other men. We got that much from the woman on reception, not that she wanted to be involved.'

'The hotel?' Bridget said.

'Palmer could have afforded better.'

'Let's assume that Wolfenden followed Palmer out to the hotel.'

'So why was he following him?' Wendy said.

'Keeping your nose clean sometimes means that you're pushed into a corner,' Larry said. 'Wolfenden was not a strong-willed character; honest and decent, but not the sort of person to stand up to anyone. He could have been threatened, not sure how to react.'

'Badly,' Wendy said. 'He would have taken the easier option.'

'Which means?'

'If McIntyre pressured him, he'd follow.'

'Follow who? Palmer or McIntyre.'

'Do we know how McIntyre found out about Bob Palmer?'

'I've given it some thought,' Larry said. 'The barman said that Wolfenden was upset, shaking like a leaf after Palmer had accosted him in the street. After he had calmed down, he made a phone call.'

'McIntyre?'

'It's possible. I ran it past the barman now that he's willing to talk.'

'Change of heart?'

'The man's not too fussy as to who goes in the pub. Underage drinkers, after-hours drink fests, God knows what else. I showed him a photo of Armstrong. He confirmed the man had been in one time, had looked around, said little and had left.'

'Wolfenden's phone records, Bridget?' Isaac said.

'I've not got the number.'

'According to Fred Wilkinson, McIntyre had grown up in the area. Both Wolfenden and Wilkinson knew the man well. It could have been purely social if he had phoned him, but that seems unlikely,' Larry said.'

'Why would he do that?' Bridget said.

'You're either on McIntyre's side, or you're not. Wolfenden would have known that. He made a choice. Let the man know before he found out that Palmer had been speaking to him. It would save himself explaining later to a man who wouldn't have been listening.'

'The hotel, the two men holding the third,' Isaac said. 'What do we know about them?'

'Nothing that helps,' Wendy said. 'I followed up with the woman. She said she hadn't seen much, but then she probably turns a blind eye to a lot of things.'

'Prostitution?'

'It goes on there, I'm sure of it. The woman tried to emphasise that it was an excellent hotel, no trouble, good food, but I went up to Palmer's room, found his keys and his belongings, not that he had many. He had paid in advance, and if he wasn't there, no need to clean the room or change the sheets.'

'She was unable to identify either of the two men?'

'She probably didn't see them, not that closely; too busy watching the television or fiddling with her nails. I'd say she had known the hotel intimately when she was younger.'

'Turning tricks in there?'

'No doubt.'

'We're assuming one of the men is Wolfenden. He's cornered, doesn't know what to do. On the one hand, he's keeping McIntyre off him, but on the other, he's now involved. Could he have made a run for it, staying low?'

'It's what we would like to believe, but if Bob Palmer were closing in on this woman, McIntyre wouldn't allow anyone to hide.'

'Who's he got working for him?'

'Gareth Armstrong, the man's butler, general dogsbody. He's got a criminal record, no violence. He and McIntyre have known each other for a long time. One rose up in the criminal echelon, the other stayed with minor crime. Armstrong wasn't a master criminal; got to know the insides of a few prisons before McIntyre employed him.'

'Any chance of CCTV cameras?'

'Not in the hotel,' Bridget said.

'How about on the street?'

'I'm still trying.'

'We know that Palmer left the hotel at close to ten minutes past three in the afternoon.' Isaac said.

'That's the closest the woman could give us,' Wendy said. 'One of her favourite programmes was on television; it had just started.'

'We were in Oxford,' Isaac said, looking at Wendy. 'We saw Armstrong leave at just after one in the afternoon.'

'He took off in a hurry. Someone must've phoned him,' Wendy said.

'How long to get from Palmer's house to that hotel?'

'Under two hours, depends on the traffic. We were back in Challis Street before three.'

'Could the third person have been Armstrong?'

'There was blood in Palmer's room, an attempt by someone in the bathroom to clean him up.'

'Wolfenden wouldn't have hit him, too scared to.'

'Armstrong could have,' Larry said.

'This assumes the three men left the hotel and got into McIntyre's Mercedes.'

'Can we trace it? What do you reckon, Bridget?'

'It depends on the woman in the reception, getting the time correct.'

'Give her the benefit of the doubt, for now,' Isaac said.

'Can we trace the car's movements?'

'It's an easy car to spot, a Mercedes,' Bridget said.

***

Confirmation had been received that the blonde hairs found in Diane Connolly's car and on Liz Spalding's clothes were a perfect DNA match.

Samantha Matthews was at home when Larry and Isaac knocked on her door. Initially, she had been polite, inviting them in, offering them a cup of tea. But neither of the police officers was in the mood to mess around with her. This time Fergus Grantham was in the main room of the house. He was drinking a glass of red wine.

'What is it, Officers?' he said.

'Are you Mrs Matthews' lawyer? Isaac said. He realised they had intruded on an intimate moment; Grantham's shirt, the top two buttons undone, a flushed look on Samantha Matthews' face.

'I am if it's required,' Grantham said. 'Your knocking on the door of this house is becoming a bit of a habit, isn't it?'

'Then, Mr Grantham, I suggest that you advise your client.' Isaac walked over to Samantha Matthews. 'I'd like you to accompany us to Challis Street Police Station.'

'What for?'

'Mrs Matthews, I'm arresting you for the murder of Liz Spalding,' Isaac said.

Grantham attempted to intercede, Isaac taking no notice of him.

'This must be a joke, Chief Inspector,' Samantha said.

'It's no joke. We can place you at the scene of the murder. You stole a car in St Austell, drove to Polperro, committed the crime. After that, you returned to St Austell.'

'You can't arrest my client,' Grantham said.

'We have a warrant for her arrest.'

'My client, Mrs Matthews, has an unblemished record. She's raised three children, all upstanding citizens. She's active with the local church. How can she be guilty of a heinous crime?'

'Mr Grantham, I suggest you accompany your client to the station. Once there, we'll conduct an interview. She will have a chance to put forward her defence. You will be able to advise her. Outside the house is a police car. She will go to the station in that vehicle. Is that clear?'

Samantha Matthews looked at Fergus Grantham.

'What can you do?'

'Nothing at this time,' he said. 'We'll have you out before the end of the day.'

Isaac knew he was taking a calculated risk. The truth was that they didn't have proof that Samantha Matthews had thrown the other woman over the cliff.

What they had was a suspect that Palmer and the police believed was the murderer, the small tattoo clearly visible. They had matched DNA in Diane Connolly's car and on Liz Spalding's clothes. What they didn't have was a match to Samantha Matthews' hair.

***

Hamish McIntyre's reaction was not unexpected when Samantha phoned him from the house.

'Fergus?' McIntyre's response after the initial shock.

'He's here with me. Don't worry, nothing will happen.'

'What's the charge?'

'The police say I murdered a woman. It's pure conjecture.'

McIntyre did not comment. She could lie to the police as much as she liked, but not to him. He would have preferred that she hadn't committed the act, but guilty or not guilty, he would ensure that no jury would ever convict her.

'Give Fergus the phone,' McIntyre said.

Samantha handed over the phone, Fergus put it to his ear. 'I'll deal with it, don't you worry,' he said.

But Hamish McIntyre did. If you commit a crime, trivial or not, you make sure there is never any evidence. But his daughter wasn't a criminal. Did she have the inherited knowledge to ensure that no evidence would be found?

'I'll be at the police station,' McIntyre said.

'I'll have your daughter out soon enough,' Grantham said. He hoped he was not going to be drawn into the crime due to his relationship with Samantha. And if he was, how far would he go to protect her, especially if the police had done their homework? He was treading a narrow line, he knew that.

One wrong action on his part, one missed opportunity to devalue the police case against Samantha, and her father, a man who would not accept failure, would react.

Grantham got into the back of the police car and held Samantha's hand; it was clammy, she was worried, and he knew she had every reason to be.

At the police station, the interview, the formal charging, explaining what was going to happen.

'My client wishes to state her innocence,' Grantham said.

'Duly noted,' Isaac said, Larry at his side. He looked at Isaac, knew full well that his DCI was pushing the envelope. The evidence was substantial, not cast iron, not yet.

'Mrs Matthews,' Isaac said, 'we have proof that you were in St Austell on the day that Liz Spalding was murdered. Do you deny that?'

Samantha looked at Grantham.

'My client withholds any answers until she knows what evidence you have against her,' he said.

'We have video proof that Mrs Matthews' car was parked at the railway station in St Austell, Cornwall, on the day that Liz Spalding, an acquaintance of hers and Stephen Palmer's, was murdered. True or not?'

'The video evidence?' Grantham said.

Isaac opened a folder and showed the accused woman and her lawyer a photo taken from the video.

'I need time to consult with my client.'

Isaac halted the interview. Both he and Larry left the room.

Outside in the corridor, DCS Goddard was waiting. 'Are you sure about this?'

'It's the only way,' Isaac said. 'We can place her in St Austell.'

'After that?'

'Not yet.'

At the entrance to the police station, a commotion. 'Samantha Matthews' father has arrived,' Larry said.

'He can wait,' Isaac said.

Ten minutes after the temporary halt, the two officers re-entered the interview room.

'My client doesn't deny that she has been to St Austell in the last few weeks,' Grantham said. 'What she will not agree to is the date that you mentioned.'

'The video is time-stamped,' Isaac said.

'That may be the case, but has it been checked and calibrated recently? It could be faulty, or maybe the railway staff didn't maintain it.'

Grantham had a point. It wasn't a CCTV camera mounted on a traffic light looking for cars running a red light. It was a camera installed inside the railway station's small car park. It wasn't there to apprehend murderers. Its purpose had just been to monitor movement and to deter the budding Leonardo da Vincis who felt that spray painting graffiti onto the station walls was artistic licence.

'If your client parked at the railway station, the question is why?'

'I was tired,' Samantha said. 'I had driven down from London, hoping to get to Penzance.'

'Any reason?'

'I like to get out into the country sometimes. I'm a free agent, the children have left home, except for the youngest but she's at boarding school most of the time.'

'You must have checked how far it was.'

'Not really. We used to go down to Penzance for our holidays when I was younger.'

'Okay, you park at the railway station, then what do you do? Look around Penzance?'

'Not that much. It wasn't as I remembered it. I took the train back to St Austell, picked up my car and drove home.'

'There was an old blue Subaru parked next to you.'

'I can see it on the photo,' Samantha said.

'Where is this heading?' Grantham said.

'The woman in the Subaru was in a hurry to get up to London on a day return. She left the car open, the keys in the ignition. We've interviewed her. She's a reliable witness. She has told us that she spoke to the lady in the car next to her, Mrs Matthews' car, that is. Told her briefly her plans for the day.'

'It's flimsy evidence,' Grantham said.

'Inside the Subaru, Forensics has found strands of blonde hair. On Liz Spalding's clothing also. A DNA match has been confirmed.'

'I'm not sure where this is heading,' Samantha said.

'You were at the funeral of Stephen Palmer. Is that correct?'

'A long time ago, but yes, I was.'

'Liz Spalding was a rival of yours for his affections.'

I believe that I've already admitted that I was having an affair with him.'

'Don't you find it strange that you were close to where your rival was murdered?'

'A coincidence, what else?'

'I think we're wasting our time here, don't you, Chief Inspector?' Grantham said.

'Your client has been charged with murder. We will require a DNA sample from her.'

'You can't do that.'

'It is within our legal rights,' Isaac said. 'Mrs Matthews, you have been charged with the murder of Liz Spalding. You will be held in our cells for now. Is that understood?'

Samantha Matthews looked at Fergus Grantham. He said nothing, just gave a slight sideways shake of his head.

Chapter 32

Jim Greenwood, aware of what had happened in London, focused on proof of Diane Connolly's car having been in Polperro. He had spoken to Mrs Venter again, but she had to be deemed unreliable.

'I saw a car down by the harbour,' she said. 'I'm certain it was blue.'

'Do you remember the woman?'

'I think I saw her up the lane, not far from where the poor woman died. But I can't be certain, the mind wanders sometimes.'

As Larry had explained to him on the phone, 'Even if we tie the woman into St Austell and to the Subaru, there is still an element of doubt. A smart defence lawyer, the witness unreliable and easily discredited, the jury disregarding the testimony. And even if we make the connection, Samantha Matthews could claim that she had gone down there just to chat with the woman and that it was an unfortunate accident.'

'I'll keep checking,' Greenwood said.

Samantha Matthews sat in the cell at Challis Street; Fergus Grantham was with her. He was not concerned about a successful outcome, but he worried that he was too intimately involved with Hamish McIntyre. His record of success in defending the indefensible was excellent. There was no shortage of clients willing to pay him handsomely. He had never interfered with a witness or tampered with the evidence or swayed the jury other than by his eloquence, but he wasn't naive, he knew that a word in the right quarter would often get the desired result.

'Your father's here,' Fergus said. 'He's doing what he can.'

'He can't do any more than you, not yet,' Samantha said. She knew she'd had to go to Cornwall.

She still couldn't understand why the discovery of Marcus's body had brought the need for resolution of the past. It had been Marcus and her marriage to him that had kept her from Stephen. She knew her father had removed Stephen from her. But he had given his word at the time that he hadn't been involved, and then soon after there was another child on the way and a husband she couldn't get rid of. However, her hatred for her father then could never be enough to break the bond between them.

But, like her, Liz Spalding had been sleeping with Stephen; the two women sharing the one man, him enjoying every moment of it.

She knew he would never have been a reliable husband, always casting an eye here and there, but she could have dealt with it.

Isaac spoke to McIntyre, told him what was going on, received an oblique threat in return.

'I remember my friends,' McIntyre said. Standing alongside him, the blue-suited Gareth Armstrong.

Intimidation was not going to work with Isaac.

Larry was upstairs in Homicide with Bridget. 'McIntyre's downstairs, his car's parked around the back of the building. It might help to have a look at it.'

Bridget had known that the car was a 2018 Mercedes S63. She had looked on the internet, found the exact model, but to see the actual vehicle could help.

She went down with Wendy, the two women looking around the car, peering in the window.

'What do you think you're doing?' Armstrong, who had just gone outside for some fresh air, as police stations didn't suit him, shouted out.

'Just looking,' Wendy said. 'It must be great to drive.' She hoped the man would be satisfied with her explanation, but wasn't too concerned either way.

Back in Homicide, Bridget scrolled over the screen on her laptop. Automatic number plate recognition had done its job.

Isaac came over after having extricated himself from his conversation with Samantha Matthews' father. 'What is it?'

'Not sure where the car's headed. It looks to be a late night for me.'

'I'll stay with her,' Wendy said as she walked in the door. 'I'll make sure she's fed.'

Jim Greenwood was in a restaurant in Polperro, just off the main street. Popular with the locals, it also drew in the tourists like bears to a honeypot.

'It was my car that was scratched, bloody tourists,' the restaurant owner said as he sat down at Greenwood's table. The police inspector liked the food, not the owner. He was a swarthy man, continually complaining, driving his staff to despair. It was the reason that the food was excellent, but the prices on the menu were high, and staff turnover was above the industry average. 'It's all right you sitting there eating your meal, but what about my car?'

'What about your car?' Greenwood said.

'A car side-swiped it, left a blue streak down one side. I can tell you the exact time. It'll be an insurance job; there goes my no-claims bonus.'

Greenwood, his interest piqued, finished his meal and went outside. The man's BMW was parked close to the wall.

'It's on the other side,' he said.

Greenwood walked around; the scratch mark was clearly visible on the silver-coloured car.

'Where was it parked when this happened?'

'I can show you where.'

'Don't move the car. I need to get Forensics down here.'

***

Bridget confirmed that the Mercedes had been picked up by a CCTV camera on the motorway heading north-east out of London, one hour after Palmer had disappeared from the hotel. It had taken her less time than she had thought, but it was still close to midnight, and both she and Wendy were exhausted.

'What do you reckon?' Isaac said when he was woken. He didn't mind the late hour. To him, policing was 24/7.

'I did a check on Hamish McIntyre before,' Bridget said. 'The man owns a lot of property. He's got somewhere not far from Epping in Essex, near the village of Thornwood, a farm.'

'Wendy, you and Larry get out there tomorrow early, take some uniforms, check around. I'll phone Larry, let him know what's going on.'

'We're leaving the office now,' Bridget said.

Larry picked up Wendy at 6.10 a.m. She'd not had enough sleep, but she could doze on the way up.

It was early morning; the traffic hadn't yet built up. It took Larry just over seventy minutes to pass through Epping and then Thornwood, turning left into Upland Road. A mile on the right, the entrance to the farm. A patrol car was parked across from the entrance of the farm, checking who was going in, who was coming out.

'It doesn't look to be much,' Wendy said.

They drove eighty yards up the track, rutted in places, muddy puddles in others; it was making the car dirty.

The farmhouse, tired and unloved, a window open, a door hanging off its hinges, was neglected. Outside an old tractor that looked as though it hadn't moved for a few years.

To the right of the farmhouse, an old barn. Larry and Wendy walked over to it, the uniforms remaining behind to check around the house.

It was Wendy who saw it first. 'A car's been up here, look at the tyre marks.'

'There must be two ways into the farm,' Larry phoned the patrol car officers to come up to the barn. Intuition told him it was where they should be looking.

It was a potential crime scene. All four donned coveralls, gloves and shoe protectors.

'Better safe than sorry,' Wendy said. She took a photo of the tyre tracks clearly imprinted in the drying mud and sent it to Bridget who forwarded it to Gordon Windsor.

'It's the same tread as the Mercedes in the car park,' Bridget said. 'I took a few photos when we were out there looking at it.'

Larry opened the barn door; it creaked. He smelt the hay. At the back of the barn, the ropes that had been used to restrain someone, the drag marks on the ground. He retreated from the barn, careful not to disturb possible evidence.

'Anything?' Wendy said.

'Phone Gordon Windsor, tell him to get his team here.'

***

Isaac saw one flaw in the investigation. He was standing, unusual for him as he preferred to sit when conversing, but everyone except Bridget was out of the office, so he was on the speakerphone in the conference room.

'We've lost focus,' he said. 'If Jim Greenwood and Forensics make the connection, provide unassailable proof that Samantha Matthews is guilty of the murder of Liz Spalding, if Gordon Windsor finds evidence of foul play at McIntyre's farm, there still remains the initial murder, the death of Marcus Matthews.'

'Have we?' Larry said. 'I don't want to dispute you, but aren't these all pieces in the puzzle, the final piece yet to be found and placed?'

'I'd agree, but it doesn't alter the fact that we've got nothing. A room at the top of a house, a dead man, an owner who keeps feeding us dribs and drabs, hoping we'll go away…'

'Which we do,' Wendy said.

'Jim, you're online. What's the latest from your end?'

'Forensics have been down, impounded the restaurant owner's car, not that it stopped him complaining.'

'A problem?'

'Not for me. He can keep on bellyaching for all I care. We're close on this one.'

'Proof?'

'Diane Connolly's car has had a rough life. The woman, even though Mike Doherty's got a thing for her, set himself up a date, is a lousy driver. The vehicle is a harlequin quilt, more than one or two scratches down the sides, a dent on the front wing.'

'Where's this leading?' Isaac asked.

'Sorry, a little excited. My first Homicide and it looks as though we've got a win.'

'Understood, but it's premature for me to offer you congratulations.'

'Miss Connolly, who didn't look after her car, barely roadworthy, had an accident ten months ago. That time it wasn't her fault, a truck caught her on the right-hand side of the car, damaged it enough for it to spend time at a panel beater's in St Austell.'

'Where's this going?' Larry said. As good a man as Greenwood was, he could talk.

'The panel beater did a matchup of the car's colour. He's still got a sample of the paint that he used. At least he did have, as Doherty's been there with someone from Forensics; it's now evidence and up in Plymouth for analysis.'

'The paint on your friendly restaurant owner's car?'

'Samantha Matthews caught it fair and square. A six-inch streak on the left-hand side of the rear of the car.

Forensics have already conducted some analysis, a spectrophotometer, and the paint at the panel beater's and down the side of the man's car are a match.'

'Conclusive?'

'Ninety per cent. Forensics won't put their name to it, not just yet. Later today they should, after they've conducted further tests.'

'No sightings of the woman in the village?'

'None that can be relied on. Just too many tourists in the place and she wouldn't have stood out.'

'Which means,' Isaac said, 'even if we can prove that she was in the village, she could still claim that it was Liz Spalding who became aggressive; that it was an accident.'

'Which we know it wasn't.'

'Knowing and proving are two different things. She'll claim, even at this late date, and after so many denials, that it wasn't her fault.'

'Lying will go against her,' Larry said.

'It doesn't matter, not much, not if Grantham is representing her. He'll say that she was frightened, unable to comprehend what had happened that day. Her husband's body had just been found.'

'The daughter of a gangster,' Wendy said. 'Another reason she'd not want to state the that, guilt by association.'

'It's unlikely that Grantham will use that, not unless he has to.'

'He will,' Larry said,' if McIntyre's daughter's freedom's at stake.'

'We might not see a conviction for first-degree, but it'll be hard to wriggle out of second-degree,' Isaac said.'

'We need the proof today,' Larry said. 'We can't hold her indefinitely, not with Grantham on her case, and her father will bring up heavier guns if he has to.'

'An inappropriate term,' Isaac said.

'More senior legal advisers are what I meant to say.'

'Money's no object as far as his daughter is concerned. Larry, you're with Wendy and Gordon Windsor. Good job by the way.'

'Does McIntyre know we're here?'

'Not from us, not yet. Any reason to let him know?'

'It might faze him if you confront him with the fact.'

'He's not in the station at present, although he'll be back soon enough. How soon before one of you two can be back in the office?'

'I can be there in ninety minutes,' Wendy said. She knew what was likely to be discovered at the barn. She had seen her share of bodies, and judging by the blood and Hamish McIntyre's reputation, they would be barely human, more reminiscent of the offal at a slaughterhouse.

'I'll stay,' Larry said.

'Wendy, ninety minutes. We'll caution McIntyre, bring him into the interview room, lay the facts out for him, look for the reaction, and see how far he'll open up.'

'What are you hoping for?' Wendy said.

'If he wants to protect his daughter, he might be forced to open up more than he'd like. There's a possibility he'll open himself to prosecution.'

***

Armstrong, immaculately-dressed as usual, steered the Mercedes around London, McIntyre in the back seat. Outwardly calm, inwardly fraught with worry, Armstrong tried to focus on what his boss was saying, watching out for the traffic at the same time. He was not handling either well.

'What is it?' McIntyre said. 'You're not yourself today. A conscience over deeds committed?'

'I'm fine, Hamish.'

McIntyre knew that something was amiss with the man, but he wasn't his priority. Samantha was in serious trouble, and her protection was paramount.

That was why Stephen Palmer had died, as had his brother and Jacob Wolfenden, a man who had never wronged him, never said a word out of turn. He knew that Wolfenden had known things about him when he was starting out in crime. The man could have fingered him back then, but he never had. He had to admit to feeling remorse over his death.

'Are you sure you completed those tasks successfully?'

'I did what was asked,' Armstrong said, although after the event, and still basking in what he'd done, he had driven back past the area, seen the police car at the end of the track.

'I'm sorry about Wolfenden,' McIntyre said. 'The man never did me any wrong.'

Armstrong offered no comment.

Hamish McIntyre realised he was getting old, sentimentality had crept in. 'Take me back to the house. Samantha will outsmart them, I'm sure of it.'

***

It was late in the evening, and Challis Street Police Station had adopted its night-time look, with most of the offices in the building closed, the lights dimmed. The only places where activity continued were in Richard Goddard's office and in Homicide. Goddard was dealing with the onerous task of the monthly report, justifying the station's expenditure, the results that had been achieved, the reasons they hadn't, and what he was doing to rectify matters.

A political animal, he knew how to finesse the wording, to make the positive take precedence, yet it had been a bad month. Crime in general was up in the area: an upsurge in drug-related crime, a terrorist incident averted.

Homicide offered the best hope for the report to glow, rather than simmer. That was where he was headed.

In Homicide, Isaac sat in his office, his hands clasped together behind his head. He felt exhausted from the weeks of burning the candle at both ends: the early-morning meetings, late home every night, the necessary seven days a week schedule.

'Tough going?' Goddard said. Isaac opened his eyes to see his senior sitting opposite him.

'Just thinking, going through the case.'

'You were catching up on lost sleep, don't deny it.'

'We're waiting.'

'What for?'

'Gordon Windsor's got lights out at McIntyre's farm. They'll be working late. Down in Plymouth, DI Greenwood is staying with his people, waiting for Forensics to sign off that Diane Connolly's Subaru was in Polperro.'

'I need you to come up trumps within the next day.'

'You say that every month.'

'You never let me down. What about Windsor?'

'Larry's there. We'll phone him for the latest.'

'Is the man going to make it?'

'So far, so good. He's kept off the alcohol and the all-you-can-eat breakfasts. I hope so.'

'They don't often, you know that. We see too much sometimes, the need to forget can be overpowering.'

'I'll protect him as long as I can.'

'I know. Call your inspector.'

A stifled yawn from Larry Hill as he answered. 'Sorry about that,' he said.

'How about the others?' Goddard asked.

'No one's giving up, sir.'

'What have you found?'

'Two items of significance. We can thank Bridget and Wendy for one of them.'

'How's that?'

'Bridget took photos of McIntyre's Mercedes when it was at Challis Street, including the tyres. Wendy took a photo of the tyre marks next to the barn. Bridget easily confirmed they were one and the same. But now the crime scene team have confirmed that the rear off-side tyre, scuffing on one side of it, is a match to Bridget's photo. We'll need the car, but it's conclusive.'

'Why hasn't that been done yet?' Isaac said.

'It's the second item that's more important,' Larry said. 'A good job that Wendy's not here, not with her sensitive stomach.'

Isaac understood what his inspector was referring to. He'd been out at crime scenes with her. A body decaying, or one that had been subjected to a violent and cruel death, and she'd be outside, vomiting.

Isaac knew that he had lost more than one girlfriend, that is before he had met Jenny, because of his apparent ambivalence over what he had seen, his unwillingness to discuss what had happened during his workday. At the scene, he could be tiptoeing around the blood and guts, feeling nothing, and that night he could be at home eating his meat and potatoes, drinking a glass of Chablis, the day's horrors forgotten.

One girlfriend had been persistent, and he had opened up. Five minutes after he had started describing the scene, the horrors inflicted by the perpetrator on his victim, and she was in the bathroom in tears. The next day she had moved out, and now nothing would possess him to tell anyone else what he had seen, although Jenny never asked, and he was thankful for that.

'What is it, Inspector?' Goddard asked.

'A 44-gallon drum outside. They lifted the lid, a revolting smell. There's a body inside, or should I say, was.'

'What's the state of decomposition?' Isaac said.

'The CSIs reckon it's sulphuric acid.'

'Identification?'

'Not by looking at what remains. Although I know who it is.'

'How?'

'Bridget compiled a report on Jacob Wolfenden after he disappeared: where he lived, phone number, height, weight, anything relevant. Wendy also did some searching around. The two of them know who it is.'

'What did you find?'

'The remains of a heart pacemaker.'

Wendy, who had been listening at the door, said.
'That's correct. The man had a medical condition.'

'Bob Palmer?'

'We'll get Forensics to see if they can get a
number off the pacemaker to trace it, but it's Jacob
Wolfenden,' Larry said. 'The man never caused trouble,
and he ends up dead in a drum of acid. No justice in this
world, is there?'

'None at all,' Isaac agreed. 'McIntyre sleeps easily
in his bed, most nights that is, although he may not sleep
tonight.'

'Proof that his daughter murdered Liz Spalding?'

'We're waiting for a phone call from Jim
Greenwood.'

In the background, raised voices at the farm.

'What is it?' Isaac said.

'I'm heading over there,' Larry said. 'It sounds
important.'

'We'll hold on the line,' Goddard said.

A retching sound came back down the phone.
The sound of a man clearing his throat, his voice weak.
'They've found Palmer. I thought it was only Wendy, but
it's me as well.'

'Identity confirmed?'

'The man's been chopped up, a chainsaw by the
looks of it. He's been buried in a compost heap.'

'We'll take the identity as Bob Palmer unless
confirmed otherwise. Any other evidence out there? Is
this Hamish McIntyre's handiwork?'

'The chainsaw was found earlier, burnt, though. There's another fire, but only ash and debris, the remains of a shoe.'

'McIntyre?' Isaac said.

'It's his farm, his car. That would be the logical deduction.'

'Logic's not what we want; it's proof,' Goddard said.

'That's why we're staying here, sir. We need to put a name to this. If we can do that, the person can't wriggle out of it. Liz Spalding's death may be open to debate, but this is murder, clear and unequivocal.'

Chapter 33

Diane Connolly's car had been in Polperro at the time of Liz Spalding's death, Jim Greenwood had phoned to confirm. It was enough to convince Homicide that Samantha Matthews had been there and her denial was invalid. She would remain in the cells at Challis Street until she was remanded to await her trial.

Fergus Grantham had put forward arguments in the interview room when the woman had been told of the latest developments. Her reaction had been to say no more. To Isaac, that was either supreme arrogance or a belief that the two men in her life would see her free soon enough.

Richard Goddard was delighted and did not delay in updating his superiors. Isaac, however, could not rest on his laurels. One murder had been wrapped up, although he couldn't help but feel that the woman would wangle her way out of the more serious charge due to a technicality, and would eventually accept the lesser charge of manslaughter, a tragic accident, when two women who had disliked each other intensely over the years had let their anger run free.

The trial, Isaac knew, would dwell on the events of the past, Samantha's affair with Stephen Palmer, his death, and then the recent discovery of the body of her husband.

Isaac had seen Grantham's waning interest, as though he was trying to distance himself. It was either, Isaac thought, the natural affectation of a man who preferred to be on the winning side, or a convicted woman who would not long hold his affection, even if it had ever been that.

Isaac had met other 'Granthams' in his time; always wanting to be on the side of good over evil, the innocent over the guilty, the righteous over the malevolent.

And even if the woman could squirm her way out of a murder conviction, she was tainted goods, and an ambitious man would not allow it to be seen that he was still with her.

He'd dump her soon enough, Isaac knew, as a lover and as a client, if he could.

***

At eight in the morning, two marked police cars pulled up in front of Hamish McIntyre's mansion. They were followed by Isaac and Larry in Isaac's car. Another vehicle brought four crime scene investigators.

Armstrong answered the door on the second knock, although he would have seen and heard the vehicles outside. Imperiously he looked at the two police officers. 'Yes, what is it?'

'We have a warrant to search these premises,' Isaac said gleefully, another charge of murder in the forefront of his mind.

'I'll let Mr McIntyre know that you're here.' The door closed.

'Let them have their moment,' Larry said.

The crime scene investigators were kitting up at the back of their vehicle. Gordon Windsor had entrusted the search to Grant Meston, his second-in-charge.

The door reopened after five minutes. Hamish McIntyre stood there in a dressing gown. 'I've spoken to Fergus Grantham,' he said. 'He'll be here in forty minutes. If you'd care to wait, I'm sure we can deal with this misunderstanding.'

'Unfortunately, Mr McIntyre, we can't. We believe that proof will be found on these premises relating to the murderer of Bob Palmer and Jacob Wolfenden.'

'There's nothing to be found here.'

'Then you'll not object.'

'Why, Chief Inspector, should I?' An ingratiating tone in the man's voice. It sounded false.

'We'll start with Armstrong's room,' Isaac said.

'What's this all about?'

'You've been told of the two bodies at your farm?'

'I own more than one farm.'

'This farm is neglected.'

'A long-term investment strategy.'

'The same as Charles Stanford?'

'If you mean Judge Stanford, then it may well be. I can't say I'm familiar with the man's investments, not having seen him for many years.'

'Not since he found a colleague of yours not guilty, is that it?'

'Baiting will do you no good, Inspector. You've put together a weak case against my daughter, but rest assured, it will not stick.'

'Gareth Armstrong's room?' Larry said.

'Up above the garage.'

'You never answered the question about the farm,' Isaac said.

'If bodies are found on a farm that I never visit, then how can I be responsible?'

'The Charles Stanford defence. Are you certain you've not had any contact with the man?'

'Believe me, Inspector Cook, I'm not a man without influence. My memory is long, and I never forget.'

'Then you can tell us what happened to Stephen Palmer,' Isaac said. Larry could see Isaac testing the man; it was a technique he'd used before, often successfully, but McIntyre was the most dangerous person they had dealt with. 'Samantha has told you about her affair with Palmer.'

'It does not need me to revisit a painful memory in her youth.'

Isaac and Larry left the front door and walked around to the garage. At the side of it, a set of stairs. The crime scene investigators were upstairs already.

'You know what you're looking for?' Meston said.

'Size 44 shoe, a Blake-stitched sole, "Made in Italy" stamped on them,' one of them said.

'He keeps the place tidy,' Meston said. 'It shouldn't be too difficult to find them.'

Larry had kitted up and entered Armstrong's residence. 'Anything?' he said to Meston.

'Anywhere else?'

'I'd try the boot of the car. The man's hardly the master criminal judging by the number of times he's been to prison.'

Downstairs, the car was unlocked. One of the CSI's opened the boot, pushed a blanket to one side, a couple of bags. He picked up a pair of shoes and put them into a large evidence bag.

'Underneath?' Larry said.

'A pair of shoes. They'll match the shoe prints we found at the barn.'

Samantha Matthews might be able to put forward a robust defence, but now her father's farm was the scene of two murders, and the CSIs were still looking for more bodies.

The handcuffs had been applied, Armstrong protesting his innocence. He was soon on his way to Challis Street. There he would be subjected to a lengthy interview, the chance to plead his case, to admit to his guilt.

Isaac wondered if McIntyre would be as generous to the man as he had been to his daughter, and that Armstrong would have Grantham as his lawyer.

***

The optimism that the Homicide team had had earlier, and which Isaac had cautioned against, was starting to affect him. Three murders out of five had been solved. There were two to go, but each of them had question marks against them.

Only two men could lay claim to the murder of Stephen Palmer, and one of them was dead, and the other one was under pressure, but he wasn't a man to give in without a fight.

The team revisited the CCTV evidence from the time of Stephen Palmer's death. It proved to be no more useful the second time.

Isaac had to admit that the probability of a conviction for that crime was low.

Down in Brighton, Wally Vincent was keeping in contact with Charles Stanford. Not that anything new was coming from that quarter, and the man, though not yet back to his old miserable self, was heading in that general direction.

'We had a complaint,' Vincent said. 'The yapping dog again. The owner said that Stanford had sworn at the dog and at her. Not that I can blame him. I was there a few days back, and the dog's going on at me.'

'What did you do?' Larry said.

'The owner wasn't looking so I gave it a swift kick. Did better than Stanford's rock-throwing, stopped it making a noise. When I came out of his house later, the dog made off, looked at me sideways from behind a gate. The damn animal's a nuisance, but the law's on the dog's side, not his.'

'You're up to date with the other murders?'

'So's my superintendent. He's on to me to shape up and start solving murders. Not sure how I can from down here, not unless Stanford's involved. Are you sure he's innocent?'

'Of murdering Marcus Matthews, yes. Give me time to get down there, and we can go and see him again,' Larry said. 'Lay everything at his feet, tell him about the two arrests we've made, the three murders solved, the fact that we're looking to solve the fourth.'

'What do you hope to achieve?'

'Stanford's played us for fools. He's been a barrister, a judge, a QC. He's seen every trick in the book, met with every devious character, even McIntyre. If he's lying about something, although why makes no sense, he would be convincing.'

'It's a long shot.'

'It's the only shot we've got. If McIntyre's behind it, he'll not talk, and at this time, he's preoccupied protecting his daughter, distancing himself from the murders at his farm.'

The two men met outside Stanford's house two hours later, Larry no longer feeling intimidated by Vincent's appearance.

Across the road, a small dog looked across suspiciously. Wally looked over at it, bared his teeth and growled; the dog took off.

'Life would be easier if we could sort out all the criminals like that,' Larry said.

'It's not the dog, it's the owner who hasn't trained it.'

The door of the house opened. 'Are you coming in, or aren't you?' Stanford said.

'Into the devil's lair,' Vincent said under his breath to Larry. Larry knew what he meant.

'That dog's not so keen on barking,' Stanford said.

'I've dealt with it for you'

'What is it you want?'

'We want to update you on our murder investigations.'

'Why? Should I be interested?'

'We'd appreciate your perspective,' Larry said. However, he thought that the truth would be more advantageous.

'Up to you. I can give you an hour.'

'We've arrested Hamish McIntyre's daughter for the murder of Liz Spalding. It's first-degree murder, but she'll probably not be sentenced for that, more likely second-degree, possibly manslaughter.'

'McIntyre won't allow her to go to prison.'

'What makes you say that?'

'Who are your witnesses?'

'We can prove she was close to the scene of the crime. CCTV cameras, DNA evidence, and a damaged car. They're one hundred per cent.'

'No such thing in a trial. Expert testimony, doubt thrown in, a dispute over the DNA testing. A myriad of possibilities. What else do you have on the woman?'

'We found a sample of the woman's hair on the dead woman's clothing.'

'That's better. If you can place McIntyre's daughter at the scene of the crime, then fine. But her defence could argue that it was coincidental, they'd met somewhere, had a cup of tea together, were great friends. How do you contradict that? Has the charged woman said that she hated her?'

'Not in so many words.'

'You see, one hundred per cent becomes ninety, becomes eighty. There'll be a jury of her peers, good and honest burghers.'

'People who don't understand they're being manipulated, is that it?'

'The defence chooses a jury based on who they think will be to their advantage. They don't want people who are going to reason it through; they want malleable minds. Who's her lawyer?'

'Fergus Grantham.'

'Never met the man, but I've heard about him. He's sharp, knows all the tricks.'

'We've arrested McIntyre's butler. He murdered two men at a farm owned by his boss. Stewed one in acid, the other he chopped up and put in a compost heap.'

'Charming.'

'Not if you were there.'

'One hundred per cent?'

'We can prove that McIntyre's car had been there no more than two days before the discovery of the bodies. We've also got the imprint of a shoe, matches with the shoe we found in the boot of the vehicle.'

'Assume that's provable, and the CSIs and Forensics will probably find more evidence, it's a stronger case than the other one, McIntyre's still not guilty of any crime. I am right, aren't I? It's him you want.'

'We have the murderers of three people, both of them closely linked back to him. But no, not directly. We're not concerned about who and why he had murdered in the past. We're only interested in finding out why Marcus Matthews was in your house, and, if we can, solve the murder of Stephen Palmer.'

Larry was looking for a change in Stanford's countenance, an inkling that the man realised the net was closing in on him. All that Stanford had done so far had been to state the obvious.

'Palmer's murder goes back twenty years, according to Inspector Vincent,' Stanford said. 'Witnesses long dead, memories distorted due to the transit of time. You'd need a confession for that unless you've got DNA evidence. Clearly, you haven't, and back then forensics wasn't as good as it is now. You can't prove that, and even if you could, it's unlikely that a jury would convict. Who was the murderer?'

'Marcus Matthews and Hamish McIntyre.'

'One dead, the other getting on in years: poor health, a tired old man.'

'A defence ploy to protect him?'

'The truth. It'll be used to maximum effect.'

'How do you know this?'

'There was an attempt to pin the murder of a drug dealer onto McIntyre. This would have been in 1999.'

'Devon Toxteth.'

'The investigation didn't go far, and no one's been found guilty of the crime.'

'You mentioned that McIntyre was in poor health?'

'The man was a heavy smoker, lung cancer.'

'He seems fit enough,' Larry said.

'He might be, but you've not seen him move fast, have you?'

'He spends most of his time with his orchids.'

'A complex man. No wonder the daughter is as mixed up as he is.'

'Do you want to see him convicted?'

'If I had a gun, I'd shoot him myself,' Stanford said. The intensity of the man's admission shocked Wally Vincent, shocked Larry.

'Are you capable of murder?'

'I suppose not, but the man brings out strong emotions in me.'

Larry was more than ever convinced that Stanford's house in Bedford Gardens was not chosen idly by Marcus Matthews and his murderer; there was a reason.

'Mr Stanford, we've solved three murders. That must convince you that we're not easily dissuaded. Something ties your house in London to Marcus Matthews. We'll continue until we understand what it is. You do realise this?'

'I realise it. You're like that damn dog across the road that Vincent dealt with. Do you suspect me of holding out on you?'

'We always have.'

'I visited Yanna White in prison. It was two weeks before her death.'

'That's never been mentioned.'

'Yanna was a very secretive woman; I've always respected her wishes. In death as in life, she didn't want anyone to ever know her true story.'

'Are you about to tell us now?'

'For some reason that day, she spoke to me as a friend. She told me things that were never mentioned in court; what had happened to her in Romania and in England. And how she had got away from them and found her way, eventually meeting her husband, forging a career for herself, loving her children. She never wanted them to know.'

'What are you going to tell us?'

'Hamish McIntyre was up to his neck in the trafficking of women, not that it could ever be proved.'

'How did she know?'

'She saw him with her captors once.'

'How did she get away?'

'Whatever his deal with them, she never knew. But McIntyre had seen her, and she became part of the agreement. He set her up in a place, not far from Tower Bridge. For a while, he'd come over once or twice a week, but he soon tired of her. And then one day, he gave her some money and let her go.'

'He acted honourably towards her.'

'To her, but what about the others? Yanna was special, the others weren't. Can you understand the untold misery that she and others were subjected to?'

'Was your visit the catalyst for her killing herself?'

'I can't say. Maybe she saw it as an unburdening of her soul, I don't know. I only know how I felt after that visit, how I felt after her death. I couldn't continue as a judge.'

Both Larry and Wally Vincent felt lumps in their throats at the thought of the torment the woman had suffered, the sadness of what they had just heard.

'And all these years you've dwelt on that,' Larry said.

'I have.'

'There's a flaw in what you just said.'

'I know.'

'It's the house in Bedford Gardens. What's the truth of it?'

'It's a time for confession, I suppose,' Stanford said. 'There's more to this sorry saga, not that it matters anymore.'

'Why's that?'

'I confronted McIntyre after Yanna's death. I had nothing to lose, and believe me, he could have had me killed if he had wanted.'

Stanford stood up and moved over to the window. He said nothing, just stood looking out.

It was Wally Vincent who broke the silence. Even though the man had caused him trouble over the years, he felt sad for him, even a begrudging friendship. 'What happened?'

'It was in London, a place he owned in Mayfair.'

'Security?'

'I knew he'd be alone. I told him what I knew and that I would go to the police.'

'His reaction?'

'He laughed in my face, told me to stop being silly.'

'Were you?' Larry said.

'I had no proof, that was the problem. If the police had been interested enough, they could have found proof of the place he had set her up in, but what else? He'd not be the first man who had installed a mistress to be there at his beck and call.'

'His connection to the trafficking?'

'It was another angle for the police to investigate, but they had tried before to find him guilty of one crime or another, but never a conviction.'

'So, let's get this straight. You visit him, threaten to go to the police.'

'That's it.'

'What could you hope to achieve? You know the law better than I; better than Vincent. What hold did you have over him?'

'I had none, but I did soon after.'

'How?'

'Devon Toxteth.'

'What's the relevance?'

'Toxteth may have been a low-life, scum, but the man had good eyesight. He operated out of a factory unit close to where Stephen Palmer had died. Lived there as well, I'm told.'

'Are you saying he was killed to keep quiet?'

'Toxteth was a stupid man. He thought he could extort money from McIntyre in exchange for keeping his mouth shut.'

'How do you know this?'

'I'm coming to that.'

'Why are you telling us?' Vincent asked.

'It's gone on for too long. The death count continues to increase.'

'Stephen Palmer's brother and another person who kept quiet, not for money, are the latest,' Larry said.

'You've not charged McIntyre?'

'Guilt by association is not proof, not even with his own farm as the murder location. You must know that.'

'Only too well. Toxteth had the proof but not the intellect of what to do with it.'

'Where did he confront the man?'

'In one of his clubs. At least that must have been where. After that, I had no idea what happened to Toxteth, not until they fished out what remained of him down past Greenwich.'

'Yet, you know all this.'

'Toxteth had been up on a charge of distributing drugs five years earlier. I took on his case, legal aid paying for it. I got to know the man, and as disreputable as he was, he was charismatic. I didn't like what he did, although he justified it by saying that he had a wife in London, three kids, and another family back in Jamaica. He was proud of his extended family and genuine in helping them. His heart was in the right place if nothing else was.'

'You've not explained why you know so much about his death.'

'The man approached me eight days before he died. I'd moved on from when we had first met. I was no longer a lawyer dealing with petty criminals. I was a QC

286

about to become a judge. I didn't want to become involved.'

'What did he tell you? What did you tell him?'

'He told me he had dirt on McIntyre, his words not mine. He was frightened, even naive about what he was intending. McIntyre's reputation was known far and wide.'

'You advised him to be careful?'

'To my chagrin, I said very little. I was more concerned about my position than that of Toxteth's. On reflection, I acted badly.'

'Did you tell him to go to the police?'

'He told me he had witnessed something. I didn't ask for details, only telling him to document it and to present himself to the police with the evidence.'

'Did he?'

'He wouldn't have followed my advice. The man was always scurrying around for the next deal, the chance to make some extra money. Apart from the two wives and their children, he was also partial to the ladies of the night, a few too many drinks.'

'How do you know so much?'

'He left me, letting me know that he'd not be deterred, and what he had would protect him. It was nineteen days later when they found him.'

'You said he visited the club eight days after he met with you.'

'Devon Toxteth, barely literate, sent me a letter in the post the day he intended to confront McIntyre. Even he, although he had ignored my advice, limited as it had been, had thought it through. He asked me if it didn't work out to let his families know that he had always cared for them.'

'Did you tell them?'

'After his body had been found. I phoned both of
the wives, although the one in London had been told by
the police. The other one in Jamaica had not, and there
was a lot of wailing when I told her.'

'This letter?' Larry asked. 'Do you still have it?'

'It's barely legible, childish in how it's constructed.
It's further proof against McIntyre, but it wouldn't be
admissible, and even if it were, it wouldn't hold up.'

'Why didn't you tell the police?'

'I was more interested in protecting myself.'

'Why are you telling us now?' Vincent said.
'You've had plenty of time before.'

'You'll be asking me about Bedford Gardens
next.'

'We will,' Larry said.

'The deaths will not stop, not until I tell you all I
know,' Stanford said. 'It was a long time ago. I defended a
colleague of McIntyre's. I got to know them both well.
The colleague died a few years later, shot in the back, a
gang war, a dispute over territory. He wasn't missed by
anyone, least of all by me.'

'McIntyre?'

'I confronted McIntyre after Toxteth's death,
accused him directly. It was the same as it had been with
Yanna White. He laughed in my face, although he was no
longer a local hoodlum and I wasn't a lawyer starting out
on his career. Now, he was a major crime figure, and I was
about to become a judge. Both of us had plenty to lose,
although I had more.'

'He had a hold on you?'

'It was the man's colleague from years before. I
had advised McIntyre, naively, that a certain witness

would cause trouble, and it would help if he changed his testimony.'

'You told McIntyre to deal with the man?'

'It was early in my career; I'd lost three cases in a row, and I was desperate. I wasn't advocating anything, just saying that it would help. Probably a little too passionately.'

'The witness?'

'He didn't turn up the next day, or any day after that.'

'Murdered?'

'What else?'

'Bedford Gardens?'

'McIntyre told me he wanted the place for private discussions, to store certain items.'

'What did you think?'

'I should have gone to the police, but my reputation was at stake. I knew what had happened to Stephen Palmer, to Devon Toxteth. I didn't want it to happen to me.'

'But now you are telling us.'

'I never committed a crime, only made a comment in error, early in my career. It's haunted me ever since.'

'Marcus Matthews?'

'I can't help you there.'

Larry and Wally left the house a lot wiser than when they had entered it. Yet Larry was still concerned about whether it had been the whole truth. Each time Charles Stanford was confronted, a little more was revealed, although the last visit had given more than the previous ones, and in Larry's hand, Devon Toxteth's hand-written note. Faded as it was, the large letters, the poorly written content, still represented proof of McIntyre's murder of a man in a warehouse twenty years previously.

Chapter 34

Gareth Armstrong sat in a cell at Challis Street. He looked around at the walls, expecting to see graffiti, a drunk's attempt at humour, but there was none. To him, it was sterile, but it was no better, no worse, than others he'd been in.

It was, he knew, the start of a lengthy prison sentence; not much chance of release before he was old and decrepit. He should have felt sorry for himself, but he was beyond that. The thought processes that had served him in prison were resurrecting themselves; take one day at a time, keep on the side of those who were in charge, keep his nose clean. Little victories each day had been his creed; he would adopt it again.

In the interview room, two hours and fifty-five minutes after arriving at the station, two hours and six minutes after the door had slammed on the cell door, Armstrong sat on the chair indicated.

On the other side of the table, Isaac Cook and Wendy Gladstone. On Armstrong's side, Fergus Grantham. The man did not seem pleased to be there.

'Mr Armstrong,' Isaac said after the formalities had been dealt with, 'you've been charged with murder. How do you plead?'

'My client exercises his right not to answer,' Grantham said.

'It's first-degree murder, and we have proof. If Mr Armstrong doesn't want to help his case, then that's up to him.'

'My client understands why he's here.'

Wendy looked over at Armstrong. 'We're confused here. We can prove Mr McIntyre's vehicle was at the murder scene.'

Armstrong said nothing, looked at Grantham.

'You'll not get an acquittal on this,' Isaac said.

Grantham looked at Isaac and then cast a glance at Wendy. 'My client is innocent until proven guilty. A vigorous defence will be conducted.'

'Vigorous it may be, but we've got your client cold. We can prove the vehicle was there, and we have witnesses that will testify he was in the company of the two men on the day in question.'

Wendy preferred that Isaac hadn't mentioned the witnesses.

The woman at the hotel reception, upon learning that one of the three men had been murdered, changed her tune. 'Oh, yes, now you mention it, I can remember what they looked like, and the man in the middle, I did speak to him.'

The woman, since identified as Joyce Langley, had numerous charges against her for prostitution, heroin addiction, a propensity for making complaints about clients who either hadn't paid or had abused her. She wouldn't be credible, not in a court. The Mercedes had been picked up by CCTV not far away, and the only person identified had been Jacob Wolfenden.

'I'm awaiting further instructions,' Grantham said.

'From Mr Armstrong or Mr McIntyre? Who are you representing here?'

'Mr Armstrong.'

'Let me put it to your client, and I suggest that you, Mr Grantham, take note as well. A claim of coincidence can't be used here. Mr Armstrong was seen in the Stag Hotel, and a frequent customer of that establishment is Jacob Wolfenden. He, we all know, had been a friend of Hamish McIntyre when they were younger. Bob Palmer is on record as having been in the hotel asking questions about a woman with a tattoo on her inside right arm.'

'Where's this leading?'

'The woman is Samantha Matthews, McIntyre's daughter. She's been charged with the murder of Liz Spalding. Both had been involved with Stephen Palmer who died twenty years ago. Not only that, we have Mr Armstrong out in Thornwood, two dead bodies found at McIntyre's farm. One of the two dead is Bob Palmer, the other is Jacob Wolfenden. It's hardly a conspiracy to lay the blame at your client's feet.'

'Okay, I did it,' Armstrong blurted out.

'Leave this to me,' Grantham said.

'What's the worst that's going to happen? A maximum-security prison, three meals a day. Hamish treated me well, but now I can't help him, not anymore, and my lawyer will dump me soon enough, you just watch.'

'I need time to talk to my client,' Grantham said, his hand on Armstrong's arm, trying to make the man shut up.

'Forget it. I'm pleading guilty.'

'Why did you kill the two men?' Isaac said.

'I did it for Samantha. I fancied her, who wouldn't.'

'Do you believe she's guilty of murder?'

'Palmer did, that was enough for me.'

'How did you know he was looking for her?'

293

'Hamish told me, not that he said for me to do anything. He wasn't worried about it, regarded the man as an irritant, no more than an ant. He said to me, out in his conservatory, "Keep an eye out. If the man gives us any more aggravation, I'll get someone to beat sense into him".'

'He said that the man would be beaten up?'

'Yes.'

'By whom?'

'He didn't say, and I didn't ask. He'd do anything for his daughter.'

'Do you believe she killed the woman?'

'I don't know either way nor do I care.'

'That's hardly charitable,' Wendy said. 'A woman died, aren't you concerned?'

'I've learnt to mind my own business. I never knew her.'

'Why murder the two men?' Isaac asked.

Grantham sat back, only glancing at his client occasionally.

'Hamish was wrong. A beating wasn't going to stop Palmer. I made the decision to deal with the man; Wolfenden knew more than he should. I couldn't trust him.'

'Are you saying that Hamish McIntyre is not involved?'

'I'll sign a confession, first-degree murder for Palmer, second-degree for the other man.'

'It'll make no difference. You'll be going to jail for a long time.'

'I'll never know freedom again, but, as I said, three meals a day, no worries about making a living. I might even get a job on the prison farm.'

'Nowhere near the compost heap, I hope,' Isaac said.

Armstrong laughed out loud at Isaac's quip; Grantham did not.

***

Forensics had been given Devon Toxteth's letter. They had scanned it, given a copy to Larry, offered a preliminary comment that it looked as though the paper had been torn out of a notebook. They didn't expect to gain much from it. The envelope had been given to them as well, a stamp in the right-hand corner, duly franked, so the age of the letter had been clearly established.

Down in the West Country, Jim Greenwood was still basking in the pride of his first homicide arrest, even though Larry Hill had reneged on his deal to allow him to make the arrest, the possibility of having Chief in front of Inspector strong in his mind.

Mike Doherty, a minor player in the investigation, was enjoying his success in St Austell, and both he and Diane Connolly had become minor celebrities in the small town. Diane didn't enjoy it, not on their first night out together, but she knew that he did. Or maybe it was because he was with her… Regardless, she knew she'd be seeing him again.

The death of Devon Toxteth, a long time in the past, was still a low priority at Challis Street. They weren't there to deal with cold cases, or only if they related to recent events. Stephen Palmer's did, although the letter by Toxteth held little value, legally that was. However, it gave the team a reason to visit McIntyre.

Isaac and Larry made the trip out to McIntyre's mansion, only to find that the gate at the front of the property had been locked, and each side of it stood a heavily-built man. No longer the haven of a retired businessman, now it was the gangster's compound.

Isaac could see the irony. 'The man's showing his true colours,' he said.

A television crew were stationed twenty yards down the road, not surprising given the coverage that McIntyre's family was being subjected to. Larry walked down to meet them, while Isaac dealt with the heavies.

'We were warned off,' Tony Cable, an athletic-looking man in his mid-thirties, said. Larry recognised him from the television, not that he was an avid watcher, although his wife was. She'd be excited that he'd met the man.

'Not like you to be out of the studio,' Larry said. There was a biting wind, and he had dressed accordingly, although Cable hadn't.

'The man's big news now. Something's going to break, and besides, it's good to get out occasionally. The studio's fine, but here's where the action is.'

'Not yet.'

'Inspector Hill, isn't it?'

'It is.'

'A comment?'

'You'll need to talk to my DCI. I'm just a beat inspector, doing my job.'

'You underrate yourself. You were up at the farm, weren't you?'

'Yes, but yet again, no comment. And don't go recording our little chat, will you?'

'Not if you give us any breaking news first.'

'I can't make promises like that, and besides, why are you the only TV crew here?'

'There are another two down the pub. We were just about to join them, that is until you and DCI Cook turned up. We'll hang around here for now.'

'You'll not get much from standing here. Have you tried talking to Mr McIntyre?'

Cable looked up the road at Isaac in discussion with the heavies. 'They made it clear that if we hung around for too long, they'd come and smack us.'

'You're still here, though.'

'As I said, we're off down the pub. What about you two? An arrest imminent?'

'No comment.'

Larry left Cable and his two offsiders and walked back to the mansion gate.

'It's not much fun standing here, Inspector,' the stockier of the two heavies said.

'Ed Davidson, how are you?' Larry said. 'An old friend,' he said, looking over at Isaac. 'We go back a long way.'

'Who's inside?'

'Mr McIntyre and his lawyer – said his name was Grantham.'

'It's been cleared, you can let us in,' Isaac said. 'I've just spoken to Fergus Grantham.'

'That's as may be, but until I receive a call, I can't open the gate.' The man's phone played a tune. He looked down at the message. 'Let them in,' he said to the other heavy, a sullen man with tattoos covering his hands as well as his neck, and whatever else that wasn't visible under the heavy coat that he wore. Isaac had seen the bulge, though. The man was carrying a weapon, no doubt illegally. Another day, another time, he would have passed the information on to Challis Street to deal with it.

But not today. Today was for wrapping up the outstanding murder investigation.

'Davidson?' Isaac asked as he and Larry got in of the car.

'He's a part-time boxer. Fancied his chance at a crack at the title eight years ago.'

'He never got it?'

'Knocked out in the first round, light heavyweight. The man's a bodyguard these days. You'll often see him close to one or another celebrity.'

'Criminal record?'

'A few pub brawls. No idea why he's protecting McIntyre.'

'Trustworthy, that's why. The other man?'

'Never seen him before.'

Isaac and Larry drove up to the mansion, walked the short distance from the car to the front door, where Fergus Graham waited for them.

'Sorry for the inconvenience at the gate. As you can appreciate, it's a little tense here, and the media are intrusive. They've even started buzzing the place with helicopters,' Grantham said.

Inside the house, McIntyre sat quietly. If it had been anyone else, it would have been possible to feel sadness for the man, but he did not deserve that, Isaac thought.

'What now?' McIntyre said. He glanced up at the two police officers, but no handshake this time.

'Your lawyer's here, so I'll speak frankly. Devon Toxteth?'

'Who or what is that?'

'Mr McIntyre, it may be that so many have been killed on your instructions that you don't remember him.'

'I advise you to be careful,' Grantham said.

'Where's this heading?' McIntyre said. He continued to drink his whisky. Judging by the half-empty bottle, he'd drunk a lot already.

'Stephen Palmer.'

'Not him again.'

'Toxteth had a factory unit down where you and Matthews took Palmer. He's a witness.'

'Where's this liar now?'

'Long dead, almost as long as Palmer.'

'He's hardly a witness then, is he?'

Isaac took a seat opposite McIntyre. 'Toxteth left a note before he visited you at one of your clubs.'

'Get to the point,' Grantham said. The man was nervous, Isaac could see, fiddling with his tie, adjusting the collar of his shirt.

'We have that note.'

'How old is it?'

'Nine days before he died, over twenty years.'

'You're joking, Cook,' Grantham said. The man laughed, but it wasn't a bellyaching laugh, more of a nervous tic.

'He was fished out of the Thames, out past Greenwich.'

'I still don't know the man,' McIntyre said.

'He would have been offering his silence in exchange for money.'

'If I can't remember the man, how can I be held responsible?'

'We can place your car and Marcus Matthews at the murder scene. And now, we have a witness's letter. It's admissible. The net closes, as I said.'

'Enough of this charade,' Grantham said. 'My client has suffered great distress recently. I suggest that you leave.'

'It's either here or at Challis Street. Mr McIntyre, your daughter is arrested for murder, so is Armstrong. And then two bodies are found at your farm. Now, either Armstrong was a damn fool, or you told him where to dispose of them. Bob Palmer was a nuisance, Wolfenden was not. Palmer was looking for a woman with a butterfly tattoo. We believe that he intended to harm her.'

'Nothing new, just rehashing what's been said before,' McIntyre said. 'My daughter will be acquitted; Fergus will ensure that. And as for Armstrong, he was a loyal employee, a friend. He may have thought that he was doing Samantha and me a favour, but he wasn't. Fergus will defend him; I can assure you of that.'

'We still have Devon Toxteth, Stephen Palmer and Marcus Matthews.'

'I didn't know one of them, the other was fooling around with my daughter, and Marcus was married to Samantha. Which one am I supposed to have killed?'

'Toxteth, we can't prove either way. You killed Stephen Palmer with Matthews as your willing accomplice. Marcus Matthews still puzzles us. We know that you had an arrangement with Charles Stanford to use the house in Bedford Gardens.'

'This is heading into the land of fantasy,' Grantham said.

'It's not,' Larry said. 'We know about your client and Yanna White. The place he set her up in, the visits to meet with her.'

'This is slanderous,' McIntyre said.

'Is it? We have proof that Yanna White, a victim of sex trafficking out of Romania, had lived in a place you owned. We have the address, photographic proof of you and her entering and leaving the place. Do you deny this?'

'My client denies it,' Grantham said.

'Not so fast, Fergus. I knew Yanna, and yes, she was my mistress for a few months,' McIntyre said. 'It may offend your petty-minded moralities, DCI Cook and DI Hill, but it was a mutual arrangement.'

'She was tainted, the victim of human trafficking. Where did you meet her?' Larry asked.

'She came into one of my clubs looking for work.'

'Not according to her. She had seen you with the Romanians who were holding her captive. Do you deny that?'

'Proof?' Grantham said.

'Mr Grantham,' Isaac said, 'the McIntyre family and their associates are at an end. Are you going to sink with them?'

McIntyre looked at Grantham; it was not the look of someone he trusted.

'I'll grant that Armstrong's confessed, but Samantha is innocent, so is her father. There is no more to say,' Grantham said.

'Not for now,' Isaac said. 'But we'll be back. The vultures are hovering. Who will be next to talk to us?'

Chapter 35

Fergus Grantham considered his options at the wine bar he frequented once or twice a week. It was late at night, and the place, never busy even at the weekend, was unusually quiet. It was an ambience that he enjoyed, the chance to reflect, to consider his life and its possibilities.

He had to admit that men such as Hamish McIntyre had done him well over the years, and the man's daughter was an added bonus. He was in his forties, still in his prime, a BMW in the driveway, an upmarket flat. He sipped at his Cabernet Sauvignon, an Australian red from the Barossa Valley.

A time to reflect, but that night he was not at ease as much as he should be. It hadn't been only DCI Cook at McIntyre's house who had told him to think about his options. He'd been considering the situation for some time. Ever since the change in Samantha, where her lovemaking had gone from mutual pleasure to a combative sport.

He could argue against her guilt, disputing the evidence, questioning the experts, bringing doubt into the prosecution, confusing the jury. As much as he would maintain that she was innocent, there was one unassailable fact: the woman was guilty.

'If you're thinking of bailing out, Fergus,' McIntyre had said after the police had left, 'you'd better think again.'

'I'm not, but let's look at the facts.'

'Let's not. You'll defend my daughter, make sure it's an unfortunate accident.'

'Samantha's not admitted to being in Polperro.'

'Can you prove she wasn't?'

'The evidence is irrefutable. Her case is weakened if she continues to deny it.'

'Then go and see her, tell her to follow your advice.'

The barman disrupted his chain of thought. 'You're not looking yourself tonight,' he said.

Grantham downed what remained in the glass, ordered another. 'Not tonight,' he said.

'Woman trouble?'

'What else?' Grantham said. And her father, he thought. In one gulp, he drank his wine and walked out of the bar.

The next day, he was led into a room at the prison, the metal bars on the windows, the solid metal door, the feeling of despair. A CCTV camera in one corner; a prison officer not far away, Samantha sitting in front of him.

'It's good to see you,' she said.

'Prison suits you,' Grantham said.

'I've lost weight. The food is barely edible.'

'I've been with your father. We need to adopt a different strategy.'

'I've missed you,' she said.

Grantham wasn't sure if he could reciprocate but said it anyway. 'I've missed you, too.'

A brief touching of hands.

'How's my father?'

'He's Hamish McIntyre. He doesn't let anyone or anything get him down.'

'What do you want me to do?'

'Let me say my piece first before you answer.'

'I trust you.'

'If you deny being in Polperro, you'll lose credibility. The evidence places you there, and you did scrape another car; it can't be dismissed. And given time, someone will remember you, or a tourist might have taken a happy snap, you in the background.'

'I wasn't there.'

'Samantha, listen to me. Admit that you were.'

'I stole the car.'

'You were unhinged after Marcus's body was found. You weren't sure what you were doing, and yes, maybe you felt that the woman had blighted your life, destroyed your happiness.'

'I'm admitting to murder?'

'While mentally distraught. Don't worry, I'll get a couple of eminent experts to testify, quote similar cases.'

'Do you want me to admit to murder?'

'It was an accident, that's what you'll agree to. You had left London intent on harming the woman, but by the time you got to Polperro, you'd calmed down. You found the woman sitting near the cliff, you became emotional, the same as she did. There was a tussle, and the woman slipped.'

'Will they believe that?'

'They'll not believe anything you say if you continue to deny taking that car and driving to the village. This is the only way.'

'What do you believe happened?'

'What I believe is not important.'

'I'd like to know.'

'I'm your lawyer. I'll defend you to the best of my ability. What I think is not relevant.'

'I'll make it up to you after I get out of here.'

'I know that,' Grantham said. He realised he no longer felt for the woman the way he had before. She was as hard as her father, as ruthless. She acted in the prison as though it didn't exist, as if her reputation no longer mattered. He'd get her off the charge, first-degree at least.

***

McIntyre could not remember Devon Toxteth; there had been more than a few who had tried to ingratiate themselves with him, others who had tried to extort money, others who had cheated.

Toxteth, according to the police, was interested in extortion. The man's death did not concern him; after all, it was twenty years ago, the same time as Samantha's fancy man had met his end. He could remember that vividly, the man pleading for his life, Marcus cowering to one side.

'Don't do it,' Marcus had pleaded.

McIntyre had known it was the time to make a man out of his wimpish son-in-law. How his daughter could have fallen for such a man, he never understood.

He thought of Yanna, the first time he had seen her, a rose amongst thorns. There was something about her that attracted him. He knew he had to take her away, to protect her, and she had treated him well, as he had her. And then he had let her go, only for her to die in prison years later.

There was only one man who could have known of her life: Charles Stanford. And if he knew about Yanna and Toxteth, then what else did he know?

He had handed over the keys to Bedford Gardens quickly enough, not once asking why. But then the man had had no option.

Why Stanford was talking now baffled McIntyre. He had to speak to him.

He phoned Grantham. 'Throw Gareth to the wolves,' he said.

'If you're sure.'

'I've no time for fools.'

'Samantha will do it.'

'I knew she would. I've one more job for you. Set up a meeting with Stanford.'

'If you're seen?'

'Neither of us has been charged with any crime. I've considered being secretive, but that would be suspicious. Make sure it's very public.'

At eight that evening, McIntyre left his mansion in Grantham's BMW. The police had no authority to restrict his movements or to follow him. It was clear to Homicide that the man was up to something.

In Brighton, a taxi pulled up in front of Charles Stanford's house. No one saw it arrive or pull away, except for one small dog and its owner. One could not tell anyone; the other wasn't interested.

***

Isaac and Wendy sat opposite Samantha Matthews. It was the same room where she had met with Grantham less than twenty-four hours before.

'I want to make a new statement,' she said.

'Your lawyer?'

'I don't need him to hold my hand. I took the woman's car.'

'Why tell us this now?'

'Fergus Grantham counselled me. I didn't kill Liz, not intentionally. It was an accident.'

'Do we rip up your previous statement?'

'Not totally. I was confused, wanting to harm the woman, not sure why. And then I'm in St Austell, and there's a car next to me, the keys in it.'

'Why not use your car?'

'I was disturbed, mentally unbalanced probably. Marcus had been found, and I realised how much I missed Stephen and how he had preferred her to me, or maybe it was the other way around. Whatever it was, she had been in the way. I had to continue with Marcus over the years, and then he disappeared. I can't say I missed him very much, although he was like an old piece of clothing. You don't want to wear it, but you can't throw it out.'

'Had you intended to harm the woman?' Wendy asked.

'When I saw her there, I wanted to scratch her eyes out.'

'What happened?'

'It was sunny, boats out at sea. It was so tranquil. I just sat down beside her. At first, she didn't recognise me, but once she did, she was alarmed.'

'And afterwards?'

'We just talked for a while; we had a mutual history. It was convivial, but then she spoke about her marriages and how her first husband had died, and the other two had disappointed. Melancholic, that's what she was. Anyway, we're talking, not as friends, not as enemies, but something's niggling her. She started pushing me, and before I knew it, we're at the cliff edge, not that I was looking. In the end, she fell, almost took me with her.'

'You could have gone to the police,' Isaac said.

'And said what? I had arrived in the village in a stolen car.'

'You panicked?'

'Not panicked. I was in shock, I think. I don't know how but I walked away, got in the car and drove to St Austell. The reality didn't hit home for a couple of days.'

'And you expect us to believe this?' Isaac said.

'It's the truth. I'll admit that I was there when she died and that it was an accident.'

'Your lawyer's hand is involved here. Is this his strategy to get you out of a murder charge?'

'It's the truth. Charge me with stealing a car, but I didn't kill the woman.'

Isaac and Wendy left the prison. Wendy had glanced back to see a smile on the woman's face as they left the room where they had met her. 'She thinks she's got one over on us,' she said.

'She has,' Isaac's only reply.

***

Two men, both getting old, sat in a nondescript pub to the south of London. One was drinking a whisky; the other a half-pint of beer. Neither liked the other, even though their lives had been intertwined over the years.

'You've caused me trouble,' McIntyre said.

'No more than you've caused me. I had hoped that I would never see your face again, to be reminded,' Stanford said.

'You agreed to our meeting.'

'I had to know what you intend to do?'

'I protect my own, always have, always will.'

'Even if the evidence is damning?'

'Why does it concern you? I would have thought you'd had enough of that.'

'The screw is turning. Your time is rapidly drawing to a close.'

'Stanford, you might have been a good barrister once, a mediocre judge, but you're wrong. Grantham's as good as you once were. You helped me out then; he'll help me now.'

'Marcus Matthews?'

'What about him?'

'Why was he in that upstairs room?'

'I thought we had come here to talk, not to indulge in verbal fisticuffs.'

Fergus Grantham sat over the other side of the room. He watched the two old men, not sure what McIntyre's plan was.

'I gave you the house, not that I had wanted to.'

'You had no option. What did you tell the police? That you are innocent of all charges?'

'I am.'

'You knew what would happen to that witness. Wet behind the ears, you might have been, but you knew.'

'Even if I did, murdering a man in cold blood in my house was a mistake.'

'Marcus, blood! Pure yellow ran through the man's veins.'

'Stephen Palmer?'

'Why do you want to go there? The police told me about this Devon Toxteth. That's how I knew it was you who had been talking, and then they mentioned Yanna.'

'Toxteth, did you kill him?'

'If I had, I can't remember the name.'

'Are you admitting to killing?'

'What if I am? What are you going to do about it? You were responsible for Yanna being found guilty. The woman was mixed up, unable to talk about her life, to throw herself on the mercy of the court.'

'You know why.'

'She'd had a rough life.'

'No conscience?'

'None at all. And besides, Yanna didn't suffer with me. In the end, I wished her well and sent her on her way. How was I to know that she was going to top her husband?'

'How long have you got?'

'Six months to a year,' McIntyre said. 'Not enough time for us to argue, is it?'

'Jacob? He was your friend when you were young.'

'Yours as well.'

'I can't remember him. Fred Wilkinson, I can.'

'He's family on my mother's side, you're not.'

'Are you going to have me killed?'

'I should, but I don't think so.'

The two men continued to drink, even to enjoy each other's company. After all, they had been the closest of friends until the age of nine, when Stanford had left the area, eventually adopting his mother's new husband's surname.

'It's a quiet life that I want now,' McIntyre said. 'What you sow, you reap, to quote from the Bible.'

'You were always smarter than me, even as children. I barely scraped through school, not that I was much interested, but you graduated from university with honours, became a respected man.'

'Soon to be derided.'

'How?'

'I'll be condemned due to you regardless.'

'No one needs to know about our childhood. Fred's the only one who remembers, and he won't talk.'

'Marcus Matthews?' Stanford repeated.

'I never used Bedford Gardens, not often anyway.'

'Women?'

'Not for that, and believe me I wasn't involved, not that much. Sure, there was a time when I didn't care who was hurt, only that the money came rolling in. Give me a good old-fashioned English criminal anytime. Foreign criminals, especially the Romanians, are a whole different breed; it took me a while to find out how treacherous they were.'

'Yanna?'

'She told me some of it. It was the day I wished her well. Admittedly, I've been a savage bastard in my time, but what she told me sickened even me.'

'You had grown fond of her?'

'Strange, isn't it? A man like me, but underneath the exterior, there was something for that woman. I wished her well, gave her enough money to find a place to live.'

'Did you ever see her again?'

'Never. I knew she had married, a couple of kids, a dull and honest man for a husband. I never expected you to convict her.'

'I had no option. She never denied that she had killed the man.'

'If you had known?'

'Unless it were put forward as evidence, then it wouldn't have helped. Yanna was determined to pay for her crime.'

'The depth of the woman, to hold that in,' McIntyre said. 'A unique person, not like us.'

Stanford had to admit it was good to see his childhood friend one last time.

'The police will solve your son-in-law's murder,' he said.

The charmless pub had filled up while they had been sitting there. Over near the bar, a group of youths out for the night were bragging to each other about who they were going to chat up, who they were going to take home. Sitting at the next table, three women in their early twenties. McIntyre had looked over, smiled at them; they ignored him. A drunken old lecher, they would have thought, not realising they had given the cold shoulder to one of the most violent men in London.

'It was Marcus. He believed a man's word was his bond,' McIntyre said.

'You just said that's what you admired about the English criminal.'

'To an extent, but with Marcus, it was an obsession. When he had made Samantha pregnant, he visited me in prison, asked my permission to marry her. Can you believe it?'

'It's the decent thing to do.'

'Decent, it might have been, but Marcus knew my reputation. He knew I could have put him six feet under, or organised a savage beating.'

'What are you getting at?'

'I don't know who killed Marcus, that's the truth. If, as the police reckon, the man sat there and allowed himself to be shot, then it must have been someone as obsessive as him.'

'Why did you phone me to tell me about the drugs in the basement?'

'I knew Marcus was there.'

'How?'

'If you want to get the police off our backs, you've got to tell them the truth.'

'The whole truth?'

'Of course not.'

'What then?'

'It was a few months before the man was shot. He started to change, became more furtive. Before that, he was impulsive, making mistakes.'

The three women left, the young men at the bar casting glances as they went, none saying anything. McIntyre knew their sort: the sort who had come into the strip clubs he had once owned, full of themselves, big mouths, money inside the skimpy underwear of the women on the stage, but when it came to a decent woman, they were tongue-tied. The only women they'd be taking home that night would be ones they'd paid for.

'He had something on his mind?' Stanford said.

'He wanted me dead.'

'How could you know?'

'I know the look of hate; I'd seen it before, not with him, but with others.'

'Do you know why he hated you?'

'I trusted the man. He had seen things, done things which he abhorred. Toughening up as I saw it. After all, someone had to take over from me when the time came.'

'And now, you'll die in your bed, an old man.'

'I played hard. Someone else could have got to me.'

'Killed you?'

'Yes. But Marcus didn't want to take over. At heart, he was a petty criminal; I never contemplated Samantha taking over, not even now.'

'She's still in prison.'

'Grantham will get her out.'

'If you had known that Matthews hated you, why did you keep him close to you.'

'Hate's a powerful weapon, especially if you can direct it.'

'And then he died.'

'He had a plan, not that I knew what it was. He couldn't have been acting alone.'

'Do you know who?'

'Never.'

'We didn't meet here to just chat about old times, did we?' Stanford said. He looked up at the clock on the wall, realised that it was past ten in the evening; two hours in the pub with a man he had previously hated, but not any longer. For whatever reason, he was the friend that he had known as a child.

'I knew Marcus was up there.'

'A phone call? Did you recognise the voice?'

'I couldn't go to the house, but you could.'

'The voice?'

'It told me that Marcus was in the top room. At the time, I wasn't focusing that much.'

'Who?'

'Someone close, but I've no idea, and that's the truth.'

'A man?'

'The man who had shot him.'

'Do you know why?'

'He wanted my fingerprints in that room. He wanted to implicate me.'

'Is this what it's all about? Marcus had wanted to kill you?'

'He couldn't have done it, but I knew that he wanted to. I had known that for years. I had forced him to do something a long time ago. He never forgave me.'

'He killed Stephen Palmer.'

McIntyre put down his drink and stood up. 'It's been good seeing you, Charles. We'll never meet again, I'm sure of that. I've told you all I know, now I suggest you use it wisely.' And with that the man walked out of the pub, the group of men still bragging, getting progressively drunker.

Outside the pub, Fergus Grantham stood at the passenger door of his BMW. 'Good to see an old friend?' he said.

'A friend, yes, I'd have to agree with that,' McIntyre said as he sat in the car and drew the seat belt across himself.

Chapter 36

The Stag Hotel, usually empty apart from a few regulars, was full, standing room only.

Isaac stood to one side and looked around the room. In his hand, a pint of beer; the occasion, a get-together of friends and acquaintances of the late Jacob Wolfenden.

'Good turn out,' the barman said. 'Where's Inspector Hill,' he asked.

'His night off,' Isaac said.

'There are a few I don't know.'

'What do you mean?'

'The drinks will start flowing; someone will stand up, offer to buy drinks for everyone. There are a few freeloaders, not that they'll stay long.'

'Are you sure?'

'Look around, what do you see?'

'Most of them are getting on in years.'

'The freeloaders want young women, and there are none in here, just geriatrics.'

'Was Wolfenden a geriatric?'

'The man was getting on, not in the best of health, but you know what I mean?'

Isaac did indeed, although the term 'geriatric' was used unwisely. Apart from the pacemaker, Wolfenden had been in reasonable health for his age. The acid hadn't had time to damage his internal organs, although his skin had been peeled, the consistency of gel. He had been there when the pathologist opened the body up, the smell of sulphur still noticeable. He'd seen the Y-shaped incision, the removal of the organs, the grinder removing the top of the man's skull, the brain coming out.

After he had finished, the pathologist's assistants had stitched the body together, attempted to make it look presentable. But no funeral home, no matter how skilled, could ever make the man's face recognisable. It was good that Wolfenden had lived alone, his wife having died nine years before, and there had been no children.

No one had come forward as a relative, no one had claimed the body. A sad ending, Isaac thought.

'Here's to good old Jacob,' a man said. He was standing on a chair.

'It won't be long,' the barman said.

'Before what?'

'A round of drinks on me.'

'Who's he?' Isaac said to the barman over the general hubbub.

'Alex Bridge. He's never paid his round, always outside when it's his turn.'

'A friend of Wolfenden?'

'Not that I know. He'll make a rousing speech, sing the man's praises and wait for someone else to pay.'

For the next twenty minutes, a succession of people stood up, offered a comment or two about the dead man. The bar was busy, drinks were selling quickly, and the barman was struggling to keep up.

'I knew Jacob well,' a man, better-dressed than the others, stood up and spoke. He did not stand on a chair as he was taller than most.

'That's Fred Wilkinson,' the barman said. 'He was in here when Palmer was a nuisance.

'We went to the same school, although we were two years apart. He made his mark there, as he did in the area,' Wilkinson continued.

'Nonsense,' the barman said.

'What do you mean?' Isaac said. He was on his second pint; the mood of the pub was having an effect on him.

'Jacob was a decent man, I'll grant Fred that, but make his mark? The man came in here, had a few drinks and then went home. Nobody knew much about him, and he never came in here with anyone else.'

Wilkinson shouted over to the bar. 'The drinks are on me.'

'There we go,' the barman said. A surge from the freeloaders. Isaac moved away and went over to where Fred was downing the last dregs of his beer.

'DCI Isaac Cook,' he said as he shook Wilkinson's hand.

'Inspector Hill?'

'He's busy trying to wrap up the investigation.'

'All because of Palmer, that's what this is.'

Two pints appeared: one for Isaac, another for Wilkinson.

'Stephen or Bob?'

'Both. The first one couldn't keep away from McIntyre's daughter; the other one stuck his nose in where it wasn't wanted. Jacob's dead because of them.'

'You're related to Hamish McIntyre.'

'It's important to him, family, that is.'

'To you?'

'I would appreciate it if you don't mention my cousin, not here, not tonight.'

'When did you last see him?'

'Ten, eleven years.'

'Where?'

'Not far from here. I was walking down the street, a car pulls up alongside me, and he's inside.'

'You got in?'

'Just sociable, nothing else. He took me to a restaurant, prices out of my reach, although the food was good. He spoke about our parents, growing up together, how well Samantha was doing.'

'That's all?'

'With Hamish, the family's all-important. It's about his only redeeming feature. In fact, I can't think of any other. As I said, I've not seen him for a long time; I hope I don't see him again.'

'Why?'

'I don't like what the man became.'

'He sees himself as a businessman.'

'I know his idea of business; either you're with him or you're dead.'

'Samantha?'

'You arrested her for the murder of Liz, so I read.'

'What do you reckon to that?'

'I preferred Samantha to Liz, not that I knew either of them that well.'

'Why Samantha?'

'Liz was flighty, too liberal with her favours. Samantha, however, was studious, always thinking of others. Hamish brought her up well, never wanted her involved in what he did, the best schools, quality friends.'

'Capable of murder?'

'Not the woman I knew. But then, blood is thicker than water. She was more like her father than her mother; genetically disposed, maybe that's what it was.'

'She'll claim it was an accident, two women arguing, a cliff, and one went over.'

'Will it hold, her defence?'

'It might.'

'I'm pleased about that, but if you'll excuse me, we're here for Jacob.'

The far side of the bar, another person on their feet. 'A round of drinks on me.'

The barman looked over at Isaac as he left, moved his eyes towards the group of heavy drinkers, the men who had never known Wolfenden.

Isaac knew what he meant.

***

Nobody expected Charles Stanford to walk into the police station in Brighton, least of all Wally Vincent. But there he was, and he was asking for him.

'I suggest you get Inspector Hill down here,' he said as he sat in the small cafeteria at the station.

'He'll take ninety minutes, give or take five to ten minutes either way,' Vincent replied. 'This is important, isn't it?'

'It's information which you've never had. It's the information you need.'

Vincent felt like saying not again, but he didn't. He phoned Larry, who was at home watching the television with his wife.

'It's after ten in the evening,' Larry said. 'You're still at the station?'

320

'There's not much at home for me. The quiet hours give me a chance to catch up on the paperwork,' he said, not that he believed it. His wife had walked out two weeks previously, and the house felt empty without her, even though they had barely spoken for months, and they had been in separate beds for longer.

'What is it?'

'Mr Stanford's here. He wants you down here as well.'

Larry looked over at his wife.

'You should go,' she said.

Outside, it was raining and the night was dark; an ominous sign, Larry thought.

Upon his arrival in Brighton, Larry went up to the second floor at the station. Both men were waiting for him.

'The interview room, gentlemen,' Stanford said. 'I want this recorded.'

Larry couldn't remember seeing the man so calm. The drive down, the police station, a man about to reveal hitherto unknown facts. It was surreal; he knew that.

'You can dispense with the formalities,' Stanford said. 'I know them well enough, and I'm not about to make a confession.'

'Very well, Mr Stanford,' Vincent said. 'The ball's in your court.'

'I met with Hamish McIntyre.'

'When and where?'

'Twenty-four hours ago. The where is not important, but it wasn't at his house.'

'Why did you meet him?'

'He asked me.'

'Personally?'

'It was Fergus Grantham who set it up. There's something you don't know about Hamish and me.'

'What is it?' Larry asked. He wanted to yawn but stifled it.

'I have made my peace with the man. I'm ambivalent as to his fate; you must understand that.'

'We do, but Mr Stanford, with all due respect, you're being obtuse.'

Stanford looked up and around the room before focusing his gaze back on the two police officers. 'As a child, I lived three doors down the road from McIntyre,' he said.

'We never knew that.'

'Nobody knows.'

'We would have checked your background,' Vincent said.

'My parents divorced when I was young. My father, who I can't remember, other than a vague recollection, was not at home often. He was in the Merchant Navy, extended periods at sea. Up until the age of nine, my surname was not Stanford.'

'Why haven't you told us this before?' Larry said.

'I took the name of Stanford, my mother's second husband's surname. My father died when I was eleven, a drunken brawl somewhere in the Far East.'

'There should still be a record.'

'No doubt there is, but it's never been mentioned by my mother or me, not until she died, that is. It wasn't an aim to conceal the fact, not originally, but then Hamish started to make his mark. He remembered me from our childhood the first time that I defended one of his men, as I did him.'

'Who else knows this?'

'Nobody that I know of.'

'Fred Wilkinson, Jacob Wolfenden?'

'Wilkinson's mother and mine used to talk over the garden fence. Supposedly he had an older sister who used to babysit me, but I can't remember her.'

'Does he know you as Charles Stanford?'

'Not to my knowledge.'

'Wolfenden?'

'I can't remember the name, but I was only young when I left.'

'What are you here for, Mr Stanford? It's not to talk about old times.'

'Hamish didn't kill Matthews; I know that now.'

'How?'

'The man opened up to me. He's dying.'

'Should you be telling us this?'

'He has left it at my discretion. He wants to be left in peace, his daughter to be free.'

'Neither is likely,' Larry said. 'If he's looking for us to leave him alone, you know that won't happen.'

'He knows that. He told me he had received a phone call around the same time as I had. Only the person told him that Marcus was in the room at the top of the stairs.'

'What else is there?'

'He suspected for some time before Matthews died that the man was planning something, incapable of doing it. Hamish had forced him to do something in the past which he hadn't wanted. To make a man of him, Hamish said.'

'What did he do?'

'I asked him a direct question. He wouldn't answer.'

'The question?'

'Did he kill Stephen Palmer?'

'Are you saying Marcus killed him?'

'I'm not saying anything. I'm only repeating the question, interpreting the man's reply. Make what you want of it.'

'We can't charge a dead man, not even McIntyre,' Larry said.

'No point, not now. The man hasn't got long to live, three to six months; he only wants to protect his daughter.'

'Then who killed Matthews?'

'The person who phoned him.'

'Did he recognise the voice?'

'He said he didn't.'

'Do you believe him?'

'I can't be sure, but there's a clue, isn't there?'

Larry looked at Wally Vincent, a bemused look on their faces.

'Not that we can see,' Vincent said.

'Marcus Matthews must have harboured an intense hatred of his father-in-law for years, but he was incapable of doing anything about it. Hamish was scathing about the man's lack of a backbone.'

'We need someone with an as intense hatred; willing to enter into a pact with Matthews.'

'An agreement either to kill McIntyre or to be killed,' Larry said. 'Matthews did have unusual ideas about wrong and right. Could he have believed in a Samurai code?'

'If he had, then we need someone equally determined to remove the parasite McIntyre,' Vincent said. 'Bob Palmer would have killed the daughter.'

'Palmer had no backbone, the same as Matthews. He wouldn't have killed her,' Larry said.

'Is there any more?' Vincent said.

'I believe that's all,' Stanford said. 'I've made my peace with Hamish; forgiven him for his past misdemeanours, forgiven myself for not protecting that dear woman.'

'We'll be in touch.'

Stanford walked out of the station. He had done what had been necessary. Now there remained only one more thing to do.

***

Finding people who had hated Hamish McIntyre was not difficult, the man had made plenty of enemies, but Homicide was looking for someone unique.

The team spent two days in the office going through the evidence, checking and double-checking, looking for suspects. A visit out to McIntyre was thought to be of little value, as, for once, Stanford had been believed.

Bridget had checked the street where McIntyre had lived, confirmed that three doors down there had been a woman with a young boy, a husband in the Merchant Navy. Charles Stanford was found to have been Charles Bailey at birth, although it had never been registered, nor had he been baptised. Bradley Stanford, a solicitor with a practice in Hampstead, had been the first person to recognise the young Stanford, legally that is.

'The Wilkinsons lived next door, that's confirmed,' Bridget said. 'Fred Wilkinson lives there to this day.'

On the third day, Larry, finally tiring of the regimen of the office, left. 'I'll scout around,' he said. 'See if anyone has strong opinions about McIntyre. Maybe there's someone obsessive, the sort of person who could make an agreement with Matthews.'

Isaac wasn't sure where his inspector was going or what he hoped to achieve. The person they wanted would be concealed in plain sight.

Isaac and Wendy, taking Larry's lead, left the office soon after. Their first call, Fred Wilkinson. The man opened the door to his house. It was a Sunday morning and from the rear of the house came the smell of bacon.

'An unexpected visit,' Wilkinson said. A large dog stood to one side of him, its teeth bared. 'Just pat it, it's harmless,' he said.

Isaac, never a dog lover, followed the man's advice. Wendy didn't, having no intention of being bitten.

'We need to talk to you about your childhood; in this house, according to our research.'

'I was born here, and yes, all my life here, apart from my time in the Army.'

Wilkinson's wife – she looked older than him, although probably wasn't – was standing in the kitchen, a frying pan in her hand. 'There's more,' she said.

'A cup of tea will do,' Isaac said. Jenny had fed him well that morning, and he wasn't hungry. He looked over at Wendy, knew she wouldn't refuse usually.

'Thanks, but I'm fine. Next time, maybe,' Wendy said, which was what Isaac had wanted. The visit, outwardly sociable, was anything but that.

'Tell us about the Army,' Isaac said as the four sat at the table in the cramped kitchen, the utensils hanging from hooks to one side of the oven, the cutlery standing up in a pot.

'It's a few years back now. I signed up out of school, a fervour of patriotism, although in truth, the economy wasn't so good, not around here it wasn't. I've never wanted to leave, and most of us out of school ended up at Downings.'

'Downings?' Wendy asked.

'They made car parts for all the major car manufacturers in England. But it was the time of the Japanese invasion of the country with their Toyotas and Datsuns. Downings was an old-fashioned company, been around for over one hundred years, and then the place is boarded up. Not many of the old-timers still around.'

'You came back here, though,' Isaac said.

'I did. For a few years, I scraped a living, the odd job here and there. I had the house, so I didn't have to worry about somewhere to live. I met Gwen soon after I got back from the Army.'

'I was in admin for a car dealer, dealt with the finance, the payroll. That's where I met Fred,' Gwen Wilkinson said.

'You were buying a car?' Isaac said, directing his conversation to her husband.

'A Toyota, even after all I'd said about them. It wasn't new, but it did the job.'

'Did you find a job eventually?'

'A small company making furniture, good quality too, not like the rubbish you see for sale now. It's still there, getting by.'

'You've retired?'

'I stayed as long as I could, and as I said, the house never cost me anything. Gwen and I, we're not rich, never wanted to be, but we're comfortable.'

'You've known Hamish McIntyre since you were a child.'

'He lived four doors down, our mothers were sisters.'

'How do you feel about him?'

'The man went his way, I went mine.'

'He's a criminal, you know that?'

'He was a friend as a child; that's who I remember. What caused him to do what he has, I don't know. I prefer not to dwell on him, no more than I have to.'

'It's not so easy now, is it? What with Marcus Matthews and his wife, Jacob Wolfenden, the Palmers. Do you remember a Charles Bailey?'

'The name doesn't ring a bell.'

'He lived next door, your mother and his used to talk over the garden fence, your sister used to babysit him when he was young.'

'She might know, but she's fourteen years older than me, not in good health.'

'You know Samantha Matthews, though.'

Gwen Wilkinson fussed around, clearing the plates from the table, topping up the cups of tea. She acted as though she wasn't listening, but Wendy could see she was.

'Samantha lived not far from here. She used to go in the Stag occasionally, and if we saw her on the street, we'd have a chat. That's all.'

'Yet you knew what her father was.'

'You can't blame the sins of the father on the child, can you? That'd be uncharitable.'

'Charles Bailey moved away when he was nine or ten. He changed his name, became an eminent person.'

'A criminal?'

'He became a Queen's Counsel, a judge.'

'And he lived next door?'

'His father was in the Merchant Navy.'

'I can't remember much back that far,' Wilkinson said. 'Too busy running around the neighbourhood.'

'Mrs Wilkinson?' Wendy said.

'Don't ask me. I grew up thirty miles from here. If it hadn't been for a job here, I'd still be back there.'

Isaac struggled with Wilkinson's answer. The man wasn't senile, far from it, and even if it had been almost sixty years, the man should have remembered something of the past.

'Marcus Matthews, you knew him?'

'I knew that he was with Hamish. I couldn't forgive him for that, but he was a decent enough person.'

'Did he hate his father-in-law?'

'I don't think we spoke about him. He liked a pint, the same as I do. I didn't pry.'

'You were indiscreet with Inspector Hill, told him about Bob Palmer, what he was asking, who he was looking for.'

'Maybe I'd had a few drinks, the alcohol talking.'

'You knew what you were saying, certain that your relationship to McIntyre gave you some immunity.'

'I don't like the man, what's wrong with that?'

'Nothing. Were you helping us to make a case against your cousin? Would you have been pleased if he had been arrested?'

'The man's corrosive. His daughter, who had never harboured an evil thought, commits murder. It's in the man's blood; he destroys those who are close to him.'

'You've not answered the question.'

'Lock him up, throw away the key. That'd be too good for him.'

'Marcus, we believe, wanted to do the same. Do you remember Stephen Palmer?'

'Where's this heading?'

'Marcus killed Stephen Palmer.'

'Not Marcus? A crook he may have been, but murder, that's another thing.'

'Hamish McIntyre forced him to kill Palmer. We know that now. Your time in the Army, did you kill a man?'

'I was a soldier in Northern Ireland, elsewhere.'

'Is that a yes or a no.'

'Gwen doesn't like me talking about it. She thinks that war is cancer, that we should love our neighbour, turn the other cheek.'

'Did you kill?'

'I did my duty, the same as any other soldier would.'

'The answer's yes, isn't it?'

'War's a dirty game, sometimes it's unavoidable.'

***

Larry returned to Challis Street at one in the afternoon, not long after Isaac and Wendy. His face was flushed, his breath heavy with the smell of beer.

'You can give me the lecture later,' he said to Isaac. 'And besides, I kept it to two pints, no more.'

Isaac didn't believe the two pints, but he'd let it pass for now. He'd done all he could with his inspector. If the man wanted to head down the slippery slope to recurring alcoholism, that was between him and his wife, not Homicide. His team, Isaac knew, needed dependable and sober people, not men with addictive personalities. Once the current investigations were completed, he'd consider the options, decide if Larry was to be moved out.

Bridget handed Larry a black coffee in a mug. 'You'd better get this down you,' she said. 'And suck on a mint.'

'People are willing to talk, more than they were before,' Larry said. 'That's why I was in the Stag Hotel, talking to another barman. He goes back a long time, and he does relief when the regular man takes a day off or calls in sick.'

'What did he have to say?'

'Marcus Matthews used to go in there regularly.'

'Anything interesting?'

'He knew him well enough, remembered when he disappeared. He reckoned it was strange at the time, as the man had seemed contented enough.'

'What else?'

'He also remembered Stephen Palmer. He said it wasn't until the man's body was found that he thought back to when he had last been seen. He said that Matthews had been in the pub nine or ten days after the man had been murdered, not that he knew that at the time. Matthews had kept to himself, slowly drinking, getting drunk. Once or twice, he'd gone outside, lit up a cigarette, and vomited. Not that it stopped him drinking though.'

'What are you telling us?'

'Matthews wasn't a drinker, but after Palmer had been murdered, the man's there drinking away, trying to forget. It confirms what we've been told.'

'We've been working with that premise. How does it help our case?'

'The barman said that Marcus, once he had stopped drinking himself into oblivion, started to become friendly with Fred Wilkinson, long chats together.'

'Is Wilkinson involved?'

'Wilkinson, a model citizen; Matthews, a man who had been forced to kill. There's enough there to raise the possibility.'

Isaac looked over at Bridget. 'Wilkinson was in the Army. His records should be accessible. Check it out, and see if there are fingerprints.'

'It was a long time ago; they may not be on a database.'

'If they're not, then find out if they're stored on microfiche somewhere.'

Two hours later, Bridget came back. 'It would be easier if you get them from the man himself. It depends where he served, if the records are still available, and if they've been stored correctly.'

'Leave it to us,' Larry said.

'Are you suggesting we make the man give us his fingerprints? We've not charged him with any crime,' Isaac said.

Larry, who had in the interim taken the opportunity to sober himself up and to wash his face, comb his hair, replied, 'Yes.'

'We'll need to find him, ask him if he'll agree. And if he doesn't, then we'll charge him. This could go pear-shaped. There's no evidence against him, other than he was friendly with Matthews, and he disliked his cousin.'

'DCI, it's not the first time you've acted on a hunch.'

'It's my skin, your hunch.'

'It's ours, skin, that is.'

They found Fred Wilkinson in the Stag Hotel. The man was sitting with his wife; she was drinking a sweet sherry; he held a glass of beer in his hand.

'We need to eliminate possible suspects,' Isaac said. 'Mr Wilkinson, we need your fingerprints.'

'I've no objection. Where? Down at the police station?'

Larry produced a mobile fingerprint scanner and placed it on the table.

'What's this for?' Gwen Wilkinson said.

'Technology's caught up with us,' Isaac said.

Fred Wilkinson said nothing, only looked at his wife and the two police officers. He complied and placed his fingers on the scanner.

'Thank you, Mr Wilkinson,' Larry said.

The man hadn't been charged, and he had previously not been a suspect. He picked up his glass of beer and took a drink from it. He said nothing.

Larry moved away from the table and found a quiet spot in the bar. He then sent the prints via his mobile to Forensics, a person there waiting to receive them.

'I think we should go,' Wilkinson said to his wife. 'I'm not feeling well.'

The husband and wife stood and headed to the door of the pub. It was Larry who stood in their way.

'What's the result?' Isaac said.

'They're a match. It's your arrest,' Larry said.

'It was your hunch, it's only right that you do it.'

A deathly hush settled over the pub, all eyes focused on the Wilkinsons and the two police officers, as Larry arrested Fred Wilkinson and put the handcuffs on him. Gwen Wilkinson, the loyal wife, stood by, unable to comprehend the situation, a tear rolling down her right cheek. Another woman who had been in the pub put her arm around her and led her away.

A marked police car arrived after a few minutes, and Fred Wilkinson was placed in the back.

Neither Isaac nor Larry were pleased with themselves. A man who had caused no harm to anyone, had even served his country with distinction, was going to jail for a very long time.

'The villains still get away with it,' Larry said later that night back at Challis Street, the cell once again occupied.

***

Fred Wilkinson sat in the interview room; his wife waited outside. The man explained how he and Marcus had formed a friendship over many years, the result of hatred for one man. How, in time, a pact was agreed that one or the other would kill the man, the other assisting as he could.

'It had been thirteen years. Marcus said that he would complete the task within one year, and if he didn't, then I was to kill him.'

'But why? That makes no sense,' Isaac said.

'You'd not understand, but Marcus did. I knew about his early life; I knew about the death of Stephen Palmer.'

'Will you testify that Hamish McIntyre was present when Palmer died?'

'It would be pointless. I shot Marcus; I'll admit to that. But it wasn't murder, it was an agreement between two men who held strong views.'

'Your Army training?'

'In part. But I had grown up with Hamish; I knew what the man had become.'

'It's bizarre,' Larry said. 'We could arrest McIntyre with your testimony.'

'He'll die in his bed. I'll die in a prison cell. Marcus died in the room at the top of a house. I only hope that my wife is looked after.'

Fred Wilkinson sat there and wrote out his confession. He had not requested legal aid. In the end, he stood up and was taken back to his cell.

Isaac knew that the man was right; he'd die in a prison cell, alone but not unloved. His wife would always be at their house, waiting for the day he would come home.

***

Wally Vincent and Larry visited Charles Stanford's house in Brighton.

Outside the house, an eerie silence. In the house, no lights were visible, nothing to indicate that the man was at home.

Larry knocked on the front door; nothing could be heard from inside.

The two men walked around to the back and tried the back door; it was locked.

'I'll break a window,' Vincent said.

'He may have a key hidden,' Larry said.

They looked under a potted plant to one side of the door.

'I've found it,' Vincent said.

Inside the kitchen, the hum of the refrigerator.

'Something's up,' Larry said.

They put on shoe protectors. Both men had gloves on. Progressively they moved through the house, careful what they touched. They used the torches on their phones to guide their way.

On the second floor, the man's bedroom. On the bed, the body of Charles Stanford.

'There's a letter,' Vincent said.

'Leave it. This place is for the crime scene investigators. It'll be a confession about how he became involved with Wilkinson and Matthews.'

'And I thought he'd told us everything.'

'He was always smarter than us. How did he die?'

'Poison, probably. It doesn't matter, not now, does it?'

Outside the house, a dog walked by on Stanford's side of the street. Unable to run away, it started yapping.

Wally Vincent knelt down and patted the dog on its head. He didn't have the heart to give it a swift kick; not that day.

The End

ALSO BY THE AUTHOR

DI Tremayne Thriller Series

Death Unholy – A DI Tremayne Thriller – Book 1

All that remained were the man's two legs and a chair full of greasy and fetid ash. Little did DI Keith Tremayne know that it was the beginning of a journey into the murky world of paganism and its ancient rituals. And it was going to get very dangerous.

'Do you believe in spontaneous human combustion?' Detective Inspector Keith Tremayne asked.

'Not me. I've read about it. Who hasn't?' Sergeant Clare Yarwood answered.

'I haven't,' Tremayne replied, which did not surprise his young sergeant. In the months they had been working together, she had come to realise that he was a man who had little interest in the world. When he had a cigarette in his mouth, a beer in his hand, and a murder to solve he was about the happiest she ever saw him, but even then he could hardly be regarded as one of life's most sociable people. And as for reading? The most he managed was an occasional police report, an early-morning newspaper, turning first to the back pages for the racing results.

Death and the Assassin's Blade – A DI Tremayne Thriller – Book 2

It was meant to be high drama, not murder, but someone's switched the daggers. The man's death took place in plain view of two serving police officers.

He was not meant to die; the daggers were only theatrical props, plastic and harmless. A summer's night, a production of Julius Caesar amongst the ruins of an Anglo-Saxon fort. Detective Inspector Tremayne is there with his sergeant, Clare Yarwood. In the assassination scene, Caesar collapses to the ground. Brutus defends his actions; Mark Antony rebukes him.

They're a disparate group, the amateur actors. One's an estate agent, another an accountant. And then there is the teenage school student, the gay man, the funeral director. And what about the women? They could be involved.

They've each got a secret, but which of those on the stage wanted Gordon Mason, the actor who had portrayed Caesar, dead?

Death and the Lucky Man – A DI Tremayne Thriller – Book 3

Sixty-eight million pounds and dead. Hardly the outcome expected for the luckiest man in England the day his lottery ticket was drawn out of the barrel. But then, Alan Winters' rags-to-riches story had never been conventional, and some had benefited, but others hadn't.

Death at Coombe Farm – A DI Tremayne Thriller – Book 4

A warring family. A disputed inheritance. A recipe for death.

If it hadn't been for the circumstances, Detective Inspector Keith Tremayne would have said the view was outstanding. Up high, overlooking the farmhouse in the valley below, the panoramic vista of Salisbury Plain stretching out beyond. The only problem was that near where he stood with his sergeant, Clare Yarwood, there was a body, and it wasn't a pleasant sight.

Death by a Dead Man's Hand – A DI Tremayne Thriller – Book 5

A flawed heist of forty gold bars from a security van late at night. One of the perpetrators is killed by his brother as they argue over what they have stolen.

Eighteen years later, the murderer, released after serving his sentence for his brother's murder, waits in a church for a man purporting to be the brother he killed. And then he too is killed.

The threads stretch back a long way, and now more people are dying in the search for the missing gold bars.

Detective Inspector Tremayne, his health causing him concern, and Sergeant Clare Yarwood, still seeking romance, are pushed to the limit solving the murder, attempting to prevent any more.

Death in the Village – A DI Tremayne Thriller – Book 6

Nobody liked Gloria Wiggins, a woman who regarded anyone who did not acquiesce to her jaundiced view of the world with disdain. James Baxter, the previous vicar, had been one of those, and her scurrilous outburst in the church one Sunday had hastened his death.

And now, years later, the woman was dead, hanging from a beam in her garage. Detective Inspector Tremayne and Sergeant Clare Yarwood had seen the body, interviewed the woman's acquaintances, and those who had hated her.

Burial Mound – A DI Tremayne Thriller – Book 7

A Bronze-Age burial mound close to Stonehenge. An archaeological excavation. What they were looking for was an ancient body and historical artefacts. They found the ancient body, but then they found a modern-day body too. And then the police became interested.

It's another case for Detective Inspector Tremayne and Sergeant Yarwood. The more recent body was the brother of the mayor of Salisbury.

Everything seems to point to the victim's brother, the mayor, the upright and serious-minded Clive Grantley. Tremayne's sure that it's him, but Clare Yarwood's not so sure.

But is her belief based on evidence or personal hope?

DCI Isaac Cook Thriller Series

Murder is a Tricky Business – A DCI Cook Thriller – Book 1

A television actress is missing, and DCI Isaac Cook, the Senior Investigation Officer of the Murder Investigation Team at Challis Street Police Station in London, is searching for her.

Why has he been taken away from more important crimes to search for the woman? It's not the first time she's gone missing, so why does everyone assume she's been murdered?

There's a secret, that much is certain, but who knows it? The missing woman? The executive producer? His eavesdropping assistant? Or the actor who portrayed her fictional brother in the TV soap opera?

Murder House – A DCI Cook Thriller – Book 2

A corpse in the fireplace of an old house. It's been there for thirty years, but who is it?

It's murder, but who is the victim and what connection does the body have to the previous owners of the house. What is the motive? And why is the body in a fireplace? It was bound to be discovered eventually but was that what the murderer wanted? The main suspects are all old and dying, or already dead.

341

Isaac Cook and his team have their work cut out, trying to put the pieces together. Those who know are not talking because of an old-fashioned belief that a family's dirty laundry should not be aired in public, and never to a policeman – even if that means the murderer is never brought to justice!

Murder is Only a Number – A DCI Cook Thriller – Book 3

Before she left, she carved a number in blood on his chest. But why the number 2, if this was her first murder?

The woman prowls the streets of London. Her targets are men who have wronged her. Or have they? And why is she keeping count?

DCI Cook and his team finally know who she is, but not before she's murdered four men. The whole team are looking for her, but the woman keeps disappearing in plain sight. The pressure's on to stop her, but she's always one step ahead.

And this time, DCS Goddard can't protect his protégé, Isaac Cook, from the wrath of the new commissioner at the Met.

Murder in Little Venice – A DCI Cook Thriller – Book 4

A dismembered corpse floats in the canal in Little Venice, an upmarket tourist haven in London. Its identity is unknown, but what is its significance?

DCI Isaac Cook is baffled about why it's there. Is it gang-related, or is it something more?

Whatever the reason, it's clearly a warning, and Isaac and his team are sure it's not the last body that they'll have to deal with.

Murder is the Only Option – A DCI Cook Thriller – Book 5

A man thought to be long dead returns to exact revenge against those who had blighted his life. His only concern is to protect his wife and daughter. He will stop at nothing to achieve his aim.

'Big Greg, I never expected to see you around here at this time of night.'

'I've told you enough times.'

'I've no idea what you're talking about,' Robertson replied. He looked up at the man, only to see a metal pole coming down at him. Robertson fell down, cracking his head against a concrete kerb.

Two vagrants, no more than twenty feet away, did not stir and did not even look in the direction of the noise. If they had, they would have seen a dead body, another man walking away.

Murder in Notting Hill – A DCI Cook Thriller – Book 6

One murderer, two bodies, two locations, and the murders have been committed within an hour of each other.

They're separated by a couple of miles, and neither woman has anything in common with the other. One is young and wealthy, the daughter of a famous man; the other is poor, hardworking and unknown.

Isaac Cook and his team at Challis Street Police Station are baffled about why they've been killed. There must be a connection, but what is it?

Murder in Room 346 – A DCI Cook Thriller – Book 7

'Coitus interruptus, that's what it is,' Detective Chief Inspector Isaac Cook said. On the bed, in a downmarket hotel in Bayswater, lay the naked bodies of a man and a woman.

'Bullet in the head's not the way to go,' Larry Hill, Isaac Cook's detective inspector, said. He had not expected such a flippant comment from his senior, not when they were standing near to two people who had, apparently in the final throes of passion, succumbed to what appeared to be a professional assassination.

'You know this will be all over the media within the hour,' Isaac said.

'James Holden, moral crusader, a proponent of the sanctity of the marital bed, man and wife. It's bound to be.'

Murder of a Silent Man – A DCI Cook Thriller – Book 8

A murdered recluse. A property empire. A disinherited family. All the ingredients for murder.

No one gave much credence to the man when he was alive. In fact, most people never knew who he was, although those who had lived in the area for many years recognised the tired-looking and shabbily-dressed man as he shuffled along, regular as clockwork on a Thursday afternoon at seven in the evening to the local off-licence.

It was always the same: a bottle of whisky, premium brand, and a packet of cigarettes. He paid his money over the counter, took hold of his plastic bag containing his purchases, and then walked back down the road with the same rhythmic shuffle. He said not one word to anyone on the street or in the shop.

Murder has no Guilt – A DCI Cook Thriller – Book 9

No one knows who the target was or why, but there are eight dead. The men seem the most likely perpetrators, or could have it been one of the two women, the attractive Gillian Dickenson, or even the celebrity-obsessed Sal Maynard?

There's a gang war brewing, and if there are deaths, it doesn't matter to them as long as it's not their death. But to Detective Chief Inspector Isaac Cook, it's his area of London, and it does matter.

It's dirty and unpredictable. Initially it had been the West Indian gangs, but then a more vicious Romanian gangster had usurped them. And now he's being marginalised by the Russians. And the leader of the most vicious Russian mafia organisation is in London, and he's got money and influence, the ear of those in power.

Murder in Hyde Park – A DCI Cook Thriller – Book 10

An early morning jogger is murdered in Hyde Park. It's the centre of London, but no one saw him enter the park, no one saw him die.

He carries no identification, only a water-logged phone. As the pieces unravel, it's clear that the dead man had a history of deception.

Is the murderer one of those that loved him? Or was it someone with a vengeance?

It's proving difficult for DCI Isaac Cook and his team at Challis Street Homicide to find the guilty person – not that they'll cease to search for the truth, not even after one suspect confesses.

Six Years Too Late – A DCI Cook Thriller – Book 11

Always the same questions for Detective Chief Inspector Isaac Cook — Why was Marcus Matthews in that room? And why did he share a bottle of wine with his killer?

It wasn't as if the man had amounted to much in life, apart from the fact that he was the son-in-law of a notorious gangster, the father of the man's grandchildren. Yet, one thing that Hamish McIntyre, feared in London for his violence, rated above anything else, it was his family, especially Samantha, his daughter; although he had never cared for Marcus, her husband.

And then Marcus disappears, only for his body to be found six years later by a couple of young boys who decide that exploring an abandoned house is preferable to school.

Murder Without Reason – A DCI Cook Thriller – Book 12

DCI Cook faces his greatest challenge. The Islamic State is waging war in England, and they are winning.

Not only does Isaac Cook have to contend with finding the perpetrators, but he is also being forced to commit actions contrary to his mandate as a police officer.

And then there is Anne Argento, the prime minister's deputy. The prime minister has shown himself to be a pacifist and is not up to the task. She needs to take his job if the country is to fight back against the Islamists.

Vane and Martin have provided the solution. Will DCI
Cook and Anne Argento be willing to follow it through?
Are they able to act for the good of England, knowing
that a criminal and murderous action is about to take
place? Do they have an option?

Standalone Novels

The Haberman Virus

A remote and isolated village in the Hindu Kush
mountain range in North Eastern Afghanistan is wiped
out by a virus unlike any seen before.

A mysterious visitor clad in a spacesuit checks his
handiwork, a female American doctor succumbs to the
disease, and the woman sent to trap the person
responsible falls in love with him – the man who would
cause the deaths of millions.

Hostage of Islam

Three are to die at the Mission in Nigeria: the pastor and
his wife in a blazing chapel; another gunned down while
trying to defend them from the Islamist fighters.

Kate McDonald, an American, grieving over her
boyfriend's death and Helen Campbell, whose life had
been troubled by drugs and prostitution, are taken by the
attackers.

Kate is sold to a slave trader who intends to sell her virginity to an Arab Prince. Helen, to ensure their survival, gives herself to the murderer of her friends.

Malika's Revenge

Malika, a drug-addicted prostitute, waits in a smugglers' village for the next Afghan tribesman or Tajik gangster to pay her price, a few scraps of heroin.

Yusup Baroyev, a drug lord, enjoys a lifestyle many would envy. An Afghan warlord sees the resurgence of the Taliban. A Russian white-collar criminal portrays himself as a good and honest citizen in Moscow.

All of them are linked to an audacious plan to increase the quantity of heroin shipped out of Afghanistan and into Russia and ultimately the West.

Some will succeed, some will die, some will be rescued from their plight and others will rue the day they became involved.

Prelude to War

Russia and America face each other across the northern border of Afghanistan. World War 3 is about to break out and no one is backing off.

And all because a team of academics in New York postulated how to extract the vast untapped mineral wealth of Afghanistan.

Steve Case is in the middle of it, and his position is looking very precarious. Will the Taliban find him before the Americans get him out? Or is he doomed, as is the rest of the world?

ABOUT THE AUTHOR

Phillip Strang was born in England in the late forties. He was an avid reader of science fiction in his teenage years: Isaac Asimov, Frank Herbert, the masters of the genre. Still an avid reader, the author now mainly reads thrillers.

In his early twenties, the author, with a degree in electronics engineering and a desire to see the world, left England for Sydney, Australia. Now, forty years later, he still resides in Australia, although many intervening years were spent in a myriad of countries, some calm and safe, others no more than war zones.